BETRAYED

The Dragon's Game
Book III

H. N. Henry

Presse Dragon Libre
Free Dragon's Press

Trois-Rivières, QC, Canada

FREE DRAGON'S PRESS
Huard, Norman Henry
220 B Farmer
Trois-Rivières, Québec, Canada, G9A 3E6
www.hnhenry.com

Publisher's Note: This is a work of fiction. Names, characters, places, and incidents are a product of the author's imagination, except for his use of the Cree language in Roman orthography to number and title chapters and as one of the languages spoken by certain characters; and also for his use of certain Tai Chi exercise names. Locales and public names are sometimes used for atmospheric purposes. Any resemblance to actual people, living or dead, or to businesses, companies, events, institutions, or locales is completely coincidental.

Book Layout © 2014 BookDesignTemplates.com

BETRAYED The Dragon's Game Book III by H. N. Henry—1st edition

ISBN 978-0-9958367-8-5

Dedication

To my sister, Corinne.

If you have done terrible things, you must endure terrible things; for thus the sacred light of injustice shines bright.

—SOPHOCLES

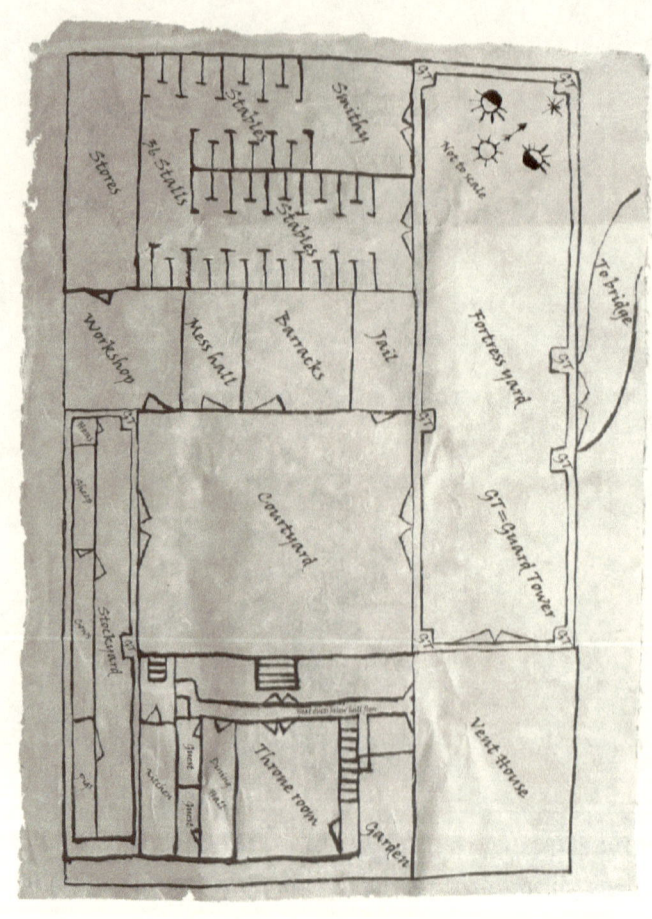

Hand-drawn map of the Isle of Smoke Fortress
Dangor will show the raiders upon arrival.

CHAPTERS

The Hundred *Mitâtahtomitanaw* 1

The Dragonwood *Paskwaskisiw sakâw* 13

The Warning *Neyak Wihtamâkewin* 25

The News *Âcimostâtowin* 33

The Reunion *Awîyak Kanakiskaht* 47

The Plans *Itasiwewin* 55

The Capture *Kahtinikewin* 79

The Rescue *Pimâcihiwewin* 101

The Oath *Kihcipikiskwewin* 117

The Hunt *Mâcîwin* 127

The Illusion *Mahtawinikewin* 135

The Secret *Ka kaskamoci kanaweyihtamihk pîkiskwewin* ... 145

The Key *Âpâpiskahikan* 155

The Wolf *Mahihkan* 183

The Island *Ministik* 191

The Fortress *Sohkîsihcikewin* 203

The Cage *Kipahitokamik* 221

The Rider *Otêhtapiw* 241

The Dream *Pawâtamowin* 259

The Chains *Sakâpihkan* 271

The Bridge *Âsokan* 285

The Cave *Kawihkwehcipayik* 293

The Lesson *Wapahtihikosiwin* 307

— † —

FROM BANISHED
THE DRAGON'S GAME
BOOK I

Legend tells us dragons fly so high they can see the future.

Reason tells us that to know the future is a curse.

*Our hearts tell us the seeds of hope are sown in the reality of
the present.*

— † —

FROM BRANDED
THE DRAGON'S GAME
BOOK II

Reality tells us that to lose hope is to welcome death.

— † —

The Hundred
Mitâtahtomitanaw

— † —

Hope tells us light lives even in the darkest places.

— † —

Back then, dragons no longer flew over that land, but the one that hoped to fly in those skies again watched over Nagora, for she was the one the dragon now needed most.

On that day, Nagora, as Edana, the dragon-warrior princess, looked up above the gates of the stone wall that protected Skull Bay from invasion by land. There stood Godomor the Terrible, King of the Land of Skulls, with the splayed fingers of his hand over his heart in the dragon-chord salute. He extended his hand to salute Edana.

2 · H. N. HENRY

Below the wall Nagora returned Godomor's salute before turning her horse, Storm, to follow Godomor's Hundred Best warriors who had volunteered to fight for Edana's Cause.

As Storm turned, Nagora reached into the opening at the neck of her cape, grasped the dragon tear amulet she wore, closed her eyes, and held it to her lips. *Dragon, Edana is on her way. I will free you. You will no longer be Raganora's captive.*

She opened her eyes and held onto her amulet.

The double column of the hundred horse-mounted warriors and their pack mules stretched out ahead of her, a hundred and sixty animals in all. At that moment, the mantle of responsibility she had taken on fell on her like the weight of all those warriors and their animals. *But I'm not alone in this enterprise.*

Tagnyoriva, my mum, Sagora, my twin, you ride at the head of the line with Godomor's son, Gabe. Mum, all your years of planning for The Cause, and working to win Godomor's support for it, have finally paid off. I know you'll only believe it when we cross into the Land of the Danu.

Gabe, you lead the Hundred Best. Sixty archers and forty warriors armed with swords, axes, spears, and shields. Gabe, this is your opportunity to earn the title "the Terrible" like your da, grand-da, and great-grand-da before you. It's your chance to prove yourself to be a worthy leader of warriors in battle so you can become Gabyndor the Terrible, the future King of the Land of Skulls and its people.

Godomor, I feel your eyes on my back. In my short time in your land, you became a father to me. Our last words together at the celebration in your Grand Hall still ring clear in my mind.

…

Godomor had pulled the big blade from its sheath and pointed to the etched Tiwaz symbol. "For a higher cause. It will inspire my best warriors to follow you, Lone Wolf."

"Father, I wear the Tiwaz. But that does not make me their leader. Gabe will lead them."

"He will. But you will lead their hearts."

"But I am not a leader."

Godomor placed his hand on hers. "Edana, they know your story. They have witnessed your actions. They have chosen to be part of your story."

Nagora held tight to Godomor's hand with both of hers. "Father, my wish tonight is that they return with a story that will make you proud of your daughter." For a moment she was lost in his smile, savoring the strength it gave her.

Godomor, your words still give me strength, despite my actions. Nagora's shoulders shook for a moment. She took a long breath. It had all worked out for the best. So far I've lived up to Edana's reputation.

Raynhard, as you asked, I'm bringing the Hundred Best so I can, as Edana, help you win back your crown and punish Raganora for all the evil she's done to the Land of the Danu and its people. First, we act on the promise you made me, then we free the dragon.

Raynhard, I hope you will have good news of my da on our return. Mum and Sagora have rarely mentioned him since my arrival. Do they know something I don't? Have they been keeping it from me, like so many other secrets that have been kept from me? It must be something you know too. I've guessed what it is. All the pieces point to it. I hope it's true. I hope Da is alive.

Nagora looked at her amulet. I've worn you since birth. In these past two years you've revealed so much to me. I understand now, but at times I was sure my mind was playing tricks on me.

A voice spoke words that set me on this path. Words, though they were strange, I understood as if they had always been part of me. That voice called me *Ka Peyakot Mahihkan*, Lone Wolf, the name Godomor used when he spoke to me in private in the tongue of *The People*. He had confirmed it's the same tongue the dragon speaks. Now I know I speak their tongue. What other powers will you reveal?

To fight for The Cause is my destiny. Hag, you foretold it the first time we met. "Child, a dragon awaits you." Even today your words chill me. Not for fear of the dragon, but for my wish to exact revenge on you. Hag, I know you're an evil witch. I know you fear me and the powers my amulet give me. You're Raganora's witch, and I will destroy you.

Nagora's uncle Dangor rode at her side. Uncle, you trained me. You raised me and taught me all the warrior skills I possess. You trained me and Sagora to ride on horses with flaming hooves to deliver Edana's message. You're the person I trust the most. Thanks to you I've learned to trust in myself.

Lars rode on her right, followed by his two giant wolf-hounds, Aydan and Lyam. Lars, you're my *masinaskisow nitisan*—branded brother and my *onâkateyimowew*—protector, as the voice told me. I believe our hearts were destined to meet. Unknowingly, we both chose the Tiwaz brand. Yes, we will fight for a higher cause. That is our destiny.

With these thoughts, the mantle's weight lightened. It became bearable. But deep in her heart, it was the promise she had made that lit the fire within her. I will be your justice. I will be your vengeance.

The Hundred Best battled the wind and rain on their first day along the coastal road and into the forest. All were wet and cold, soaked to the marrow. Cooking fires, lean-tos, and dry bedrolls were their only consolation.

The following morning, the rain gave the respite necessary to down a warm, hearty breakfast and repack their gear and break camp. They had just left the meadow where they had camped when the rain came again, steady and unrelenting, but without the wind.

Nagora peeked out from the hood of her rain-soaked, waxed woolen cape. It no longer kept her dry. "Sagora, your salve is a gift from the stars. It's doing wonders to soothe my cold wet backside in my saddle. Our second day on the trail and already my arse is being rubbed raw."

Sagora shook her head. "Yours and just about every warrior's butt."

At the end of the afternoon, the sky broke open, and the sun poured down on them. Gabe signaled a halt to set up camp early. Lars was happy as he dismounted. "Good move, Gabe. It'll give us, our animals, and gear a chance to dry out." He didn't waste time as he lashed spears together to make racks for their saddles. Lars stripped as soon as he finished setting his saddle on a rack.

Nagora looked at his muscled back as she brought her saddle to the rack. Would she strip? Why not? Everyone else is. Lars looks damn tempting. Get busy, girl. Hang your clothes to dry.

A warm mist and gentle breeze surrounded the warrior encampment as the sun went to work drying trees, vegetation, and warriors.

Most had not eaten since breakfast, so they lit cooking fires for an earlier meal.

The breeze strengthened and helped dry their clothes and gear. Even the shaggy coats of Aydan and Lyam were almost dry.

In the evening, just before sunset, the wind shifted, promising a cold night. By nightfall all had dressed.

Nagora and Dangor were among the ten pairs of warriors that rotated through watch duty that night.

As they turned in after their watch, Dangor confirmed what she had been thinking. "I'm impressed. These Hundred travel well and their camps are secure." For him to say so, he had to be pleased how the warriors kept guard on their watch. He had always taught her it was important.

On the afternoon of the fourth day, the Hundred Best made Godomor's hunting lodge in the hills bordering on the Land of the Danu. Gabe met outside the stone lodge with his three commanders and Tagnya, Sagora, Dangor, and Nagora. Nagora learned that as soon as the support of Godomor's warriors had been confirmed, Tagnya had sent a missive to

Geirador for Raynhard. The message had been picked up, but neither reply nor messenger waited at the lodge.

Could a different message have gotten through about Vorpinger trying to stop the Hundred from leaving, about what Nagora had done, and not how it had all worked out? Could her actions have caused more problems?

Tagnya obviously expected to find a reply at the lodge. "I'm worried something has gone wrong. What should we do?"

Dangor didn't hesitate. "No sense waiting for a message that might never come. Gabe, I propose Nagora and I go ahead with four warriors of your choosing to find out what's happened. We could travel light and fast without mules. We'll find out what's caused the delay and send back word to you as soon as we know."

Uncle's right. I hate waiting around, especially when I have to count. It seemed she was always counting time, though, now she did it without effort. A day's work was twenty-four counts, and a day was three times that. With the help of the sun, it was even easier. But waiting around and counting just to mark time was a waste.

"Good thinking, Dangor. When will you leave?" asked Gabe.

"Soon as you give us the four warriors. We'll ride until nightfall and continue on our way at first light tomorrow."

"Take Lars and his dogs." Gabe explained the situation to his three commanders and asked each of them to choose a warrior to scout ahead with Dangor and Nagora.

They each made their pick and said their choices would be ready in a count.

Tagnya reached out and touched Nagora. "Dangor, Nagora, be careful."

With her uncle she would have no choice. "We will, Mum."

Dangor gave Nagora's mother a reassuring smile. "Tagnya, we won't pick any fights without the rest of you." That made her smile.

The three riders were ready before the count was up. Their smiles told Nagora they were happy to have been chosen for this task, a welcome break in their routine. Dangor instructed them on the signals they would be using on the trail and what he expected of them. "I'll lead, followed by you, Lars. Nagora and the others will follow. You are all to keep within sight of the rider ahead of you." Lars translated and made sure the three chosen riders understood.

Just before they mounted, Dangor gave each of them a whistle arrow to use as a possible warning signal for danger. Nagora had used one a year ago in Windhaven to create a diversion and witnessed its effect. Shot straight up into the air, when it reached the end of its upward climb, it tipped to come back down, opening the wooden reed of the whistle near its tip. As the arrow gained speed, the whistle screamed louder and only stopped when it hit the water. It had frightened the large crowd at the harbor, too many people to be able to run for cover. All they could do was cover their heads and duck.

When Dangor was sure the warriors had understood, he gave the signal to ride. They would go as far as their mounts would take them before nightfall.

Dangor set the pace and rode for two counts. They crossed the Blood River into the Land of the Danu, leaving behind them the silent skulls that stood atop stakes as warning sentinels along the riverbank border of the Land of Skulls.

When Dangor stopped at the top of the rise, the others dismounted and watched as he took a stick and sketched a rough map of their destination in the dirt on the trail. It was the notch in the cliff face where Nagora and her uncle had spent their first night on the way to the Land of Skulls.

Lars conveyed the destination to his three companions.

Nagora, Lars, and the warriors rode in silence, following Dangor's pace, which he set for the horses' comfort and the terrain. He always stopped to dismount before going over a rise on the trail to check for signs of possible danger. When the way was clear he signaled with his hand for them to move on.

As Dangor had planned, the group arrived at the cliff with enough light to set up camp. They made a small fire to boil water for forest tea sweetened with honey to drink with their dried venison, nuts, and berries.

Dangor set the night watch according to their ages. Nagora had first watch. Lars was next and the three others followed. Her uncle had the last. The early riser got his way. He smiled at the two big hounds at Lars's side. Yes, Uncle, they'll keep watch too.

By dawn's earliest light the riders had broken camp and were leading their mounts to the trail. Until the sun had risen on the horizon, they rode in single file behind Dangor, separated by five horse lengths apiece. Then Dangor picked up the pace.

The riders arrived at the spot near the ledged cliff where Nagora and her uncle had hidden their pack mules the day before leaving for the Land of Skulls. Dangor led them to the high ground above the cliff where Geirador lived on the outskirts of Cairnmase.

On the way there, he led them along a path that led to the cache of fire arrows. At the cache, Dangor lifted a corner of the tarp to show the bundles of arrows stacked and waiting to be tied to the pack mules the Hundred led.

Lars's eyes grew wide. "There must be thousands of arrows!"

Dangor smiled at the warriors who were obviously amazed. "Ten thousand, as promised. Before we leave for the campaign, the Hundred will stop here to get their fire arrows. Each one is ready to have its tip touched to a hot flame and have an archer send it on its fiery way."

Lars conveyed the information to his companions. "That's more than enough to set a kingdom ablaze."

Visions of the fire arrows Nagora had shot at the Temple of Fire came back to her. *Hag, I came close to setting you on fire. If you hadn't pulled free from your cloak, you would have become a torch.*

Strips of cloth, soaked in liquid tar, were wound tight and left to dry in place just behind each arrow's tip. The strips of cloth closest to the arrow heads were still damp with liquid tar. It was what made them so lethal once lit. A simple dousing with water would not put one out. One had to pull it from where it struck to immerse in water or jab into the ground. Stomping on one to put it out guaranteed the stomper a flaming foot as the molten tar stuck to the sole of the boot.

Next, Dangor led the group on foot up the tree-covered slope. When they arrived near the top of the cliff, they all followed his lead and crouched as they approached the edge. Geirador's home sat below.

Sure enough, from this vantage point, they could see Geirador's shop, the stable, corrals, pastures, and the road from Cairnmase that led to the smithy.

Further beyond, the rocky, tree-covered projections of Cairnmase stood as silent witnesses—tall cairns around which the stone dwellings of the hamlet were built. From this vantage point it was clear how Cairnmase got its name. For strangers venturing there, it must truly be like entering a maze to find one's way.

But today a smoky haze hung over the hamlet. Most of the stone dwellings with thatched roofs had been burnt. Fire had also scorched a field of barley near one of the lodges on the edge of Cairnmase.

Nagora's stomach took a turn. "There's no one in sight. There's not one animal in all the corrals. What's happened?"

Dangor propped himself higher. "No bodies on the ground. I'm guessing the people went to hide in the Dragonwood."

Lars frowned. "Dragonwood?"

Dangor pointed a thumb over his shoulder. "Aye, Lars, a haunted plot of forest many will not dare enter. Human and animal bones of all kinds hang from the trees at its perimeter. Story is a ghost dragon lives there with the Little People."

"Is that true, Uncle? I've seen it from afar, but have never been there," said Nagora.

Her uncle raised an eyebrow and showed the hint of a smile. "What's a place like Cairnmase without a legend to be used to good effect?"

"Are we going there, Uncle?"

"It's our best chance to find Geirador to learn what happened here."

Uncle doesn't seem too concerned. That might change when we get there.

From the way the warriors reacted to what Lars had told them, venturing into the Dragonwood worried them.

Nagora swallowed as her stomach tightened again.

On the way back down the slope, Dangor stopped at a stand of hazelnut trees where he cut a branch. He left the leaves and young fruit growing on the forks and skinned the lone branch below the fork. "Cut yourself a branch like this. When we get to the Dragonwood, stick it in the back of your shirt so the fork branches stick out on either side of your head. You won't be visible to the ghost dragon and the Little People won't bother you."

Nagora caught a wink from her uncle as the others got busy cutting their branches. Oh! I get it. He wants me to play along. "Uncle, I've heard about this place. Why have I never been there?"

"Again, for your safety and that of our cause. You'll understand when we get there."

The Dragonwood
Paskwaskisiw sakâw

When the group arrived at the edge of the Dragonwood, Dangor shot a whistle arrow. As it began its descent, the sound was a distant hum that turned into a sharp scream as it raced back to the ground.

"If Geirador is in there, he'll find us. We're going in. Single file. Keep a horse length between us. Slow and steady and don't panic. Make no abrupt moves. Don't draw your weapons unless I tell you. And Lars, signal your dogs to stand down." When Dangor was sure Lars had made the message understood, he led the riders past the hanging bones.

Despite Uncle's wink earlier, was it the bones or the quiet that had Nagora on edge? How does Lars feel right now? And the others?

A lone crow cawed from the canopy of leaves above them. The surrounding silence chilled Nagora as they moved deeper into the Dragonwood.

Pare, are you in here? Has something happened to you?

Dangor signaled a halt. He remained motionless in his saddle.

He must be listening. Did he hear something?

Nagora looked around at the others. Their eyes tried to look everywhere. They were expecting the worst.

What would someone watching six warriors on horses with hazelnut branches sticking out of their shirts be thinking? Laughter of every kind burst out all around them.

Geirador's familiar whistle sounded. The laughter died down and he stepped into view from behind a tree. "Welcome to the Dragonwood. Good to see you." I'm happy to see him. I'll be happier when I see Pare.

Dangor leaned forward in his saddle. "Good to see you, Geirador. What happened at Cairnmase?"

Geirador held up his hand. He would get to his friend's question in a moment. He called out, "All clear. You can show yourselves. They've come in peace. Two of them you know."

At least thirty people appeared from behind trees, all armed with bows. They were putting their arrows away.

One fellow with a huge grin on his face stepped forward. "We like your antlers. You can doff them now."

Dangor did and wore a big smile as he looked at the others. The tension on the warriors' faces faded into bashful grins upon realizing Dangor's prank on them had been for a good reason. They all dismounted.

Geirador approached and shook Dangor's hand. "I take it these are your friends."

Dangor nodded. "From Godomor's Hundred Best from the Land of Skulls. Lars, this is Geirador, the man who saved

Gabe's life, who made our blades, and who trades mead with Godomor."

Lars and Geirador shook hands.

When Lars translated the introduction, the warriors reached back and touched their blade gifts in appreciation. Lars spoke for them. "We are pleased with the gifts sent in the name of your rightful king. Your skill in making these blades is beyond compare. What we are most pleased with is the medicine you sent. It helped Tagnuska heal Godomor, our king."

Geirador smiled at Lars and his companions. "I'm glad you like the blades and I was most pleased to read of the success Tagnya had in caring for my friend, your king, Godomor. I look forward to meeting his son, Gabe, again. He must be a man now. I don't think I would recognize him."

Lars held up five fingers and brought them down to his thigh. "He still wears the scars the bear left him, and the bear's paw."

Geirador turned to his forest companions and waved a hand at them. "These are good folk from Cairnmase." And he addressed them. "Looks like we'll have guests for our evening meal. Let the cooks know. In the meantime get back to your work. There's a lot to do."

They obeyed Geirador and dispersed in small groups, heading off in different directions.

I recognize most of them and know the names of the ones I once trained with.

As Geirador turned back to the riders, his look became more somber. "I've been taking care of the people from Cairnmase. We've set up here temporarily. We lack nothing and as you know, Dangor, we're well armed and ready to fight on our terms here.

"So when you didn't find me or my reply message at Godomor's lodge, you scouted ahead."

"That's right. Gabe, Tagnya, and Sagora will be along with the Hundred. Slower going with the pack mules. They should arrive in a few days."

Something's bothering Geirador. What's he keeping from us? I want to know. "Geirador, what happened in Cairnmase? Was anyone killed or hurt?"

Geirador took a deep breath. "We got a return visit from Prince Acindor's guards, led by the captain of one of Queen Raganora's units. This time they came looking for more than news of a maiden who may have escaped with her life from the prince's dungeon sea cave."

Dangor's look was one of concern. "Were they looking for armed rebels?"

"Aye. The day you two left, I set about moving anything that could link us to the weapons we've been making, all our molds and patterns and samples. I brought them here and hid them. Then I moved and hid all the weapons we had stock-piled here. Just in case someone from Cairnmase had sold us out. If that's what happened, Acindor will have a hard time pointing to the proof."

"Where's Pare?" asked Nagora.

Geirador pursed his lips and breathed deep through his nose. "I was here on their second visit, three days ago. Paruline was out riding with three younger girls. Three others were waiting at the corral for their turn to exercise the horses. The prince's guards left with the three girls and a dozen hors-es."

Nagora's fists clenched. "Oh! No!" If they fall into the hands of Acindor and his jailor, their lives will be in danger.

"And they searched most of our homes. Ransacked them. Set fire to the ones with thatched roofs. One of the barley fields caught fire."

Three days ago. We can't wait longer. We should do something! "Have you planned to free them?"

Geirador's chest expanded. "Paruline insisted she go Prince Acindor to intercede on behalf of the parents of the three girls."

Dangor was shaking his head. He looked worried. "She'll be questioned."

"Aye, we figured as much. We planned what she should tell if questioned about you and Nagora. We think she'll have a convincing story that'll free the girls."

Pare is so brave. "When did she leave?"

"Yesterday morning."

Nagora imagined the worst for her friend. "And if she doesn't return?"

"We knew you were on your way and that if she didn't return, we could rescue her with your help."

She stepped closer to Geirador. "You must be worried for Pare."

"Paruline can hold her own. She'll explain who she is and that I'm the one who's done much of the finer ironwork in the prince's fortress. And that I provide the best trained horses for the queen's mounted force. She'll explain that she helps train the horses and that we often use young people to exercise the horses. That's why the three young girls were at the corral, waiting their turn to ride with Paruline. If Raganora's captain and Acindor have the least amount of sense about them, no harm should come to her."

Dangor ran a hand through his hair as he looked at Geirador. "You hope."

"Aye, I hope."

"Is Raynhard at the fortress?" asked Dangor.

Geirador shrugged. "He could be. I'm guessing not. He left seven days ago to meet with area leaders loyal to The Cause to establish the latest number of rebels who support our cause. Word is the numbers have been growing. He wanted to get the information firsthand to report to us before we start the campaign."

"That means he'll be missed at the fortress. That length of absence won't be normal," said Dangor.

Geirador raised an eyebrow and shrugged. "He's done it before. How he pulls it off, I don't know. He could be back already. I know he wanted to be back before your arrival."

Dangor placed a hand on his friend's shoulder. "Geirador, if we have to, we'll free Paruline. Don't worry. We'll come up with a plan."

Geirador smiled and placed a hand on Dangor's and his other on Nagora's shoulder. "What happened to you, Nagora? I thought you were coming back with your twin sister, not a twin brother."

Nagora forced a smile. "We are twins, in a manner of speaking. Our brands are the price paid by twins returning to the Land of Skulls. Lars is a returning twin. Lucky for me, he set the precedent for the branding."

Geirador looked into her eyes. "I know there's quite a story behind that. I look forward to hearing it. Though, those many years ago had I known your mother was carrying twins, I would not have sent Tagnya there to seek refuge."

Nagora patted his arm. "Don't fret about it. I think it was in my star's path to happen. Mum can't wait to see you again."

"Nor I, her. Come, we'll walk a ways. I'll give you the tour of our temporary home and show you to your lodgings."

Geirador led them on foot deeper into the Dragonwood. Nagora and the others led their mounts. When they came to a stream, they followed its shore until it turned into a cascade and then into a waterfall. There, they left the stream and went into a valley with massed mounds of earth and huge boulders spread among the forest trees. She spotted a Cairnmase trainee atop the highest boulder.

Guard duty.

They arrived at a horse line where a dozen mules and three horses were tied. "You can tie your mounts here after you remove your saddles." They passed guarded, penned corrals made of dead trees that had been felled, stacked, and tied together to hold pigs, sheep, and a few goats. Further on was a tighter fenced-in area where a simple coop held hens.

Geirador pointed to the big tarp strung from overhead tree branches. "The outdoor cooking area provides shelter for the cooks and the food they handle. The cooks baked the first batches of stone bread today. Much appreciated by all."

Past the cooking area they came to a honeycombed array of cave openings in the biggest mound. Geirador held out his arms. "Here is where we live. Each family has its own sleeping area. We have plenty of caves like these for all of us."

A little further on Geirador showed them a bigger cave. "You'll spend the night here with me. You can bring your saddles in there. Dangor, I've got what's necessary for you to write a missive for Gabe and Tagnya. I expect you'll have that ready for whoever returns with the news tomorrow."

"Aye, that'll be Lars and his companions. I'll set to work on it soon. I don't like writing by candlelight."

Once the scouts had unsaddled and taken care of their horses, Geirador brought them to what he called the common area where people met and ate their meals in shifts, given the few tables and benches set up so far. "We're comfortable, though eager to get back to rebuild and fix our homes. That'll be soon. Perhaps we'll head back before the force arrives. People are itching to get even."

Dangor raised an eyebrow and smiled. "That could be sooner than they think."

Geirador shrugged. "Things could have turned out worse. We could have fought back, but with the force coming, we knew it wasn't worth risking lives. Had it been closer to winter, no question we would have."

Cairnmase was a second home to Nagora. Playing with the younger trainees had shown her all its advantages. "Archers in the cairns could have picked the prince's guards off, every one of them."

"Aye, Nagora, that's so," said Geirador. "But then a garrison would show up to put down a rebel force. Not the time to have that happen. Not yet, at least. But we've planned for that eventuality."

Dangor had just set down his saddle. "Geirador, where shall we all meet when the force arrives?"

"How about that cliff face with the ledges where you and Nagora brought the pack mules before leaving for the Land of Skulls? There's a nearby meadow for the force to set up camp. We'll pitch a meeting tent near the cliff. Raynhard thought it would be a good place. He should be there with us waiting for the Hundred to show up."

"I agree. We rode by there earlier. I'll show Lars tomorrow and put that in the missive too."

After having eaten, Dangor set to work on the message by himself at the mouth of the cave.

Nagora and Lars told stories of their adventures as twins in the Land of Skulls to Geirador's eager ears. When they had finished, Geirador dropped a last log onto the embers of his fire. "Had I heard your stories from strangers, I would never have believed them. Reality can be stranger than the stories we make up. Nagora, Lars, all I can say is I'm happy to see both of you alive. You must tell your stories to Paruline. She'll not believe me if I tell them. They'll have me dreaming tonight."

After their morning meal, at first light, Dangor gave Lars the missive for Gabe and Tagnya. Geirador rode with them to where they had entered the Dragonwood the day before. Nagora and Dangor accompanied Lars and his three warrior companions to the ledged cliff face so Lars could get his bearings.

"Lars, we'll be waiting for you here. If we aren't here, it won't be a good sign. Come for us at the Dragonwood with your friends." Uncle pointed to the three warriors. "Use a whistle arrow like I did. Someone trustworthy will meet you.

"The meadow where the Hundred can set up camp is just yonder." Dangor pointed.

Lars gave a thumbs-up. "I remember. We let the horses drink at the stream near there."

"Aye, that's it."

Lars nodded as he looked to the meadow. "Our Hundred can camp on the perimeter of the meadow and let the horses and mules graze there. At night we'll tie them to horse lines near the stream."

When the group arrived at the trail, Nagora dismounted to have a last tussle with Aydan and Lyam. Lars dismounted and walked over to her. "You're making me wish I were a dog."

She smiled. *If we could have had more time together, alone.* "I want you to take them both, Lars. They brought you back the last time we were apart. I know they'll do it again."

"We'll be back in a few days." He reached his big arms around her. His body armor combined with the pressure of his embrace brought her big blade, quiver, and bow in contact with her back. *With you at my side I'm invincible. And I want you in bed at my side.*

Nagora looked up into his eyes, reached for his face, and brought his ear close. "I can't wait to hurt you again. Go now, so you can come back sooner." She stood on tiptoes, gave him a quick kiss, and punched his embossed leather breastplate. In return, she got what she wanted, his grand smile.

He helped her mount Storm.

Dangor's eyes follow the four warriors until they disappeared on the trail. *Was he thinking of Umma?* "Would you be planning to get wounded in this campaign so you can return to the Land of Skulls on sick leave?" asked Nagora.

Dangor turned in his saddle to face her. "No, when I return I want to be as fit and able-bodied as possible. But you've given me something to consider. I'll go back with the wounded to make sure they get all the care they deserve until every one of them fully recovers." He adjusted Umma's scarf at his neck. He had been wearing it since they left.

Nagora smiled at him. I'm happy for you. "Where to, Uncle?"

The Warning
Neyak Wihtamâkewin

"How about we ride through Cairnmase, then we make a run home to see the situation there? And then we'll check on the beach hut," said Uncle.

"Can we spend the night at home?" asked Nagora.

"We'll see when we get there."

At Geirador's corral, Dangor turned to Nagora as he dismounted. "Lassie, you have a look in Geirador's home. I'll check on his shop."

Nagora nodded and rode on. What is Paruline doing right now? Is she okay?

As soon as Nagora left Storm at the hitching post not far from the door, images of Paruline kept slipping into her mind. Pare cutting fresh chives from the clump that grew near the door step. Pare at the door, waving to her. Pare setting the table, preparing vegetables, making bread, starting a fire, climbing the loft ladder, heading into the cold room, picking stored fruit.

Nothing in the home had been disturbed to spoil these images from her memory. Nagora left to go report to her uncle. "They must have decided to ignore what looked like a small hut, as seen from the corral."

"Aye, and with horses and the three young girls, they had a worthwhile take. They had done enough damage before in the village."

"Uncle, those girls must be terrified. They'll have been questioned. When I first learned to ride, knowing my story was the first thing Geirador taught me in case we were ever stopped. He always tested me on it."

Dangor sighed. "Fear, under actual questioning, can throw anyone's story off. Let's hope Paruline kept it all together and what she tells them matches what they know."

Nagora and Dangor rode on into Cairnmase. A lookout waved them through.

Dangor waved back to him. "Geirador said a half dozen would be working here today, sorting through the rubble to see what can be salvaged and taking stock of the repair work to be done."

Nagora's eyes scanned the insides of the roofless huts. "Some will have a rough go of it, cleaning charred and soot-stained stone walls. Not exciting work at the best of times." She had cleaned soot and smoke-stained stones around their fireplace with beach sand brought home for that job. It helped occupy long winter days. Rub wet sand into the dirty stones. Let it dry in place. Brush it off. Repeat until no soot left its mark on a clean hand pressed to the stones. Tar piss! A thankless job! "It'll be a memorable winter for the children strapped with that chore."

Dangor looked at her. "And you thought you had it rough!"

"Do you think some people just won't bother?"

"Could be. They'll live with the smell year-round and it'll become part of them."

"Like when we tar the seams on the curraghs?"

"Aye. And you know how hard you work getting that off you when you go for a swim at the end of the workday."

"Do I ever."

"Because you get to wash yourself so often, you notice those that don't. Nothing like seawater to clean out your nose and make smells sharper."

"Speaking of smells, Uncle." Nagora pointed.

They came across a charred and bloated carcass of a dog and its six pups in the middle of the road. A man with a shovel and a barrow approached. "So far the only dead victims we found. The bitch brought out one of her pups. Went back in for the others. Got trapped with 'em. The young lad has the lucky one with him in the Dragonwood. Can you guess what the pup's name is?" The man pointed. "I dug a hole on the other side. Rather I bury them than my own young."

Dangor nodded. "Aye. I hope you grow old and never have that task."

Nagora stared at the carcasses. Her nose tried to sort out the odors. She tried to recall the smell of her own flesh being branded. There was a memory of it. It was not among those that assaulted her nose at the moment. Perhaps my nose didn't catch it in the wind and rain.

The dull feeling of the burn remained in that spot where she could go to summon it. Though, finding her way there was becoming more and more difficult as that spot in her mind receded in the distance. Even with the aid of her reflection in a mirror, the visual remnant of the branding, her chosen Tiwaz, was taking over and becoming as familiar as its feeling against the tips of her fingers.

No more pain. Something I can see. Something I can touch. Something I chose. Something others see on me. Something I see them react to.

"Lassie, we're going home."

Home, that place where Nagora had lived with her uncle all those years still brought back that same image to her mind.

When will "home" have a new meaning?

Dangor set an urgent pace. Or is it because we're not in our cart being pulled by Patches?

Disbelief, incomprehension, pain, and anger—they all assaulted Nagora at once as they left the forest trail and came upon the remains of their home on the meadow's edge.

Words would not come to her mouth as Dangor dismounted. Uncle, tell me what I see is real. The way he walked with his hands hanging at his sides, motionless, told her his pain must match hers, or worse. Nothing remained standing of their lodge he had built with his own two hands and the help of friends.

Someone had torn out everything made of wood, piled it outside, and set it on fire. Did they set the fire before or after tearing the stone walls down and scattering the stones? Every part of their lodge that hid the rocky outcrop, against which Dangor had built it, now lay somewhere flat on the ground, humbled. Whoever had destroyed their home with such utter force had done so with calculated and deliberate intent.

Dangor finished his walk through the rubble remains of their home and returned to his mount. "It's a message."

"From who? Acindor?"

He held the reins in his hand as he gazed around at the remains. "Queen Raganora. She knows the girl with the dragon tear amulet lived here."

Nagora clenched her teeth. Aye, well, when that girl gets her hands on your son, Raganora, she'll make him pay. "How would she know?"

Dangor pulled himself up into his saddle and sighed. "She has her eyes in the land, everywhere. Someone has told what they know, and what they know could have been enough to point to you."

"Does she know I'm alive?"

Her uncle shook his head. "She has no proof you're truly dead, taken by the sea. I doubt she has proof you're alive. In case you are, she has left you a message." Dangor pointed to the charred remains of the fire and the scattered stones. "'This is what I'll do to you, if you show up.'"

When I show up, Raganora, you won't believe what I'm going to do to you. "But you lived here with me too."

"It's also a message to anyone aiding the Dragon Warrior Princess."

"Uncle, had you been here, they would have wanted to question you about me, like the two soldiers who came here the day before we left. Perhaps they came looking for those two missing soldiers. Perhaps they went to look for you in Cairnmase. They're probably still looking for you."

"Could be. If they've been thorough, they'd have spoken to anyone who's done business with me and they'd have asked about you too. That I have gone to cut ash in the forest to make curragh frames will have become an old story by now. Those in these parts who know me will have been questioned and asked to report my return, no doubt. As for the two soldiers we dispatched, unless someone witnessed our actions, they can't link us to their disappearance."

"Could they have someone watching for us, even now?"

"If they have, I haven't spotted them. Let's go see the hut." Dangor kneed his mount. "We'll have a look from the clifftop. It could be a likely trap, depending on how hard Raganora is pressing Acindor for information."

As far as Nagora could see from the cliff above, nothing had changed at the hut on the beach. The two curraghs above the highwater line had not moved. The one on its anchor at the water's edge needed to be emptied of the rainwater that had accumulated in it. She couldn't detect movement in the hut.

Dangor turned away from the edge of the cliff. "When Raynhard gets back, we'll have a better idea of the situation. And if Paruline returns, she'll give us more information too."

"Uncle, I know where Raynhard could be hiding. I'll go there to find out."

"You won't. Did he give you specific instructions about his hideout?"

"Yes, but—"

"He did for a reason. Respect his instructions. If he's there, he'll get to us. The worst that could have happened is that he's been found out somehow. It won't be by us who know his three identities. And for all I know, he may have a fourth identity. At this stage in our planning I doubt he'll have become careless and done something to be discovered."

Nagora had first known him as The Watcher, the one who watched her from far. Her uncle had assured her he meant her no harm and that she would meet him one day.

When she thought she was meeting The Watcher, Dangor introduced her to Raynhard, the rightful King of the Land of the Danu. And that day he revealed his secret identity as Chive. That had been a shock because she had met him as Chive, Hag's idiot scrounger for wild herbs and mushrooms. Raynhard was playing the role to perfection when she was captive in the prince's dungeon, awaiting her execution. Chive had helped her escape from the dungeon sea cave. The Watcher had saved her from drowning after she had swum to her freedom. All three, the same person.

Her uncle was right. Raynhard wouldn't do something foolish to put The Cause in danger. "So back to the Dragonwood to wait?"

"Aye. We'll make sure we aren't being followed."

The News
Âcimostâtowin

Nagora looked forward to tying Storm to the horse line. She had spent most of the day in the saddle and needed to stretch her legs. She led Storm on foot and followed the lad who had greeted them on their return to the Dragonwood. He was bringing them to the caves by another route so as not to wear a trail that could be followed with ease.

They unsaddled their mounts, stored the saddles in the cave, and returned to the horse line.

Grooming and feeding the horses allowed her to reflect on her day. Someone had destroyed all the physical references to the home where she had grown up. It hurt and angered her. If Raganora can do that to my home, what will she do when I show up as Edana to free the dragon?

"Uncle, how do you feel about no longer having a home?"

Dangor rested an elbow on Kimmo's back and held the brush still for a moment. "It always hurts to see something you've worked hard to build get destroyed, especially when done with deliberate intention like that. We have to look at it as warriors at war. It's the cost that's often paid in war. The country and the homes of its people get destroyed before it can be rebuilt. That's something we wanted to avoid by taking the fight to Raganora on the plain opposite the Isle of Smoke.

"Raganora is striking out at all signs of rebellion. She's hoping to strike fear in us. Instead, she'll reap rebels with greater resolve to carry the fight to her."

Geirador's familiar whistle signaled his approach. Nagora and Dangor both looked up.

"You're back. Long day in the saddle, Nagora?"

"Long and painful. We no longer have a home."

"What do you mean?"

"Nagora speaks true. It's been torn down, not a stone wall left standing. Everything of wood has been burnt," said Dangor.

Geirador bared his teeth as he shook his head. "They must have connected you to the girl with the powers of the dragon. It confirms this was a unit from Queen Raganora come to show Acindor how to put down the local rebels."

If I only had the fire power of the dragon, I would burn Acindor's fortress to the ground, and Raganora's. "Why would she have sent them here?"

Geirador held up two fingers. "A report of a possible failed execution of the maiden with the powers of a dragon, and the continuing rumors of the coming of a Dragon Warrior Princess.

"The captain of Raganora's unit pushed the investigation further. He must have questioned anyone who had witnessed what had happened since Acindor rounded up local virgins. They had Dangor's name from the captain of Acindor's guard,

Nagora's name from the jailor. In trying to find Dangor for more questioning, Nagora's name must have come up. That linked the two of you and where you lived.

"Now they've got the girls. They were waiting for someone to go ask for their release. That someone is Paruline. They'll question her to get confirmation that Nagora is dead or alive. Either way, they'll want a body as proof."

Nagora shook her head. "But Pare doesn't have a body to give them."

Geirador nodded. "True, but she has a good story that could cause them to think Nagora is dead."

Dangor pulled on his beard and then pointed to himself. "What can she tell that will convince them I'm dead?"

"We agreed that, if she was questioned about knowing both of you, she would not deny it and stick to the story details you," Geirador pointed to Dangor, "had told the captain of the guard. And," he pointed to Nagora, "to what Acindor had learned from questioning you."

"As new information, she would tell that you were raised by your uncle, Dangor, that you worked with him to build curraghs, and that Dangor was distraught when he brought the news of your capture and execution, and that he had said that he was leaving to cut ash wood in the forest to make curragh frames to change his mind.

"But that when we found his mule wandering into Cairnmase by itself, Paruline herself went to his home to check on him. And when she didn't find him there, she went to his beach hut. He had mentioned that he had four curraghs at the beach, two with seams drying, one he was testing for leaks, and one of his own. Paruline found three curraghs at the hut. The set of oars from the hut and one of the curraghs were missing. Paruline feared that Dangor had killed himself out of grief."

"So they'll want Uncle's body too, won't they?"

"Paruline will plant the idea that he rowed out to sea, tied the killick anchor to one of his legs, capsized the curragh, and let himself go under, food for the fish."

Dangor cleared his throat. "That story would make me think twice."

The sun had just set when a lookout's whistle called. "Someone's approaching," said Geirador. Another whistle sounded, different than the first. "One of ours."

Soon a rider came into camp leading his mule. Geirador went to the rider, who whispered in his ear. He put his hand on the rider's shoulder. "Go find them. Tell them the good news and that we'll leave at first light. They're to meet us here."

Geirador was all smiles when he returned.

Dangor looked happy for him. "Looks like good news for you too."

"For all of us. Paruline is at home in Cairnmase, with the girls and The Watcher."

So he's back as The Watcher. She went to Geirador's side and hugged him. "You must be so relieved! That is good news! I can't wait to see Pare!"

Geirador hugged her back and kept his arms around her. She could feel his breath rattle in his chest as he breathed in to speak. "I'm so relieved. The parents of the girls will be too." When he released her, he wiped a tear from his eye with the back of his hammer-sized thumb.

"We'll pack a few mules tomorrow. We have a tent to set up for the meeting and animals to round up and pen for the feast to celebrate Tagnya's arrival with the Hundred."

Dangor saluted Geirador. "We're at your command, good smithy."

It was still dark the next morning. Nagora doubted the parents of the girls had slept. They were waiting with their mules ready to leave for Cairnmase. Two of the girls were sisters. Their parents each had a mule. The other parents had a single mule.

Even the friends of the girls showed up to ask their parents to let the freed girls know they would be seeing them soon. One young boy held a puppy in his arms. "Tell Mirra I only have one pup left. Tell her I'll share Lucky with her."

The mum tussled the lad's hair. "I'll do that, Tommi. She'll be sad to hear what happened to the others."

The happy parents surrounded Geirador as soon as he appeared. "How will we ever repay Paruline?"

He put a hand on a shoulder of one of the parents. "She didn't do it for payment. She loves your lasses as much as you do. Just say thank you and be sure to allow your daughters to ride with her again."

Geirador turned to Nagora. "How about some trail rations on the way? Knowing Paruline, she'll have a meal in the pot waiting for us when we get there. We'll call it a late breakfast."

Before she could answer, Dangor spoke. "Fine by me. Please get the horses, lass. We'll have the saddles ready by the time you get back."

Nagora nudged Geirador. "You know, I think my uncle's stomach is attached to his mouth, especially when it comes to anything Pare cooks."

As the group approached the meadow above Geirador's smithy, Nagora caught sight of the lookout up on the cliff.

All's clear.

Geirador stopped to speak to the parents. "Go on ahead as fast as you want. Leave the mules in the corral. Go right to the house. Your girls will be happy to see you."

The parents who shared the single mule made good time, riding several lengths behind the other two who each rode a single mule.

Before Nagora could say it, Dangor did. "I smell fresh bread." Geirador laughed.

As they brought their horses into the corral, Paruline appeared at the hut door. She whistled and waved.

Nagora waved back. She reached into her saddlebag and pulled out the sea ear. She left Storm saddled and ran toward the hut with the shell pressed to her belly.

Happy parents came out the door with their girls, warm loaves of bread, and hunks of cheese. Paruline was right behind them. She stopped when she saw Nagora.

It's my brand. "Pare, am I ever happy to see you."

"Oh! Nagora! So am I!" Paruline took her by the shoulders. Worry furrowed her brow as her eyes focused on the scars. "Why the Tiwaz on your forehead?"

"Just so you won't mistake me for Sagora."

"No, be serious."

"If you were in the Land of Skulls, I would be very serious. It's the price returning twins pay these days. In the past they were killed. I chose to be branded with the Tiwaz."

"Oh! My! Truly?" Paruline put her arms around her.

"It's a long story. I'll tell you one day soon. If I don't, well, your da will." She held out the sea ear to Paruline. "I found a birthday gift for you. I know I'm late. This makes up for the one I lost."

Paruline took it in her hands. "It's beautiful, Nagora. Where did you find it?"

"At a beach Sagora took us to. Mum has one like this in her kitchen. They're always using it. When I found it, I thought of you."

Paruline took one of Nagora's hands in hers. "Thank you so much. You can be sure I'll put it to good use.

"When did you arrive? Are your mum and sister here?"

"Three days ago. We spent two nights in the Dragonwood, but Mum and Sagora are with the Hundred. We came ahead of them to see why your da hadn't answered Mum's last missive. We found out why."

Nagora reached for Paruline's arms. "Pare, you're so brave to have gone to the prince."

Paruline sighed. "Nagora, I had to. I love those girls. I had to do something."

"Well, it worked. You deserve credit for that."

"Thank you, but Raynhard deserves credit as well."

"Is he inside?" Nagora pointed to the hut.

"No, he went to see firsthand the damage done in the village. He'll be back soon." For a moment the smile on Paruline's face disappeared as she bit her lower lip and glanced down, taking a breath before looking up with a smile.

Nagora hugged Paruline. "Your da will be happy to see you."

"I think so." She pointed and let go of Nagora. "Here he comes."

Paruline ran to her father. He held her and spun her around. When he set her down she hugged him and she hopped over to Dangor and gave him a hug too. She showed them the shell.

Pare, we're lucky to have these good men in our lives.

Further down the road, Raynhard was on his way. Nagora pointed. Dangor turned to look, as did Geirador and Paruline.

Will Pare tell of her night with the king? Did the girls sleep? Did Pare sleep? She doesn't look too tired. She seems to be in a good mood. I wonder what she'll think of Lars when she meets him. What'll Raynhard think?

When Raynhard had reached the three, he shook Dangor's hand in greeting. Then he put an arm around Paruline's shoulder and his other hand on Geirador's shoulder as he spoke to them, looking from one to the other. He took hold of one of Paruline's hands and spoke more to her. His hands then went to her shoulders, and he embraced her.

Well, Pare, if that's not taking notice of you, I don't know what it is.

As they walked toward the hut, Raynhard held on to Paruline's hand as he spoke to Dangor and Geirador.

I'm happy for you Pare. She left the doorstep to go greet Raynhard. Did Mum inform him of my branding in one of her messages? Pare had been surprised, Geirador not so much.

...

"Nagora, I am so glad to see you again." Raynhard's eyes had immediately gone to her brand and then to her eyes and back to the Tiwaz. He reached out to embrace her. His breath on her ear where it met her cheek and her neck brought back the memory of the last time he had held her, but the feeling was not the same.

"Raynhard, I'm glad to see you."

He held both her hands. "I'm a lucky king to have subjects like you and Paruline. Both of you have shown immense courage in your actions." He let go of one of her hands and took up one of Paruline's, bringing her next to Nagora. Then he bowed before them. "'My Ladies of Valor' I call you today, and I bow before you in thanks. Someday, I hope to bestow greater reward on you."

Nagora looked to Paruline and smiled. She was biting her lip again and staring at the ground.

Am I blushing too?

Geirador approached with a big smile. "The man hasn't got his crown on his head yet and he's already taking his job seriously."

Dangor nudged Geirador. "Shows he's been well brought up by King Bernhard and Queen Julianna. They would be proud of him."

Geirador scratched his beard as he looked Raynhard up and down. "True. True. I'm proud of him too."

Paruline was shaking her head. "Da, you're embarrassing me."

"Sorry, my dear, for making light of the moment. It was that or cry again. I did plenty of that last night."

"Never be embarrassed by your da, Paruline. Like Dangor would say, 'He's worth his weight in horseshoes,'" said Raynhard.

Nagora shook her head and smiled as the three men bent over laughing and pointing at each other like young boys.

Raynhard spoke first, barely getting his words out. "Sorry, Geirador, without my crown on my head, I couldn't let that one go by." Their laughter continued.

Paruline took Nagora's hand. "And they want to put him on the throne. Come."

Paruline's comments had brought on another wave of laughter and it followed her and Nagora back to the hut.

Paruline had picked up the pace and her smile left her face. "Pare, what's wrong?"

She opened her mouth as if she were about to speak, and then brought a hand to her mouth. Then she took it away. "I must be tired and all these events. What happened to the girls. What happened to you and to our village here. So many things could have turned out worse. All this has finally caught up with me."

Nagora hugged her. "I know the feeling. You'll get over it."

After their late breakfast meal, Nagora spoke to Raynhard. "Pare told me you too deserve credit for getting the children released."

"Well, yes, without knowing what had happened at Cairnmase, when I met with area leaders, I was able to arrange for a fisherman from further down the coast to visit Acindor to report that his son had found two bodies, both of young women, on two different occasions while out fishing.

"One covered in scratches with what appeared to be bite marks on the breasts, neck, and shoulders, and rope burns at the wrists and ankles.

"The other, wearing the shreds of a garment, was also covered in scratches with arms tied so," he indicated how Nagora had had her wrists tied, "above her head, her eyes open, and her mouth open as in a scream."

Good thinking, Raynhard.

"That fisherman showed up the day before Paruline went to intercede. When Acindor and Raganora's captain questioned Paruline, her answers satisfied them. The captain and his contingent were on their way back to the Isle of Smoke even before Paruline left with the girls."

"What about my smock I left hanging in the iron ring?"

"From what I've heard, the jailor had thrown the clothes of the two previous victims into the sea cave. They figured that smock must have washed back in and gotten caught there during the highest tide. Also, the jailor had found a dress on the sea cave taper."

"So you were at the fortress?" asked Nagora.

Raynhard nodded. "I had shown up drunk, two days before the fisherman. When I go looking for roots and herbs in the forest, I also set snares. I sell the hares I catch. When I get enough coins, I go on a drunk and don't come back for days. At least that's what I've been able to make Hag believe over the years. Since it's not been a regular occurrence, she's tolerated Chive's longer absences."

Dangor leaned back on his chair and patted his stomach. "Thanks to Paruline, I'm ready to put up a hundred tents today. Shall we get to it, lassie? I think Raynhard will be setting his thoughts straight for the meeting we'll have when your mum arrives. Geirador will be joining us once he's assembled the animals to be butchered and the cooking spits and utensils."

Geirador shoved past the cellar door, a keg of ale in each arm. "And the ale. I've got two more of these and a keg of mead. My cellar'll be dry after this. Next batches I brew will be to celebrate the crowning of our rightful King Raynhard."

Dangor got up from his chair. "We'll drink to that for sure. Paruline, once again, my stomach and I are in your debt. I'm sure I speak for the others here."

Paruline smiled. "I'm pleased that you liked it. Nagora, I'll see you later. I'll be adding finishing details on one of the maps for the meeting, based on what Raynhard learned from the area leaders."

Raynhard looked to Nagora. "Paruline's been busy for The Cause since you left. I truly value her work."

A sense of ease and positive complicity between Paruline and Raynhard seemed evident in the warmth of Paruline's smile, though, when she lowered her gaze, her smile disappeared. Is she just tired or is something not right? Big sister, we've been through a lot. And there's more to come.

Nagora and Dangor set up the meeting tent and prepared two firepits, a small one a dozen paces from the tent entrance, the other much bigger and farther away near the cliff where the roasting spits would be set up. They had just finished improvising a temporary pen with dead branches and small trees for the animals when Geirador pulled up with a big cart carrying the pigs, goats, sheep, a calf, and at least two dozen hens. "You two haven't wasted your time."

Dangor walked to the back of the cart. "And neither you. I'll help you pen the animals. Nagora, can you take care of the spit poles and supports?"

"Will do."

"Dangor, you figure they'll pull in by noon tomorrow?" asked Geirador.

"At the latest. No sense in pushing it to come in here in the dark."

Geirador pulled the firepit support poles from the wagon and stood them up for Nagora. "I can't wait to see your mother again."

"She can't wait to see you, either. Your name must have come up at least twice a day while I was there. She admires you greatly." Nagora bent a knee to lean the metal support poles against her shoulder to hoist them onto it.

"And I, her." He pointed to the side of the wagon. "I'll lean the spit poles here."

The rest of the day was one of trips to and from the Dragonwood, ferrying residents of Cairnmase set on rebuilding homes as soon as possible and others who would set up defensive positions and conceal caches of bows and arrows high in cairns throughout the village. Future attackers would ride into a death trap.

In the Dragonwood, Geirador showed Nagora and Dangor the locations of the weapons' caches he had personally concealed. "Just in case. Tomorrow morning, we'll bring back a number of these bows and arrows destined for rebels who'll be joining us for the battle on the plain. We'll spread them among the Hundred so not to have to bring extra mules."

A last night in the Dragonwood. Lars, tomorrow I'll see you again. I've missed you already.

The Reunion
Awîyak Kanakiskaht

The next day, Aydan came running toward the meeting tent near the cliff where Nagora was talking to Paruline. "Aydan! You big boy, you've come to get me." She submitted to a face wash. "This is the hound I was telling you about. They must be near. Okay, Aydan. I understand. We'll go meet them."

When she had finished her mandatory petting and hugging of Aydan, she left the tent and pulled herself up on Storm. "Aydan, take me to Lars." She waved to Paruline. "I'll be back with Mum."

"And your big sister."

"Yes, and Lars and Gabe."

Tagnya walked into Geirador's big arms and took his gentle bear hug. "Just look at you. You haven't changed. Just a tiny bit thicker here." She stepped back and patted his belly.

"Tagnya, the years have been kind to you. You're as fair and as fit as I remember you."

Geirador smiled at Sagora. "You must be Sagora, Nagora's big sister. You're taller than her, by a hair."

Sagora took his big hand in hers and gave it a vigorous shake. "You're right. I'm Nagora's big sister." She turned to Nagora. "See, I told you, I'm taller than you." Geirador laughed with them. "I've heard so much about you, Geirador, that I feel I know you."

Geirador reached out to Nagora and Sagora with his big arms. He looked from one to the other, gave them a hug, and handed them over to Tagnya. "Tagnya, you must be so happy to have your daughters with you. I, for one, am happy for you."

Nagora looked at his face. There's something he's not saying. Almost as if he wants to say it, but can't. What's he holding back? News of Da? Good or bad?

Tagnya gave Geirador another hug. "I can't tell you how happy I am to be with them."

Geirador pointed. Gabe was approaching with Lars.

Dangor put a hand on Geirador's back. "I think it's been a while since you've seen him."

Geirador reached out to embrace Gabe. "A while! Aye! Well, look at you, lad! Had you been this size when you met up with the bear, you could have turned him inside out before I came along."

"Geirador! My savior!" Gabe stepped back and showed his thigh with the scars. He brought the bear paw scrip that hung behind him to the front and placed its claws over the scars on his thigh. He held up the paw, opened it, and retrieved two arrowheads. "From your hunting arrows, Geirador, when you killed the bear."

Gabe reached over his shoulder and tapped the handle of the big blade Geirador had sent as a gift. "Today, I'm better armed than I was back then. Geirador, on behalf of my father, myself, and our Hundred Best, I thank you for the fine blade sets you sent us. We're most pleased.

"Father is on the mend thanks to the ingredients you sent to Tagnuska to make his medicine. You and Tagnuska brought my father back to life. For that, he is most grateful. Again, he thanks you for that cask of your mead which, he says, makes life worth living. He says he can't wait to finish taking his medicine so he can savor your most delectable mead."

Geirador smiled wide. "I'm glad to hear that he's in better health and pleased with my gifts."

Tagnya looked around. "Has Raynhard arrived yet?"

Geirador pointed. "He should be in the tent with Paruline."

Tagnya made her way toward the tent just as Raynhard and Paruline stepped out. Nagora and the others followed. Within three paces of Raynhard, Tagnya dropped to one knee, bowed, and offered her hand. "Your Majesty."

Raynhard took her hand and had her stand before him. "Tagnya, please, save your bows for another occasion, and 'Raynhard' will be fine." He opened his arms and Tagnya stepped into his embrace.

She held him by his shoulders, moved back a pace, and looked him in the face. "My! What a handsome man you are, Raynhard. If only your parents were alive to see you as I do."

Raynhard smiled and hugged her again.

Paruline had been watching. Tagnya went to her. "Paruline! Your eyes and your smile tell me it's you. You've truly become a most beautiful woman."

"Thank you, Tagnya. And you are as beautiful as I remember you. Though, today you aren't with child."

Tagnya hugged Paruline.

Nagora approached with Sagora. "Raynhard, Pare, though she needs no introduction, I want you to meet my big sister, Sagora."

Sagora stepped forward and was about to go to one knee and bow.

"No! No! Please, I should be the one bowing. Two Edanas stand before me. Two Dragon Warrior Princesses whose future deeds will make Edana famous." Raynhard held his arms open to embrace Sagora. Then he held her hand, took one of Nagora's, and looked from one to the other. "It's true, Sagora, you are taller than Nagora."

Geirador tapped Raynhard on the shoulder. "I've already told her that."

"You never miss one, do you, Geirador?" Raynhard smiled.

Nagora put an arm around Sagora's waist. "Until I found out about you, I always considered Pare as my big sister. Now I have two. So meet your big sister, Paruline. I call her Pare."

Sagora hugged Paruline. "I'm most happy you are my new big sister."

"And I, Sagora, am happy you are my new little sister. Twin sisters no less. How lucky I am."

Tagnya stepped forward with Gabe and Lars. "Raynhard, Paruline, this is King Godomor's son, Gabyndor. He prefers to be called Gabe. He leads Godomor's Hundred Best warriors. They will help make our cause Edana's cause."

Raynhard reached out to shake Gabe's hand. "Gabe, it's my pleasure to meet you. The reputation of the warriors of the Land of Skulls reaches beyond your borders. Thank you for maintaining and honoring our old alliance. Gabe, as soon as you and your commanders are settled in, we will meet in my tent to explain the situation in our land and the maneuvers we have planned for this campaign. Do you think you can be ready in four counts?"

"Raynhard, I can assemble them sooner, if you wish."

"In four counts. Let the trail dust settle and refresh yourselves."

"Very well. We'll be here then."

Gabe reached out with both hands to Paruline's. "I would not be here to greet you today had it not been for your father. I owe him a great debt. Paruline, if ever there is something I can do for you, just ask. No favor will be too big."

"Thank you, Gabe. I'm most pleased to meet you. Now the image I had of you from my da's story will change. I wish you and your da long lives."

"Thanks for your kind words."

Tagnya had a hand on Lars's back. "Raynhard, Paruline, meet Lars Marraden. No doubt you've heard of him from Nagora and Dangor."

Raynhard smiled. "Actually, Geirador told me of Nagora's twin brother. Tagnya, you must be pleased to have him as an adoptive son."

"That I am, and he comes with these two. This is Lyam and this is Aydan." The two great wolf hounds sat on their haunches at the mention of their names, looking proud. Lyam in his iron colored coat and Aydan in his rusty pelt brought a smile to Raynhard's face.

Lars held out a hand, while his other touched the crossguard of his big sword. "Raynhard, it is an honor to offer my sword in service to you."

Paruline's eyes took in all of Lars as he and Raynhard shook hands.

Raynhard placed a hand on Lars's shoulder. "From what I hear, I'm already in debt to your services for taking care of Nagora, our Edana."

"I do so not as a duty, but a pleasure."

His words, his grand smile when he winks at me that way. I must be blushing crimson.

Lars stepped toward Paruline and reached out a big hand.

Paruline took it as she gazed up into his face.

Lars bowed. "Paruline, as Nagora's twin brother, I'm happy to call you my sister. Since I dare not ask a lady her age, I'll not dwell on whether you're my big or little sister."

Paruline hesitated a moment before replying. She hadn't let go of his hand and her eyes were still riveted on his face. "Lars, my brother, I'm most pleased to meet you. If I were to call you big brother, it would regard your size, and not your age."

Lars's smile grew wider. How I love your smile, Lars.

"Raynhard," Lars nodded in Tagnya's direction, "Tagnuska has asked me to attend the meeting to help translate for Gabe's commanders. I'll see you then."

"Very well. Glad you will be there."

Gabe and Lars left. Paruline held Nagora's arm as they watched them walk to their mounts. She brought her other hand to her open mouth, touched it, then pointed, and mouthed two silent words, "Lars. Wow."

Dangor placed a hand on Nagora's shoulder. He held Sagora's hand with his other. "Well, lassies, let's leave your mum some time with Raynhard and Paruline. We'll go set up with the Hundred at the meadow."

Geirador patted Dangor on the back. "Dangor, I forgot to tell Gabe to invite the Hundred to the feast after the meeting. Tell him what we'll be roasting on the spits. There'll be a limited amount of ale and mead. Ask them to bring their bowls."

"They'll be glad to hear your invitation," said Dangor.

Tagnya had been listening and rushed to Geirador's side. "Oh! Geirador! You're ever so generous. How can I thank you?" She gave him a big hug. "You're worth your weight in gold, Geirador."

Dangor snorted. "Gold? Perhaps horseshoes, but not gold."

Geirador smiled and pointed both fingers at Dangor.

"Tagnya, it's the least we can do for guests like these. You know me. Anyone who comes to my home is welcome at my table. Officially this is Raynhard's land, but I consider myself caretaker, and so my privilege. See you at the meeting. I have a feast to prepare."

Nagora hugged Paruline and then her mother. "See you later."

The Plans
Itasiwewin

Raynhard greeted Gabe and his commanders near the tent's firepit. Gabe introduced his commanders. What Nagora had learned about them wasn't much. Tankar was a burly warrior who took pride in the axe skills of the warriors under him. Bullidor was the tallest yet lightest warrior at the meeting. He wasted neither words nor movements. Romanika, the only commander who was an archer, was known for her stealth and swiftness of foot. She was an unmatched hunter.

Lars held the tent flap aside for Tagnya and her twins. Raynhard followed with Gabe and his commanders. Dangor and Geirador came in last.

On entering Raynhard's meeting tent, Nagora examined the two big maps embroidered in colored yarn on natural wool blankets that hung from the horizontal support pole on one wall of the tent. Only Pare can produce such maps with the necessary detail clearly set out. Surely they meet with Raynhard's approval.

One map showed all the Land of the Danu. It comprised a huge peninsula, with the sea bordering on the three sides and the Land of Skulls bordering at the top. The two countries together formed one big island. Small islands dotted the coast of the Land of the Danu. Paruline had indicated coastal waters, forest and mountain areas, rivers, roads, and villages, as well as the coastal and crossroad lookout stations. All these items had separate colors and their own symbols.

As Nagora went to the next map, Gabe and his commanders moved in to look at the first one.

The other map showed the Isle of Smoke with a detailed layout of its fortress and the bridge leading to the mainland plain, where Edana would wage war with Queen Raganora's troops to free the dragon.

Also, it showed the forest hills above the plain where Edana's troops would camp before the battle.

Lars, Gabe, and the commanders sat on the first of the long benches facing the maps. Nagora sat on the next bench with her mother, sister, uncle, and Geirador.

Below the maps was a small table. Further over in the corner was a bigger table with a chair.

Raynhard wet his lips with his tongue, scratched his chin, and looked to Tagnya. "Before we get started, I must speak with Tagnyoriva and her daughters. While I do so, Gabe, Geirador will give you and your commanders an overview of the maps. We'll return shortly."

What's this about? He could have pulled us aside outside. The pit of Nagora's stomach began to knot. *Are we finally* going to get news about Da? She looked to Sagora who wore a frown and shrugged her shoulders.

Raynhard held the entrance flap aside for them, followed them out, and led them toward the face of the cliff.

Tagnya was silent and kept up with Raynhard's quick pace.

Nagora hadn't been able to see her mother's face before leaving the tent. Should I expect the worst?

About three hundred paces from the tent, Raynhard stopped at a spot with several big rocks. With his back to the cliff face, he spoke. "Nagora, Sagora, your mother has important news for you. You will want to sit while she tells you."

Why should we sit?

Sagora sat on the nearest rock and patted the space next to her. "Come, little sister."

Nagora took a deep breath and sat.

Tagnya looked at them and then to Raynhard. She reached out for his hand and looked back at them. "I've been waiting a long while to tell you this. Earlier Raynhard confirmed what I'm about to tell you. It was my wish I be the one to tell you and no one else." Tagnya paused and took a deep breath. "And it was my wish you not be told until now."

Good news or bad?

"My daughters, I beg you to reflect well on my reasons for not telling you before."

This doesn't sound good.

"Nagora, I especially beg you to try to understand why you are only being told now."

Sagora stood. "Is this about Da?"

Tagnya let go of Raynhard's hand. "Yes!" Tagnya's eyes opened wide and filled with tears as she took another breath.

Is she about to cry, or is she just very happy?

"Your da is alive! Yogari is alive!"

Nagora stood to join Sagora. "Mum, where is he?"

Tagnya swallowed, pursed her lips, and clasped her hands to her breast. "On the Isle of Smoke. He's Queen Raganora's prisoner—with the dragon."

Sagora rushed to her mother's side.

Nagora sat on the rock again as all the pieces of information fell together, confirming her guess. She had dismissed them in the past because of what she had been told about her father. How many times had the truth of his whereabouts nearly been revealed? So Da is the Dragon Talker, the Rider, one and the same! Moreena, why didn't I ask your da the name of the Rider? I had planned to, but events got in the way. Edana happened.

All these years this too had been kept from me. What would I have done had I known before?

An uncountable number of images flashed through her mind.

She shook her head. Just as well. I can't go back and change that. My path has brought me to this moment. Now I can act. Da, I'm coming to free you. A dragon awaits me.

Tagnya and Sagora stood before her.

Sagora held out her hand. "We will be a family, Nagora, a family! With a mum and a da! Four of us, Nagora! Together!"

Nagora took Sagora's hand, stood, and they placed their arms around their mother. She had to ask. "How is he, Mum? After all these years, alone with the dragon in a cave?"

"From what our source has told us, he appears fine."

"Did that person see him?" asked Sagora.

"From afar, yes. Your father is seen when he steps into the cage lowered in the vent hole to send down water jugs and food supplies for him. That's about every two weeks. Food for the dragon is sent down more often."

What must it be like down there? Could I even stand it? He must be living on hope. "Is there a way he can get news from the outside? Is he aware of The Cause? Of our plans to free him?"

"Nagora, we can't say. Our source won't take risks unless he's sure he won't get caught. And he won't tell us about anything he's been able to send to Yogari."

He's not trusting anyone. He doesn't want to be ratted on. At least he's been talking to someone in The Cause, and it's a sign he's smart. If he's smart, he just could let Da know certain things. Da surely needed something to feed his hope all these years. I know I would.

"Sagora and I will free Da. We will free Yogari! Mum, you'll be with him again. And we'll free the dragon!"

Tagnya wiped tears from her face.

Raynhard stepped closer. "Well, Sagora, this news gives new importance to Edana's role, doesn't it?"

"It does. Now we have a personal stake in The Cause, your Cause."

"And you, Nagora?"

"The sooner your meeting gets started, the sooner we'll be on our way to free Yogari and the dragon."

Raynhard smiled. "Well then, let's do that." He showed them to the tent.

The twins took Tagnya by the arm and followed Raynhard.

...

In the tent, Raynhard waited until Tagnya and her daughters sat. "Tagnyoriva asked me to share this good news with you. Her husband, Yogari, is alive in the cave with the dragon on the Isle of Smoke. Our source tells us he is well, at least he seems to be physically fit. Yogari is the Dragon Talker. If we free him and the dragon, we'll see a dragon fly in our sky once again and what Edana foretold will come to pass. The people of the Land of the Danu will rise up and return their country to its greatness."

Gabe stood and looked to Tagnya and her girls. "Tagnyoriva, that truly is good news. I'm happy for you and your daughters." He turned to Raynhard. "And you, Raynhard, will take back your rightful crown and lead your people in rebuilding their country."

"Thank you, Gabe. Let's get on with the meeting so we can move to free Yogari as soon as possible. I will start with the situation in the land. This is based on information I've been able to glean from my source who eavesdrops on Prince Acindor and the witch, Hag, in the prince's fortress here at Yhorgal Cliffs."

Good Raynhard. Keep it simple.

Lars helped Gabe translate for the commanders.

Raynhard pointed to places on the map. "We're here. This is Cairnmase where Geirador lives. Here, the town of Yhorgal, and the prince's fortress here on Yhorgal Cliffs.

"I also have information from my meeting with rebel leaders from across the land loyal to our Cause. They shared information from other neighboring leaders who did not attend. And I have information from our spies who've been able to report.

"The one key element throughout the land is that many of the people who make up the work force are no longer as docile as they once were. Whatever poisoned their water supply is no longer there or not as potent, especially in the smaller villages. People are grumbling. They realize all these years of living as subsistence farmers has left them in a vulnerable position, courting disaster with no surpluses to fall back on.

"They realize they have to care for themselves and ready themselves for winter. They must revive fallow fields to get a good planting in for enough to harvest for the winter. A small surplus would be nice. They see the sorry state many of their homes and buildings are in. As they come out of the stupor Raganora put them under to control them, they see all this extra work ahead of them. It's a discouraging task. What this has done is increase rebel support for our cause."

Tankar and Bullidor spoke to Gabe. Gabe put up his hand. "Does their support for your cause go as far as being willing to take up arms and join in a fight?"

"They are more than willing. When they get the call to arms, they'll show."

You sound very confident, Raynhard. That's good. You'll be giving confidence to Gabe's commanders.

Raynhard continued, "Next, Raganora's mercenary replacements are long overdue. Their duty rotation has gone beyond a year. All the mercenaries have recently moved to Windhaven and are holed up in King Bernhard's castle. All work site overseers, and even those commanding local troop garrisons, are there.

"That has put Queen Rag in a weakened position. She now has to find loyal leaders for her troops among the ranks of the local forces. Not an easy thing to do on short notice, considering how disdainful the mercenary commanders treated the local forces. And we know many of the locals only joined to put food on their families' tables.

"Also, word is the mercenaries are threatening to leave on the next mercenary boat that comes to harbor, or perhaps sooner, by taking over a boat that could bring them home.

"Hag sees that as a negotiating tactic to get more pay to stay."

"When did the last mercenary boat leave?" Tagnya asked.

"A little over two years ago," said Raynhard.

"Does that mean when one of their boats arrives, it brings a replacement contingent and supplies? The departing mercenaries leave with whatever Raganora has agreed to pay them in gold and silver?" asked Tagnya.

"That's been the routine," said Raynhard.

"If Queen Rag is going to negotiate with them, she'll need to make an offer they'll not refuse," said Dangor.

"I doubt she has the resources to do that, for if she did, she would not have lost them as commanders of her own troops in the local garrisons," said Raynhard.

"Where is Queen Rag right now?" asked Dangor.

"Latest report says she's on the Isle of Smoke," Raynhard pointed to the map.

"And Prince Acindor?"

He pointed to it on the main map. "At his fortress on Yhorgal Cliffs."

"It looks like our time to strike is at hand," said Geirador.

"The sooner we set our plan in motion, the better," said Dangor.

Raynhard nodded in agreement. "As soon as Raganora gets reports of Edana and her force heading for the Isle of Smoke, she'll need to deal with her reluctant holdout mercenary force, especially if another confirming report is brought to her by Acindor and Hag."

Raynhard paced before the maps. "Recently, we've seen Raganora send one of her own units here to Cairnmase to put down suspected rebel activity and teach her son a lesson in how to deal with rebels.

"If things heat up in Yhorgal, Prince Acindor will most likely want to hightail it home to Mother on the Isle of Smoke. She most likely won't leave the isle to go set up in Windhaven with the mercenary force there, unless that is part of a deal she can strike with them. Mind you, if she did that, it could change our plans."

"I don't see that happening," said Tagnya, as worry etched her face. "Raganora is a sly one. She wouldn't risk having the mercenaries turn her over to us for their safe passage out. Besides, if she moved from the Isle of Smoke, it would mean moving Yogari and the dragon, a dangerous proposition because she would have so little control over them. As it is now, on the Isle of Smoke, they're under her complete control. She can send them crashing into the volcano's vent. They're her hostages."

Tagnya briefly turned to her daughter. "From what Nagora learned, Raganora, because of an agreement with Hag, is keeping the dragon alive until Prince Acindor produces a male heir to the throne.

"Raganora will know Edana is coming to free the dragon. There has been no mention as yet of freeing Yogari. How she'll play her cards, we don't know. Personally, I don't see Raganora freeing the dragon on condition we all go home and leave her alone. She could just as well kill Yogari and the dragon. Or use them to negotiate."

Nagora stood. "We need another card in our hand. We can get that card two days from now, three at the most. We just need to act."

Gabe's commanders shifted on their bench to look at her.

Tagnya looked at Nagora. "How so?"

"Take Acindor as our hostage. Give Raganora a reason to negotiate. Remember what Hag had told Acindor about me when she saw my amulet. Here's my opportunity to come back as Edana to seduce him and take him hostage."

Tagnya shook her head. "I don't know, Nagora."

"Mum, I can do this. I have a plan. With Sagora's help, we can capture the prince, I'm sure."

"Well, what's your plan, daughter?"

"I need more time to piece it together, Mum. Let Raynhard finish briefing us. I could learn certain elements that will pull my plan together."

"Do you or don't you have a plan?" demanded Tagnya.

Bullidor raised an eyebrow.

Dangor placed a hand on Tagnya's. "Give her time. Your daughter has a good head on her, and she's taking this seriously. I'm confident as soon as she's ready, we'll know her plan."

Raynhard cleared his throat. "Dangor, I'll let you brief us on the appearances of Edana."

Nagora's mind raced with the possibilities of a plan. *We need to trap Acindor like we trapped Vorpinger. We must appeal to what he wants most.*

With the map of the Land of the Danu, Dangor explained the twelve Edana appearances they had planned. The commander's eyes were on Dangor.

Nagora caught snippets of it. It was very much as Dangor had explained to her and Sagora. " ... six by each of you ... simultaneous appearances ... every two nights over twelve days ... reports of Edana appearing in two places at once will put her farther and farther apart."

We must get him out of the fortress. We need to lure him out.

"Dangor, have you had the twins try out the fire baskets for the flaming hooves effect?" Geirador had obviously asked the for the benefit of Gabe and his commanders.

"We've had two successful trials." Dangor was pleased to provide that information.

"Well, that's good. I've added another element to Edana's appearances. I figured she would need something distinctive on the banner she leaves planted in the ground at each place. Something else to reinforce what the people see, besides the flaming hooves."

"What's that, Geirador?" asked Dangor.

Geirador retrieved the banner from the table and unfolded it to display to his audience.

"It's a horned horse!" said Tagnya. "It looks like a horse with a narwhal tusk sticking out of its head."

Romanika was pointing at the banner as she listened to Lars translate.

What's a narwhal?

Geirador nodded. "That it is, Tagnya. Only those who have been to Ice Island would recognize it as that. I call it a unicorn. Dangor gave me two narwhal tusks in a trade years ago. Every time I looked at them, I told myself they could be put to good use. Dangor had told me about the sea creatures the tusks come from. I got to thinking about what land creature could support such a tusk and came up with putting one on a horse."

Uncle has never spoken of this animal to me. I don't ever recall seeing such tusks.

"After many tries, I finally came up with a harness helm that will hold a decent length of one of these tusks onto a horse's head. The next thing was to train two that would be happy to wear these for several counts at a time. Well, I've got two white mares trained that'll wear the tusks. Believe me, seen from a distance, they make the most wondrous animals I've ever seen graze in a meadow."

Uncle had told us Geirador was working on something. So Edana, you'll be riding a unicorn!

Tankar and Bullidor looked around. They had big smiles on their faces.

They won't believe until they see it.

Geirador continued, "I've got fifteen of these flags with white unicorn heads on them and three Edana shields with unicorn heads embossed on them.

"I've trained the two mares to run alongside fire, just as the mounts of Dangor and Nagora do. Edana will make appearances at night on a white unicorn with flaming hooves.

On the spear she plants, there will be a unicorn banner. What say you?"

The pieces of Nagora's plan fell into place. A message!

"Wow!" said Sagora. "That'll draw people to the Isle of Smoke. I would go just to see a unicorn. Geirador, I can't wait to see one of your unicorns!"

Geirador wore a smile. "They're a sight to behold. Paruline made these banners and helped me train the mares. She says she dreams about them now and wishes they truly existed. She loves to watch them in the meadow in the early mist of the morning. 'The most beguiling of creatures,' are her words."

Dangor put his hand up. "Your, or rather Edana's, unicorn will fit in with the date we've chosen to free the dragon, the Feast of Maxxa, protectress of horses and of crops. Some will say that Edana rides a unicorn because she is under Maxxa's protection. Proof of this would be the unicorn's hooves of fire, like the bonfires lit throughout the land on the night of Maxxa's feast."

Before Dangor could speak further Nagora stood. "Here's my plan." All eyes were on her as she explained how Edana could make her first appearance at the prince's fortress with a banner bearing a message for Acindor. Instead of the message to join her at the Isle of Smoke, it would be a message to join her in her tent set on the road leading up to the fortress.

Sagora had been listening intently. "I like your plan little sister, but will he have the balls to come out to meet you on his own, or will he bring an audience with him, if you know what I mean?"

Romanika and Bullidor smiled once Lars translated Sagora's comment.

"Or will Hag hold him back like the first time he met you, Nagora?" asked Dangor.

Raynhard had been scratching his chin as he listened. He stood. "Nagora, since the time you spent in Prince Acindor's dungeon, he's been blaming you for his problem. He thinks you put a curse on him before the sea took you away, even though he had the problem already. If you do return, your words may very well lure him to you."

Tagnya crossed her arms, looked at Raynhard, and then glanced back to Nagora. "I'm not convinced he'll come alone."

Nagora held her mum's gaze. "Maybe he won't. But he'll be tempted. He has a special relationship with Hag, most likely sexual, from what the jailor said." She looked to Raynhard for confirmation.

He shrugged. "I can't say for certain. I know on occasion Acindor spends the night with Hag in her chambers, behind locked doors."

Nagora pointed to her head. "Acindor doesn't think with this. That useless tool between his legs is what drives him. It's his obsession. As was his perverted idea of setting up the virgins in the Temple of Fire in Windhaven for his own personal pleasure.

"If Hag fears me, he could be tempted to see if my powers can get it to work properly."

Gabe's commanders chuckled amongst themselves.

Sagora stood again. "Add this to your message, little sister: 'The fire of your desire is meant for me alone. Only with me will you sire a son for your throne.'"

"Perfect!" That'll get him thinking. My big sister has the heart of a bard.

Tagnya looked at Sagora.

"What?" asked Sagora.

"I didn't say a thing, daughter. I'm just realizing you're a woman."

"Good idea, big sister. That'll go with what Hag said about my powers of fire. If he wants to connect his desire with fire, that's all right with me. Once he's in the tent, we've got him. So, what do you think?" Nagora looked around at the others.

Dangor looked from Tagnya to Geirador to Raynhard and back at the twins. "It could work."

Raynhard was nodding his head in thought.

"I'll be in that tent, Nagora, to watch over you," said Tagnya. "We'll work out the details later on how to protect you should he not come alone."

Tagnya turned to Geirador. "Do you think this will call for a change in the message Edana will give?"

"Only on this first appearance at the fortress."

"Acindor for my Yogari? What for the dragon?"

"A unicorn," said Sagora.

"If only it were so simple," said Tagnya. "We have two unicorns and we don't have the prince yet."

Raynhard spoke. "Your plan could work. If we get him, that would leave his servants, his guards, Hag, the jailor, and the prisoners in the fortress. The question is: Will he go for it? Will he leave the fortress? Will Hag let him? If she does and we get him, Hag will want the news to get to Raganora as soon as possible.

"He's been through all the girls, but without success. Of those, we know of two who have met their fate in the sea cave. Recently, another two laughed at his shortcomings and they're now in the dungeon awaiting punishment," said Raynhard.

An image of the bruised young girl the jailor had carried out of the neighboring cell came to Nagora's mind. "The third girl, Vorpinger's daughter, Sellannye. Is she still alive?"

Raynhard pursed his lips and nodded his head. "Yes, poor child. Geirador told me how you learned who she is."

Gabe and his commanders shuffled uneasily on their bench at the mention of Sellannye.

Her beast of a father will never harm another person again. My trap saw to that. The beautiful damage an axe can do.

"Nagora, after your execution, to try to appease Acindor, Hag had Chive search the sea cave for your body or a part of your body so she could have something to use to make a charm to relieve your curse," said Raynhard.

Nagora pointed to the warriors seated before him. "You better explain who Chive is, Raynhard."

Raynhard did so for the benefit of Gabe and his commanders before continuing. They nodded their understanding.

"I was down in that cave at low tide. From the rock they had left you standing on, I could walk about ten strides until the water came up to my neck to where the cave ceiling slopes downward into the water.

"I took a deep breath and swam along for another body length to a spot where the ceiling rises again. I soon had my head back out again and found myself looking out on a calm sea. I was at the mouth of the cave that opens onto the sea like a giant arch. Since it was low tide, I figured the sea must rise at least to the top of the arch at the highest tides, three body lengths above my head or more."

Nagora raised a finger. "So in the right conditions at low tide, the sea cave dungeon is accessible from the sea, and it would be possible to free the prisoners held there. The jailor could be caught off guard and dispatched."

Raynhard pursed his lips and tilted his head from one side to the other. "It's a dangerous place. The risks are great as the state of the sea can quickly change."

"When did you go into the cave?"

"At mid-afternoon."

"So in two days from now, when would be the next low tide at night?"

Raynhard closed his eyes for a moment before answering. "Somewhere between midnight and dawn. I'll check on which count from midnight. Am I thinking what you're thinking, Nagora?"

"Those girls suffered enough at the jailor's hands. I can take him and save those girls, provided they can swim the short distance you did, Raynhard. I could use a rope and in-flated air bladders for them to hold on to in case they can't swim. I know I can do it.

"We could bring three curraghs to the mouth of the cave to help me. Couldn't we, Uncle?"

"I need more information on what you plan to do, Nagora," said Dangor.

"The same night we take the prince, under the cover of darkness, I could make my way to the nearby cliffs and dive to the waiting curraghs. The lookout to seaward won't be on the job. He'll be watching Edana's tent from the gate wall with the others to see what success his prince is having."

Romanika had turned to listen to Nagora. As Lars translated, she raised an eyebrow.

"Only if the sea conditions are right, Nagora. If the day's winds are gentle, the sea should be calm," said Raynhard.

"I want to be in one of the curraghs," said Lars.

"Good, Lars," said Dangor. "You've just made my job easier. I'm glad you volunteered. I can arrange for the curraghs to be there."

I knew I could count on you two. "Once Acindor is in our hands, give me a count to make it to the cliffs. Then make the prince vanish with Edana."

Tagnya looked worried. "Nagora, are you sure you can do this?"

"Don't worry, Mum. I've seen the plans of the fortress. They include the depth of the waters that surround the cliffs. Don't they, Geirador?"

"Aye, they do."

Tagnya had lifted her hand to her cheek. "You've taken such dives before?"

Nagora jabbed her uncle, who spoke up. "Diving has always been one of her favorite games. The higher the better. And she knows at which height to go in feet first to avoid hurting herself. As long as she knows the depth of the water, she can't be stopped."

Dangor turned to Lars. "I'll give you a length of rope as a measure of the minimum depth for her dive. Find a spot deeper than that and Nagora will be fine."

Lars gave him a thumbs-up.

Raynhard added, "I witnessed her dive. Like I said, only if sea conditions permit and the curraghs are in place to help you, and they've done soundings to be sure the water is deep enough."

Nagora raised her hand. "We mustn't forget about the other girls in the fortress. What if we do this?" She held up two fingers. "Well before sunrise, we shoot two arrows at the fortress gate. One of them is on fire to make sure we get the guards' attention. The other carries a message in which Prince Acindor orders all the prisoners be set free since he has found his princess bride.

"The prince could also order all who bear arms in the fortress to leave the fortress to follow him and his bride, Edana, to the Isle of Smoke to free the dragon. They must do this before sunrise. If they do not, one hundred Edana archers will rain arrows of fire down on them. If they pull out before the sun is up, we'll let them ride where they will."

Tagnya was shaking her head, her fingers pressing each side of her forehead. "I doubt Acindor would even consider doing that. He'd never convey orders in that way. It looks like we'll see the fortress go up in smoke. Let's hope the prisoners make it out safely, if at all."

Silence settled inside the tent.

If I get my way, at least two who mistreated prisoners will not make it out alive before the sun rises.

Raynhard spoke. "Chive will see that the prisoners escape from the fire."

Dangor sighed. "Either way, by the next day we're on the road to have Edana make her appearances as planned. The mercenaries will get news of Acindor and Edana. Will they use that to bargain with Raganora? We'll only know later on."

...

Then Dangor explained the daytime appearances of Edana and her troops near specific crossroad lookouts.

Gabe and the commanders listened with renewed attention.

Dangor also explained how the force would be divided in two. The warriors of Tankar and Romanika would go with Nagora, Dangor, Lars, and Mina; the warriors of Bullidor and Gabe with Sagora, Tagnya, Raynhard, Geirador, and Paruline.

Next, he explained the potential battle on the plain before the Isle of Smoke—a diversion for the raiders that would attack the Isle of Smoke Fortress from the sea.

Gabe's commanders looked at the Isle of Smoke map with keen interest. Tankar spoke to Gabe who translated the question. "Can you tell us how the raiders will take the island?"

Dangor explained how he would lead the small force that would land on the sea side of the Isle of Smoke, scale the cliff, infiltrate the fortress, take control of it, and if possible, free Yogari and the dragon. He pointed to Nagora and Lars. "I want these two with me."

Nagora swallowed as her heart swelled.

Dangor addressed Gabe and his commanders. "I'll need six of your warriors. Three must be archers, crack shots. The other three warriors must be able to fight in close quarters. Put that to your commanders. I would like Lars to be here with me to show the raiders the Isle of Smoke map before Geirador takes down this tent. He'll do that before sunset."

Gabe nodded and turned to his commanders and Lars. After they had consulted, Gabe gave a thumbs-up to Dangor. "In a count after the meeting ends, Lars will be here with the warriors you asked for."

"Good." Dangor pointed to Nagora, indicating she was to be there too.

Da, I'm coming to free you, to give you your knife so you'll know me. I am your daughter, Nagora. Da, Mum and Sagora would surely want to be there with me, but being healers they chose to be on the battlefield where they'll be most needed. We'll join them. We'll be a family.

Having the task to free the dragon made Nagora realize that Hag's prediction—Child, a dragon awaits you—would soon to come true. True as the realization she had no control on how the event would actually play out, and that began to eat at her.

Raynhard stood again. "Our ultimate goal is to free Yogari and the dragon. That done, we aim to capture Queen Rag and make sure all those who carried out her cruel orders are brought to justice under my rule as I take back my rightful throne. This evil queen murdered my parents, the King and Queen of the Land of the Danu. She poisoned them. I will serve justice on her.

"I will deal with the mercenary force last if they stay out of the fight. Questions?"

"What if Raganora refuses to turn over Yogari and the dragon in exchange for her son's life?" asked Gabe.

Raynhard pointed to Sagora. "Edana will give this ultimatum to Queen Rag: 'Release the dragon and Yogari before the sun reaches its highest point today. If you do not, I will rain fire down on you and your son will die.'

"If we don't get their release, the battle begins. Gabe, your archers and those I've been able to assemble will rain down fire arrows on Rag's troops on the plain."

Gabe had another question. "How many mounted troops are in Queen Rag's force?"

"Forty at most. Double that if the mercenaries take part. The troops on the plain have nowhere to retreat other than back over the bridge to the Isle of Smoke and its fortress. If we have to free Yogari and the dragon, we'll cut off that retreat.

"Depending on how all these possibilities play out, your Hundred Best, my secret rebel force of a hundred, and any who join us on the plain that day, we could be in for anything from a bloody battle to two thousand of Raganora's troops surrendering their weapons. Such is their unmeasurable loyalty and duty to Queen Rag," said Raynhard.

Gabe explained Raynhard's answer to the commanders, obviously giving the odds they would be facing. The grins on their faces showed no fear. Instead, they seemed to relish such odds that would spur them to fight with greater fierceness.

If I meet you face-to-face, Raganora, trust me, my blade will remove you from the throne, and if you are wearing your crown, I'll remove its resting place.

Gabe translated Romanika's question. "Will we and Edana not be pursued after our appearances?"

Geirador answered, "That could happen. However, given the limited number of troops garrisoned in each of these villages where we've planned the appearances, it's most unlikely they will hunt us. We could be tracked and followed from a distance. Along the way, rebels loyal to Raynhard will join us. They'll work with your warriors to form a rearguard of twelve to fifteen warriors to warn us of anyone following who could be a threat. Remember, the troops garrisoned in those areas are without mercenary commanders to push them into action. They'll report on what they see, but engage or pursue Edana, we doubt it."

"Until the day of the battle on the plain before the Isle of Smoke, you do not foresee us engaging in significant fighting?" asked Gabe.

"Based on all our information, no. But we will, at all times, be battle ready and on the lookout for forces that may seek to oppose us," said Geirador.

Gabe relayed this information to his commanders.

"You must have heard from Lars about the fire arrows. Bundles of them await you. Tomorrow, they'll be in your possession. Save your own arrows for skirmishes and the heat of the battle," said Geirador.

Gabe gave Geirador a thumbs-up and looked to Raynhard. "Until we arrive at the plain, it's travel by day. Set up camp. Help Edana make an appearance in the dark. Repeat this, along with a few daytime appearances for distant lookouts, until we set up camp in the forest surrounding the plain. There, you expect to have a day to negotiate the release of Yogari and the dragon. On the following day, if Queen Rag doesn't release them by the deadline, the battle starts?"

"Yes," said Raynhard. "However, once Yogari and the dragon are released, we will demand that Raganora and her commanders surrender. How she'll react to that, we don't know. Your guess is as good as ours. If she resists, we have a fight on our hands. If she gives up, we have a control problem to deal with. Who are those that'll throw down their arms and offer me their allegiance? And who are those that share in Queen Rag's guilt, and to what degree?

"Whatever the outcome, we show we have the power to fight and take control of the land. Justice will be swift. My country must be rebuilt."

The Capture
Kahtinikewin

Early the next morning, the force gathered at the base of the cliff where Tagnya and Raynhard had climbed onto the shelf on the rocky outcrop at the cliff's base, half a body length from the ground.

Nagora sat on Storm with Lars and Dangor at her sides behind the assembled, mounted warriors. Next to them, Geirador and Paruline were on their mounts, flanked by Sagora, Gabe, and his commanders Bullidor, Romanika, and Tankar.

When Tagnya established that all had gathered, she spoke to them. "Warriors of Godomor the Terrible, King of the Land of Skulls, here next to me stands Raynhard, the rightful heir to King Bernhard's throne in Windhaven of the Land of the Danu. As a young man, Raynhard sailed with Yogari and I. Raynhard has learned our ways and our values. Raynhard has sworn to protect my daughters and me. Raynhard is sworn to our cause—to free Yogari and the dragon.

"Then with Yogari, and with your help, Raynhard will take back his rightful throne."

Silence greeted Tagnya's words as all eyes were on Raynhard, waiting for him to speak. When he did, he paused to allow Tagnya to translate.

Raynhard placed an open hand on his chest. "I am Raynhard of the Land of the Danu, rightful heir to the throne of the Land of the Danu. That, I own by the birthright given me by my mother, Queen Julianna," he held out his left hand, "and my father, King Bernhard." His right hand joined the left.

"I am Raynhard, a warrior of the Land of the Danu." He raised a fist in the air. "That, I owe to the training given me by Yogari, the navigator who rides the sea beyond its horizon." His fist opened and drew a broad arc before him.

"To that same Yogari, the Dragon Rider who rides dragons beyond the clouds, I owe the hope he once gave my people." He pointed to the sky and then brought his hand to his chest.

"To Yogari, the Dragon Talker who guards the last dragon of our land in captivity, I owe thanks for his duty to me and our dragon." He looked to Tagnya as he spoke those words, placing a hand on her shoulder and smiling at her as she translated for him.

Then he placed a hand on each of her shoulders. "To Tagnyoriva, the healer who saves the lives of those who touch her heart, I owe thanks for her never-ending devotion and belief in our cause."

He pointed to Dangor. "To Dangor, the archer, the trainer of warriors, I owe thanks for his faithful service and wise counsel to our cause."

With two hands he pointed to the twins. "To Nagora and Sagora, daughters of Yogari and Tagnyoriva, who will ride as

Edana to free the dragon, I owe thanks to them for joining our cause."

"To Geirador, the blacksmith who forges blades and weapons for Edana and her warriors, I owe thanks for his ever loyal service and wise counsel to our cause." Raynhard smiled broadly as he pointed to Geirador and his other hand immediately pointed to Paruline who stood at her father's side.

"To Paruline, daughter of Geirador, most trusted servant in so many ways, I owe thanks for her loyal and brave service to our cause."

Raynhard paused as he pressed his two middle fingers to his palm and splayed the remaining two and his thumb in the dragon-chord salute over his heart. "To Edana, I owe thanks beyond words for the hope she has given to our people." He raised the salute high over his head.

"I will be King Raynhard of the Land of the Danu. That I will owe to you, Gabyndor, son of Godomor the Terrible, King of the Land of Skulls," he said and pointed to Gabe. "To your commanders Bullidor, Romanika, and Tankar," he said, pointing to each of them in turn; and then with arms outstretched, "And to you, the Hundred Best warriors who have volunteered to fight for our cause. Thank you for joining our cause!" Raynhard raised both hands with dragon-chord salutes. "Today we ride to free the dragon!"

The assembled warriors raised their hands in the dragon-chord salute, pumping their arms as they cheered, "Raynhard! Warrior of the Land of the Danu! Raynhard! King of the Land of the Danu! Free the dragon! Free the dragon!"

Raynhard and Tagnya climbed down from the stone ledge and mounted their horses.

...

Nagora, Dangor, and Lars fell in with Romanika and Tankar at the head of their line of warriors.

Raynhard led the force in single file to the forest trail.

As Nagora lost sight of Raynhard ahead, her mind raced with questions.

What is that spark that makes one a leader of a country?

Birthright?

The crown is his by right.

Training? How does one train a king?

Ambition? To serve the people or to serve one's own interests?

A cause? Regain his crown, free Da, his Dragon Talker, and free the dragon to rally the people to him.

A dream? Fulfill King Bernhard's dream?

Perhaps all of these?

Raynhard's signal came down the line. All were to fan out as they approached an open meadow. He then gave the signal to stay in the trees at the forest's edge.

At the far side of the meadow, two white horses in the mist nibbled on the long grasses.

Geirador gave a short whistle, and the horses raised their heads.

The unicorns! They're beautiful. Such grace. How can a single horn do that? They are so at ease wearing the tusks.

"Would our two Dragon Warrior Princesses care to ride their unicorns?" asked Geirador.

The twins smiled at him. He handed each of them a bridle. "Bareback will be fine this morning, lassies."

They must have names. "Geirador, what are their names?"

"Nadana and Sadana. Call them by name. They'll come to you."

He sent the sisters off to the unicorns.

They kneed their mounts and walked them across the meadow, to dismount near the unicorns. As they approached, Sagora pointed. "Look at their helms."

"That's Geirador's work. He's thought of everything. Attachments for the bridle. The leather of the straps and helm painted white. Openings for their eyes and ears and even for strands of their manes," said Nagora.

Which of you beauties is mine? "Nadana." The unicorn looked up and walked over to Nagora. She patted the front of Nadana's neck and rubbed her nose.

"Sadana." Her twin had a big smile on her face as the unicorn answered her call. "Nagora, I can't believe it."

"Neither can I, big sister." Nagora ran her hand down one of the straps from the helm to the girth strap that connected to the other straps around the front legs. "From a distance we can't see these straps."

She brought her hand back to the helm, which went three quarters of the way down the back of the mare's neck. The leather helm encased a wooden support for the tusk, which was strapped and buckled in place.

"Did you see the toe loop stirrup on the strap going to the girth strap? We just have to attach the bridles, place the bits in their mouths, throw the separate reins over their necks, and mount up," said Sagora.

"Let's do it!" Nadana was very docile and responded well to Nagora's commands. They set off in opposite directions and made their way around the open meadow to the side where the warriors watched them.

What are the Hundred Best thinking now?

Before the twins had reached the force's side of the meadow, every warrior had dismounted. They stood at the edge of the meadow in awe, silently taking in the beauty of the creatures headed their way.

As soon as the twins dismounted, the warriors came forward and gathered around to touch the unicorns.

Geirador and Tagnya approached. She placed a hand on his arm. "Well, Geirador, looks like you've created a magical animal, judging from how the warriors are reacting."

"Tagnya, with your two warrior daughters riding them, I would be inclined to agree with you."

Nagora gave Geirador a hug. "The work you did on their helms is amazing. You're a true craftsman, Geirador."

Sagora gave him a hug too. "And they're so docile. Did it take long to train them?"

Geirador smiled. "It was time well spent."

Dangor waved and pointed. Paruline was riding across the meadow, leading Brith and Storm. Nagora pulled on Sagora's hand, and they ran to her.

Paruline dismounted. "Do you like them?"

Nagora reached for her hand. "Pare, they're beautiful! You and your da have done a truly great job in training them. From a distance the tusks look like they're part of them."

"Wondrous," said Sagora.

"I told Da you had to see them in the morning mist of the meadow to feel the magic they impart. He agreed to let me bring them."

Sagora pointed to the unicorns. "They're truly magical. Look at the warriors. Like us, they're amazed by them."

Raynhard approached and went to Paruline. "Thank you so much for bringing the unicorns to show us. Of course, I had heard of them from your da, but not seen them. Now I'm more than convinced they'll complement Edana's appearances, and have the people of the land talking and hopefully moving to see them at the Isle of Smoke.

"Tagnya is right. Geirador has created a magical animal that will become a much sought-after prize."

Paruline wore a proud smile. "I hope they'll forever stay out of the reach of those with evil intentions." She looked up. "Da's calling. I'm to help with the tusks. Come, you two. The tusks will be in your care from now on."

The twins followed and Raynhard left.

Paruline and Geirador unbuckled the tusks from the helms. Paruline placed each one in its own leather sheath. "Here you go, one for each of you. The straps allow you to wear them on your back or tie them to your saddle. They're now in your good care. We better mount up. The column's moving. I'll take care of the mares. See you later."

The column came to a halt. Up ahead Dangor led a group of warriors up the slope to the cache of fire arrows. I think they'll be surprised and pleased.

...

Paruline came up alongside. "You look like you're lost in thought. What are you thinking?"

Nagora glanced at Paruline. "Edana will make Raganora's troops eat her fire on the plain before the Isle of Smoke. They'll wish they had never harmed a single dragon nor taken my da captive."

"Is that what you see?" asked Paruline.

"That's what I know in my heart."

The column started its slow quiet move forward again.

The force had set up camp in a wooded clearing. It was equidistant from the village of Yhorgal, the prince's fortress at Yhorgal Cliffs, and the planned spot for Edana's tent on the road to the fortress.

Nagora, along with Tagnya and Sagora, had followed the preparations to set up and take down Edana's tent. Those assigned to that duty practiced three times. They made final adjustments to make sure it went up without a problem on the fourth and final practice.

Nagora hugged Lars when he came by with Dangor, just before they left to get the curraghs ready to leave by nightfall. Dangor placed a hand on her shoulder. "Just so you know, I'll be asking Jan Trickleson and his son, Raddy, to help us tonight. They'll follow the sea cliffs to the mouth of the dungeon sea cave. Lars will sound for a safe spot for you to dive. He'll be watching for you. He'll have a candle lantern lit. Line up with that to make your dive. Let's hope the weather holds. If it doesn't and you don't get word from us, you'll know because you won't spot Lars's light."

"Got it. I'll do that. Thanks, Uncle. Thanks, Lars."

The tension mounted in Nagora's stomach. She found a spot away from the others to focus on preparing her weapons. She was sitting cross-legged on the ground, oiling her knife sheath and blades so they would resist their swim in the salty sea, when Sagora found her.

"That Raynhard is a handsome one, isn't he? I'm happy Da saved his life. Soon he'll be king."

"Someday Gabe will become king." Nagora wiped more oil onto the big sheath.

"Do you see yourself as his queen, Nagora?"

"What? Me? Why do you ask?" Where did she get that idea?

"I saw the way Raynhard looked at you."

"What way?"

"Something in his eyes."

"I saw that when he looked at you too, Sagora. I think it's my brand, that I accepted it for The Cause, his cause. Would you give up Gabe for him?"

"The question is: Would you give up Lars for him? I also saw the way you looked back at him."

"The man saved my life. So did Lars, under different circumstances. Lars and I are warriors. Both returning twins. I think our brands brought us together as well as our stars."

"You'll be in a position to give Raynhard back his kingdom," said Sagora.

"First, I want to free Da. I don't see myself as queen."

"I didn't see myself branding my twin," said Sagora.

Nagora held up her big blade, looked at her reflection on it, and shoved it into its sheath. "It's best we don't know what the future holds. That would be a terrible gift."

"Though some profess to know the future."

Her sister's words chilled her. "You're right, Sagora." Nagora reached into her scrip. "Time to paint our faces. Now we become Edana." She unfastened the lid on the container of red paint Tagnya had made. "Move closer, big sister." She applied the red stripes, one across the forehead just above the eyebrows, the next across both eyelids and the nose bridge, followed by another from one ear to the other across the lips, and finally, one across her chin. Then she painted the Tiwaz on Sagora's forehead.

Sagora looked at Nagora as she took the jar of paint from her hand and dipped a finger into it. "I can't get over how well the scar from the brand has healed. You know, even though I had no choice, I still feel bad about being the one to brand you," she said as she applied the red paint to Nagora's face.

"Don't feel bad. You did a perfect job. The three converging lines of the Tiwaz are even. You must have applied the brand in the shortest of breaths just before that clap of thunder. I swear Godomor's Grand Hall shook. I felt it through my knees on the top step."

"You're probably right, and then the rain came down in buckets. We were soaked before we managed to get you inside the hall."

Nagora made a snarling face at Sagora. "Now that we're identical with the paint, do you think we'll scare someone from the Hundred?"

"No. They know we're both being Edana. It only makes sense we look the same. But if you growl at them that way, you could scare a few."

When they returned to find their mother, Tagnya had a satisfied look on her face. "There you are. The tent sets up just fine. The lengthened guy lines make it easy to push the stakes into the ground off the road where the earth is softer.

"I'll be instructing the archers who'll be hiding in the shadows on what our signals are, and to keep out of sight unless needed. Now all we have to do is hope Acindor takes Edana's invitation."

Nagora nodded in agreement. "He'll take it."

With the coming of dusk, the tent contingent of twenty moved closer to the fortress road. By nightfall, they would be in position to pitch the tent and furnish it with a makeshift bed of furs and candle lanterns, ready to be lit.

Dangor returned with news that the curraghs were already at sea, heading along the coast to Yhorgal Cliffs.

Nagora waited next to Nadana as the warriors set up Edana's tent under Tagnya's supervision. Nadana wore a saddle. The poles holding the gourds containing the combustible hung from the yoke attached to the saddle. Further down the road, the archers were taking up their positions among the trees along each side of the road.

Sagora and Dangor were waiting further down the road to open the spigots on the gourds.

When Tagnya gave the signal that all was ready in the tent, Nagora removed her cloak, gave it to Paruline, and naked, mounted Nadana.

When Nagora arrived at the spot where she would ride Nadana on flaming hooves, Dangor and Sagora opened the spigots at her signal. She rode her unicorn down the road a hundred paces in the dark, streaming a line of the combustible mixture along each side of the road up to the position within view of the fortress where she would later stop to plant Edana's banner and shout out her message to the prince. She turned her unicorn in a circle there, streaming the remaining combustible.

On her return, Sagora gave Nagora Edana's spear that held her standard with the embroidered message for Acindor:

> Come my prince.
> Be my love tonight.
> The fire of your desire
> Is meant for me alone.
> With me you will sire
> A son for your throne.
> The sea did not put out my fire.
> Edana comes back to you tonight
> To be your Dragon Warrior Princess.

Dangor and Sagora removed the gourds and attached the fire baskets. "On your call, little sister. When you say so, we'll light the fires."

Nagora didn't count. "Fire!"

Dangor and Sagora lit their torches. Dangor counted aloud to three as he moved to his side of the horse. On three, they touched their torches to the fire baskets and then touched the streams of combustible on each side of the road.

At that moment, Nagora kneed Nadana forward and raced down the road with the flames to her position just out of reach of the fortress archers. She pulled hard on the reins and danced Nadana on her hind legs inside the circle of fire. Before the flames went out, she raised her standard and shouted out:

"Come my prince.
Be my love tonight.
The fire of your desire
Is meant for me alone."

She planted her spear in the ground and turned Nadana to ride back up the road to the tent. By the time she returned, the fire baskets had died out, but not the fire burning in Edana's heart.

Sagora and Dangor removed the fire baskets and saddle as soon as Nagora had dismounted. "Good work, Nagora," said Tagnya and Paruline in unison.

"I can imagine what that must have looked like from the fortress wall," said Tagnya.

Paruline gave Nagora her cloak. Tagnya handed her one of the two candle lanterns she held and gave the other to Sagora.

Dangor tied the unicorn to the left front corner of the tent.

Tagnya watched for Mina's arrival. It would signal someone from the fortress had claimed Edana's flag.

They all waited and watched for Mina to come running down the road. Their eyes strained to see movement in the dark. They were rewarded. "A rider came out and took the flag back to the fortress," said Mina.

Tagnya lit the lanterns the twins held. With care, they concealed them under their cloaks. Tagnya gave their cloaks a gentle tug. "Keep your eyes and ears alert for signs of attack. Don't stick around if you see the least sign of danger."

"Don't worry about us," said Sagora. "Mum, you be careful when the prince shows up here at the tent."

"Nagora, I'll be in the tent waiting for you, hidden under the fur blanket in a cavity of that big bed we knocked together for you. Now go, you two. I'll light the lanterns here."

Nagora reached out for Sagora when they reached the spot on the road where she had planted the spear. "Look, I know this is not in the plans. I'm going to go twenty paces closer before I start. You move ahead of me from there another twenty paces where you'll do your dance. I'll move ahead twenty paces, do mine, and then double back past you as you do yours again and then you can double back past me as I do my dance. They won't shoot. They'll want to hear what Edana says and they'll want to see her naked body. They've nothing to fear and won't shoot. If anyone comes out of the fortress, we disappear into the trees. If not, Edana then appears as a shadow inside the tent."

Sagora squeezed Nagora's hand. "Okay, little sister, let's do it."

Nagora put her face into Sagora's hood. "I love my big sister."

Then Nagora walked twenty strides closer to the fortress, pulled the hood of her cloak down, and slung the left side of her cloak back over her shoulder while raising the lantern to show the bare side of her body. She danced and swayed wantonly, slowly calling out to Acindor: "Come my prince. Be my love tonight," over and over, and on the fifth call, she hid herself and the candle lantern under her cloak.

Almost at the same moment Sagora showed the side of her body as she flung her cloak back over her right shoulder and raised her candle lantern in her right hand. She danced and swayed and sang Edana's song.

Nagora scooted past her sister and took up her position. She was right on time and did her song and dance. Onlookers lined the wall of the fortress. Nagora disappeared to let Sagora take over. As she snuck past her sister, she called: "We're on our way back."

As Sagora disappeared, Nagora reappeared. "No one has moved from the fortress wall. They're taken by what they're seeing."

After Sagora's last appearance, Nagora danced naked as Edana inside the tent. She imagined the shadow seen from outside, beckoning the prince to come to her.

Nagora smiled at Tagnya, who had been peeking out from under the fur blanket on the dark side of the bed. "Daughter, if Acindor doesn't show up, you'll be getting offers from every warrior out there who can see the tent."

"Don't worry. My prince will come."

Outside Sagora sang, "Come my prince. Be my love tonight."

It was the signal someone was approaching so Nagora was to take over singing inside the tent. Sagora said, "Uncle, the rider looks unsure, hesitant even."

Nagora sang. The tent moved slightly. Nadana had pulled away from the tent after Dangor untied her. Nadana most likely went to either Paruline or Geirador who waited further down the road behind the tent.

The prince's full attention is surely on the tent, on my dancing silhouette, and my singing.

Over and over Nagora sang her Edana song and danced, swayed, caressed herself, and beckoned Acindor to come to her arms.

A saddle creaked and a heavy foot hit the ground. Acindor has dismounted. The footsteps approaching must be his. He will have his sword drawn and ready to strike out.

When he arrived at the open entrance on the side of the road, he held his sword before him.

Nagora continued dancing and singing as Acindor stood at the tent's threshold. His eyes scanned the inside then came back to her body to stare at every part of it.

She turned slowly, dancing as she did, so he could admire her back. When she faced him, she motioned to the bed and said, "My prince! My love! Rest your sword here, remove your garments. Lay on the bed that I may cleanse and anoint your body so you can take mine. And if you do, you could, I am sure, sire an heir to your future throne. I have returned from the sea to be with you, to satisfy your heart's desire, to give you a son. Once you lay in this bed, I'll put out three of these candles and leave one as the symbol of the future son you will sire in our lovemaking tonight. Come, my love, to our bed."

She continued dancing, her eyes never leaving Acindor's except when he looked directly into hers. Then she coyly lowered her gaze in a submissive smile and caressed her breast.

Acindor returned his sword to its scabbard and stepped inside the tent. He unfastened the belt buckle, removed it, retied the buckle, and then placed it over the bed post at the foot of the bed. His gaze never left Nagora's all the while as he continued to undress.

As Nagora danced, she held out a hand for each piece of clothing Acindor removed. She placed each piece on the back of a nearby chair. When the prince sat on the edge of the bed to remove his boots and pants, she went to the small table that held a big bowl of water, clean cloths, a piece of soap, and a small bottle of scented oil.

Acindor removed his boots, kicked them next to the chair, and removed his pants.

Nagora soaked a cloth in the bowl, wrung it out, and then soaped it before placing it next to the bowl.

Acindor wiped the drool from his chin and smiled as he lay back on the bed and rested his head on the big fur pillow.

Anyone watching from the outside would see the silhouettes cast on the tent wall play out the scene. Now was the time to dim the lights. Acindor didn't hide his arousal as Nagora climbed up onto the bed to remove one of the candle lanterns.

Your poor little pecker looks like it's trying to prop up your mountain of a belly—a tree stump pushing into a grassy hillside. So far, so good, as long as I don't do something to throw you into a fit of rage.

Nagora stood between Acindor's legs as she reached up to take down the first candle lantern, the kind used in stables and meant to be hung from secure places. Wrought iron frames held the four glass sides of the lantern in place in such a way only one side could be moved up to allow one to clean the glass panes or replace the candle.

The bottom of the lantern was shaped like a ball cut in half to prevent the lantern from being set down on a flat surface where it could be tipped over by accident and set fire to something nearby. She had chosen that kind for a reason.

She unhooked the lantern and slowly brought it down in front of her. She bent at the knees, crouched down between Acindor's legs, rested the lantern on the bed between his knees and bent over the lantern chimney to blow out the flame.

I bet if I touched you there, you would explode.

Then Nagora rose to step off the bed and hang the lantern from the bar above the tent entrance.

Nagora climbed back up on the bed and this time straddled Acindor at the level of his hips as she reached up for the second lantern. Slowly she brought it down and held it just above the prince's rotund belly as she crouched over him just a breath from touching the bottom of his belly. While Nagora held the lantern in her right hand, she carefully tilted it toward herself so she could blow down into the chimney to put out the flame. She purposely started blowing so her breath struck Acindor's distended belly button before it hit the flame.

...

When the flame went out, Nagora stood, stepping over the prince and off the bed to bring the lantern to the bar next to the first one.

When Nagora climbed back on the bed, she straddled Acindor at the level of his chest. Once again she reached for a lantern. Before she unhooked it, she looked down at the prince in the glow of the two remaining lanterns. Acindor's face, neck, and chest were crimson red. His eyes were riveted on one spot of her body.

Nagora reached for the third lantern with two hands. She unhooked it and kept it held aloft as she returned her gaze to Acindor's face. Ever so slowly, her hips undulated as she crouched down above the prince's chest.

Acindor's face had turned beet red, his eyes bulged further from their sockets, as he groaned and licked his lips. He grabbed her ankles and at the same moment a whistle arrow screamed outside in the night. The blood drained from Acindor's face as he bared his teeth and tried to push her away.

Nagora brought down the wrought iron lantern base with all her might, right into the middle of the prince's forehead, just above the bridge of his nose. Acindor's eyes crossed before they closed with the impact. His jaw dropped as he expelled a grunt.

Hoofbeats sounded in the distance on the road. Outside, voices yelled commands in two languages. Then Nagora heard the muffled sound of warrior arrows striking targets that screamed in agony as they fell from their mounts.

Tagnya held a knife at Acindor's neck and pressed her other hand on his chest.

Nagora stood with the dead lantern, ready to strike again, but she didn't need to.

Sagora appeared at the tent's entrance. "No time to waste here. More riders from the fortress could be coming."

Tagnya pointed and grabbed Nagora's wrist. "Bring the last lantern down by me. The show is over. It was going well until now. If you're still going to try to rescue those girls, get going. Sagora, Dangor, and I'll take care of the prince."

Tagnya used her knife to cut out a depression on the ground to seat the lantern.

Paruline and Mina showed up with arrows nocked on their bows. Paruline had Nagora's cape and set of blades slung over her shoulder. "Are you still headed for the cliff? If you are, we're going with you to cover you."

"Glad to have your company. What's the situation out there?" Nagora slipped her blades on.

Paruline made a fist and struck her chest as she imitated the sound of an arrow striking. "Twelve of the prince's guard will never ride again. Hag must have sent them. I doubt others will be coming to Acindor's rescue."

Nagora, Mina, and Paruline made their way down the road to the last warrior lookout who signaled the coast was clear. They took to the woods and then skirted the field that bordered the left side of the fortress until they came to open ground with a few stone outcrops all the way to the cliffs. They would have to keep low and under their cloaks so as not to be seen by the sentries.

They made it to the open ground and moved from one rock outcrop to the next in short bursts, running alone, stopping with one knee to the ground and heads bent low.

The Rescue
Pimâcihiwewin

Nagora and her escorts made it to the cliff's edge without incident.

Nagora couldn't see the curragh waiting for her. "He could be right close to the cliff and I can't see him from here. If you can anchor yourselves well and let me hold onto your bows, I'll be able to stretch out further beyond the edge for a better look. Pare, have a stone ready to throw down below to get his attention if I still can't see him."

"Okay." They each strung their bows, sat with their feet dug into the rough stone of the cliff edge to gain purchase.

Nagora stood between them and took hold of their bow tips. "Ready?"

"Ready."

She spread her legs shoulder width and slowly leaned out over the cliff as Paruline and Mina held onto the ends of their bows.

"Throw the stone."

Paruline threw it and from where Nagora was positioned, the sound of the faintest splash climbed to her ears. Moments later the curragh appeared. Lars had rowed it into view and was flashing a lantern. She was good to go.

"Pull me in, girls."

Nagora removed her cloak and tightened the straps of her blades. "See you later," she said, as she flexed her knees and pushed off the cliff to dive into the dark waters below.

Nagora timed her twist in the air so that she struck the water feet first with her fists pressed to sides of her thighs and every muscle in her body tensed. Her vertical entry cut the water like a knife and slowed her descent. When her feet touched, she pushed off the rocky bottom and spread her arms to swim to the surface.

Nagora gasped for air as she broke to the surface and looked around to get her bearings. The sea was calm with gentle swells. The curragh bobbed ahead of her about twenty body lengths away. Lars had spotted her and was rowing in her direction. She wouldn't have to swim for long.

Nagora grabbed on to the curragh with both hands as she brought her left leg up and hooked the heel of her foot over the curragh's topside edge. "Get an oar out on the other side and brace yourself. I'm going to rock the boat so I can pull myself aboard."

"Ready," said Lars.

Nagora held onto the edge and let her body sink back into the water. She spread her legs and brought her knees up to give a strong scissor kick. At the same time, she pulled hard on the curragh's edge. She shot up out of the water and landed on her right buttock in the bottom of the curragh.

Lars steadied the little vessel as Nagora took her place at the bow. He put his port-side oar in place and rowed a few strokes before turning to grasp his shielded candle lantern. He brought it forward and handed it to Nagora.

He smiled his grand smile. "I'm happy to see you too, Lars. Row out so I can signal to my friends on the cliff above that I'm fine."

Lars nodded, turned the curragh, and rowed further away from the cliff. I should see two hooded silhouettes against the starlit sky above the cliff. Now I see them, holding their bows above their heads. Nagora raised the candle lantern to shine on herself and Lars. She waved to the two silhouettes. They waved their bows above their heads and disappeared.

Nagora raised the lantern shield. "Good. Now we can head for the cave entrance."

Lars pulled on the oars and guided the curragh back closer to the cliff and headed to the cave entrance.

Lars took off his vest and pulled his woven shirt over his head. "Here, wear this. It'll warm you. You'll need all your strength to get into that cave and bring those girls out."

"Thank you." Nagora took Lars's shirt and pulled it over her head.

He smells good. This is a clean shirt. He must have picked it to wear tonight. It won't smell like this at the end of the campaign. I'm warmer already.

Lars put his leather vest back on and checked behind him in the dark more often. He must be looking for the others he left near the cave entrance. I'll look too. They're in the darkness watching and listening. They'll show their lanterns at the first sound of rowing.

Two lanterns flashed ahead at the same time.

Nagora raised her lantern and flashed it.

The two lanterns flashed again, and then one appeared to go out while one remained lit. It was a tiny dot in the distance. Lars pulled long, steady strokes as he gazed over his shoulder to guide the curragh toward the light.

Before long, Nagora and Lars had drawn up alongside the curragh with the lighted lantern. It rode on two small killick anchors that allowed it to keep its position within three body lengths of the mouth of the cave. A second curragh was tied next to it.

"Welcome to the cave's entrance. Only Edana would try this," said a man's voice from the nearest curragh.

Nagora replied, "I came out of it once and that was at high tide. Have we reached low tide level yet?"

"In less than three counts," said the voice.

"So that means a drop of another arm's length, at the most."

Again the voice answered, "That would be about right."

"Am I talking to Jan Trickleson?" asked Nagora.

"That be me, a fisherman who knows this coast well and who only goes to sea in curraghs yer uncle makes."

"Would you be the one who traded walrus hides for three curraghs?"

"That would be me."

"Thanks for coming to help."

"Glad to be of help." The man's laugh was hearty.

"They call you 'Hook,' right?"

"Aye, they do." Jan 'Hook' Trickleson raised his lantern with a hook that protruded from his left shirtsleeve where a hand should have been. "Oh! Pardon me. This here's my son, Raddy, at the oars." He swung the lantern back to light the other curragh. Raddy gave Nagora the dragon-chord salute and a shy toothless smile as he lifted his own lantern.

"So Hook, it's true about how you lost your hand?"

"Oh! Aye! A shark did that. Fishin' through the ice in the bay. Haulin' in my hooks when I gets a good tug on the line. I pulls it in as much as I can, but it won't come up the hole. I jabs my gaff spear down to help get a better purchase. Still stuck so I hangs onto the gaff with me right hand and I reaches down with me left to see if I can move what's blockin' 'em from comin' up. I feels around and around. I figures my hand's gettin' numb from the cold icy water. When I pulls out, my hand it's clean bit off at the wrist. I jabs it into the snow next to the hole, and I yells to my son who's fishin' over a ways at his hole.

"He comes a runnin' and can't believe what he sees. I'm holdin' my wrist to stop the bleedin' as best I can. He puts me on the sled and heads for the shore hut where your uncle and his friend Geirador are cookin' somethin' warm to eat while they fish.

"That man Geirador, he can't believe I'm not feelin' pain. He ties a leather belt around my wrist real tight. Then he has me lie down with my hand held above my head. He piles up snow all around my arm. He puts his big knife in the fire. 'Aye,' he says, holdin' 'is big, red hot knife, 'this'll hurt, then again, maybe not 'cause yer arm's so cold. Believe me though, when it warms up, it's goin' ta hurt fierce. What I'm goin' to do is cook the meat on the stump of yer wrist to stop the bleeding. I'm goin' to pull on your arm so as to pull the skin and meat on yer wrist over the bone tips, then I'm goin' to touch this knife to the stump.'"

Nagora had been staring at Hook's candle-lit face in disbelief. She turned to look at Lars. He was holding his own wrist as he too was obviously taken in by the story.

"Then he tells Raddy and Dangor to get on top of me and hold me down so I wouldn't budge while he did the cookin'."

Nagora pointed. "Geirador make the hook?"

"Aye, made it and remade it until I was fine and comfortable with it."

"Was the hook his idea?"

"No. Mine. I've always been a fisherman, so I figured a hook is what I need. Serves me well. It's been seventeen years."

"Well, Hook that's quite a story. I'm glad you survived the shark bite and are here with Raddy today to help me."

"I'll never turn down yer uncle or Geirador."

"What do you have for me?" asked Nagora.

Raddy held up a coil of rope and an air bladder, like the ones Nagora used when testing the curraghs she built with her uncle. Hook explained. "Six lengths of rope, each long enough to take you from 'ere into the prison cave. Six air bladders covered in leather so they can take a beatin' on the rocks. Each has enough line so you can tie the bladder to the rope and the remainin' line around the girls. I suggest around the waist and up to one of their hands and tie that hand to the bladder. They can hold onto the loop at the bladder. That'll leave them with one hand free to push off the rocks as they're bein' pulled out. I suggest they try to keep their heads as close to the bladder as possible."

"Good," said Nagora.

"You want to go now? You can take a line in with you and then haul the bladder ropes in."

"Okay, I'll do that."

Hook stuck his arm out.

Raddy hung a large coil of rope on his father's hook.

Hook swung the coil over to Nagora.

She took it, handed most of it to Lars, and kept one end of the rope at her feet.

"I'll tie one girl on at a time and instruct her on what to do. When I give four good tugs on the rope, you'll know it's the one to pull on. Count to ten like this: one anchor, two anchors, three anchors, and so on. When you get to ten anchors, start pulling. The girl should have her breath. First one out will tell you how many are coming. From what we know there should be two, possibly three.

"Now Hook, don't fret as this could take a while depending on whether I have to deal with the jailor or not. If I don't come out right after the last girl, it means I'm busy. Give me six full counts before you start to worry. Got that?"

"Aye. Good luck to you."

Lars tossed one end of a short line to Hook so he could tie their boats together.

Nagora pulled Lars's shirt over her head, moved closer to Lars, put it in his lap, and gave him a quick kiss and a hug.

"Be careful, Nagora. If you don't come out as planned, I'll go in for you."

"I know you will. I'll be fine. Pay out the line steady." She tied her end to her waist, dove into the water, and swam into the cave entrance where its arched roof sloped inward and down to meet the water.

Nagora paused, resting her feet against the rock as she floated on her back and pulled enough line over to herself so she wouldn't have its tension to fight against once she swam down and in through the cave entrance.

Nagora took a deep breath and dove, kicking with her legs, swimming and pulling herself down with her hands as they found handholds on the cave's rocky wall. Sooner than she expected, she broke to the surface inside the wet cave.

The familiar dank smell brought back images of her last time there. Ahead, a dull reflection of light came from the dungeon chamber. She swam forward, pausing now and then to see if she could touch bottom. Just as the dull reflection became a glow, her foot touched stones. Soon she was within the center vault of the cave where the jailor had left her to die. If she stood, she would have water up to her waist. The rock pillar the jailor had stood her on now cleared the water by about as much.

Nagora kept low and swam to the pillar. The day the jailor had set her on it, she stood there with cramped feet for a long time, watching the cold, icy sea water rise up her body as she tried to escape to a warmer place in her mind.

Near the top of the third step leading to the top of the pillar, she found an iron ring pinned to the column, just like the one pinned to the cave's ceiling directly above the pillar. A hangman's noose had hung from it on that day. The jailor had bet she would choose to hang herself.

I'll pull the ropes in and tie the bladders here behind the column.

Nagora listened. Not a sound came from the dungeon. Did I hear a whimper?

Slowly, so as not to make noise, she pulled the ropes in to her. The bladders appeared, floating on top of the water, one behind the other. She tied the rope ends to the ring, and then she walked toward the dungeon steps.

Nagora crouched on the bottom step, just out of the water, letting water drip from her hair past her blades and down her back. She listened for sounds. The quiet told her the jailor wasn't there.

Unless he's asleep.

She climbed the stairs, keeping low and to the right side of the steps until her eyes were at floor level. Beyond, the big table, a lone stool, and a bench sat next to the wall near the bottom of the dungeon staircase that led to the tower above.

Above the stool on the side of the steps, a taper in its holder, nearing the end of its usefulness, feebly illuminated the jailor's chamber. The dungeon cells proper were to her right, just out of her line of sight.

Nagora reached back over her shoulder to the handle of her big blade, flipped the hilt latch, pulled it from its sheath, and held it before her. She moved up the steps, balancing on the balls of her feet and ready to meet an attack or to attack if she had to.

To Nagora's right was the jailor's filthy cot. Next to it was a bucket of piss that needed to be emptied.

Beyond, the three barred cell doors held their prisoners in the dark. She scampered forward, grabbed the metal ring that held the cell key and slipped an unlit taper from its mount above the peg board. She went to light it on the one near the steps, pausing a moment to listen for noises from above. Nothing, all's quiet. Nagora held the taper to its sister's flame until it lit. A plate with a chunk of bread, a piece of cheese, and the carcass of a cooked chicken rested on the table. The smell of stale ale from the pitcher next to the plate reached her nose.

With the taper lit, she headed to the first cell.

Nagora stuck the taper through the bars of the cell door window to light its interior. A lone figure lay naked, huddled in a corner, legs covered in straw.

The anger in her surfaced. I'll be your vengeance, your justice. They'll pay.

Dead or asleep?

Nagora couldn't tell. She couldn't see movement.

Nagora sidestepped to the second cell. A naked young girl lay on her side; her back covered in welts told Nagora of the pain she must have suffered. Her hands and forearms, cut and encrusted with dried blood, cradled her head into the corner of the cell where she lay. A finger twitched.

Nagora's stomach turned. Do I turn away? She didn't. She let what she saw feed her anger.

In the third cell, a young girl sat in her corner. With one arm she held her knees pressed up in front of her. She bit into the wrist of her other arm as she stared back at Nagora with wide-open, terrified eyes. "Sellannye, I'm here to help you." Nagora fumbled with the key and inserted it into the lock. The girl's whole body trembled. The poor girl's body shook even harder as she bit deeper into her wrist as if to stifle her own interior screams so they would not come out.

Nagora whispered, "Sellannye, I'm here to help you. I want to help you to escape." She touched the girl's arm. Sellannye pulled herself back further into the corner.

You poor child. I know the awful treatment you suffered at your own da's hands. And you've suffered more here at the hands of the prince. Will I be able to reach you? Do you have strength left somewhere in you? Any hope?

"I know you've been through a terrible ordeal, that you have suffered unbearable pain. Do you understand when I speak?" Nagora tried to keep her voice soothing for the child. "I swear to you, those who did this to you will pay. But before that can happen, I need to get you and the other two out of here. I have others outside waiting to help. If you can listen to me and talk to me, then I'll know if I can get you out."

The girl nodded, but did not loosen her bite on her wrist.

"You understand me?"

Again the girl nodded.

Sellannye, I can feel it. There's a spark of resilience in you. Let it grow. Trust me.

Nagora touched the girl's cheek, then her arm, and then gently took hold of it to pull it from the girl's bite. The girl let go and broke into loud sobs as she threw her arms around Nagora. Nagora rocked her, caressed the back of her head. "Don't worry. Be strong. I can get you out of here. Can you talk? Can you answer my questions?"

Sellannye gulped back her sobs, looked up into Nagora's face, and nodded. She reached up with a shaky finger to touch the Tiwaz on Nagora's forehead. The tip of her finger came away red.

"It's not blood. It's my warrior paint. My name is Edana. Sellannye, how do you know my language?"

"My mother from here long time. Speak language here with me at home."

"Sellannye, I am here to help you. Does the jailor leave and come back regularly?"

"He always here. Today is leave first time. Someone come get him to see something."

He could be back at any moment.

"Are the other two girls alive?"

"I think yes."

"When is the last time you have eaten?"

"Two days."

"When is the last time you have had something to drink?"

"Before he go."

"Can you help me with the other two girls?"

"Yes."

"Sellannye, do you know their names?"

"She," pointing to the cell next door, "is Tagina. The other Srina."

"Sellannye, can you stand?"

She nodded.

Nagora stood and helped her to her feet. "I will unlock the other cells. You wake Tagina. I will wake Srina."

Sellannye nodded.

Nagora unlocked the two cells.

Nagora called softly to Srina. "Srina. Awake. I'm here to take you away from this nightmare. Awake, Srina." Nagora shook her gently. The child awoke from her deep sleep, shielded her eyes from the taper's light. "Fear not, Srina. I'm here to help you. My name is Edana. I'm here to help you, Tagina, and Sellannye escape. Do you understand?"

Srina nodded.

"Are you hungry?"

She nodded again.

Nagora pointed out past the cell door. "There's something for you to eat in the plate on the table over there. You eat first, and then you'll have to do as I say so I can get you away from here."

Nagora stood and helped Srina stand.

Sellannye was holding Tagina by the hand as Nagora and Srina came out of the cell.

"Hello, Tagina. I am Edana. I have come to help you girls escape."

Tagina nodded.

"Come. There is food on the plate on the table. Help yourselves."

The girls made their way to the table as fast as they could. They kept looking to the stairs.

"Don't be afraid if the jailor returns. I can handle him."

Nagora found a bucket with clean water in it. The drinking ladle's handle stuck out above the rim. She brought it to the table, and the girls washed down small portions of bread, cheese, and chicken with several ladles of water each.

Tagina went to the jailor's cot, reached under it, and pulled out their shirts. The girls put on their shirts and finished off the scraps that remained in the plate.

Nagora kept an ear on the stairway for noise from above.

"How will we get out?" Tagina asked.

"Trust me. I escaped from here. It'll be easier for you girls. Come with me."

Nagora led them to the sea cave steps. She lit the taper on the cave wall next to the steps and placed the one she held in the holder on the other side of the steps.

She led the girls down the steps. At the water's edge, she explained about the waiting air bladders behind the column and the people outside who were in boats, ready to pull them out of the sea cave.

"Look. It's low tide. The cave is not filled with water like at high tide. That means you'll only have a short way to go underwater before you reach the surface for a breath of air. Even if you can't swim, you have the bladders to hold onto. They'll be tied to your waist and one of your hands. All you have to do is bring it close to your head and it will keep your head above the water. Believe me, it will be nothing compared to what you've endured. Surely you want to be away from this place and be at home with your families."

Two of the girls nodded. Sellannye didn't.

I know, poor child, how your mum died. Someday you'll learn how I punished your da. Perhaps you have relatives of your mum here. We'll try to find them.

Nagora led the girls to the column and tied a rope around each one's waist and the bladders to their left hands. Then she walked them as far as they could go before their feet no longer touched bottom. Nagora swam ahead of them as they held onto their bladders and kicked their legs to follow her.

...

When Nagora arrived at the spot where the cave ceiling met the water, she pulled the girls to her.

Tagina wanted to go first. Nagora said, "I'm going to give four good tugs on your rope. The people in the boat will start pulling it and won't stop until you're next to their boat. When I yell 'last breath,' take a deep breath, hold onto the bladder, and push off the rocks with your right hand. Before you know it, you'll be on the other side. Ready?"

"Yes."

Nagora did as she had said. The slack in the rope ran through her hands and approach the limit. "Last breath!"

Tagina took in a deep breath, closed her mouth and her eyes, and disappeared below the surface. Nagora counted fifteen anchors before she felt a single pull on the other ropes. "There. The signal that Tagina has just reached the boat. See, that didn't take long."

The girls smiled.

"Ready, Srina?"

"I'm ready."

"Last breath!"

Nagora counted seventeen anchors. "There! She's at the boat on the other side. Your turn, Sellannye. I won't be coming up right away. The other girls will be taken back to the beach and to their families. One of those families will take you in. Are you ready, Sellannye?"

"No, I want to stay with you."

Tar piss! Now what do I do?

"Okay, I'll go with you. Are you ready?"

Sellannye nodded.

"Hold on tight to me." Nagora gave four tugs.

"Last breath!"

Nagora kicked with her legs and pulled with one hand as she counted anchors and held onto Sellannye.

Soon they came alongside Lars's curragh. He pulled them close and reached for Sellannye's arm. Nagora grabbed onto the edge of curragh. "Lars, both her parents are dead. You'll know who she is when she tells you her name. Hook, Lars'll explain. You'll have to find a family to take her in until a search can be made for a relative. She says her mum is from here. I'm going back in. She's the last one."

"Be careful, Nagora," said Lars.

"I will."

The Oath
Kihcipikiskwewin

Nagora swam back in the cave to the stone column, bringing one air bladder with her. She listened. It's quiet. The glow from the taper's light in the dungeon casts no shadows. She walked to the steps.

Still no sign of the jailor.

Nagora tiptoed into the dungeon, listening for sounds from the stairs. At the table, she set on the floor the key, the plate, the knife, the half-empty pitcher of ale, and the bucket of water.

Then she dragged the heavy wooden table back over to the top step at the sea cave entrance.

Next Nagora went to the wooden box under the jailor's cot and pulled it out. Besides the leather straps, the box contained a variety of metal objects, half a dozen of which were wrought iron metal dogs, horseshoe shaped, but smaller and pointed at each end. She brought them over to the table to see if she had guessed right.

Nagora had. The tabletop was made of wide, long, thick boards. At each of its corners was a pair of holes. An iron dog fit into these holes and stuck out on the underside of the board. With enough tension on the chains and with the dogs threaded through a link of chain and hammered into their holes, a shackled prisoner could not free themselves from the dogs. She placed the iron dogs on the floor.

Nagora returned to the box and looked at the assortment of crude instruments of torture. She found a hammer, lengths of chain, and wrist and ankle shackles—exactly what she needed. She brought them to the table and laid them on the floor next to the iron dogs.

Then Nagora untied her sheath of blades and removed them from her back to lay them on the table. She took careful hold of one of sheaths of her throwing daggers and, with great care, removed the dagger. There, inside of the sheath on the flat side of the knife blade was a wax cylinder half the length of her little finger and not as big around. It had been a tight fit, but the dagger had held the cylinder intact in its hiding place.

Inside the tiny wax cylinder was a thorn from a hawthorn shrub, the tip of which she had barely touched to the liquid in the vial of her mother's "healer's secret," as Sagora had called the poison. Nagora had used the tweezers from her mum's medical scrip to hold the thorn and place it inside a piece of bark from a twig before filling the space around the thorn with wax melted from a candle.

Now the vial of poison is back in the pocket of Mum's scrip, and I have a secret weapon to help me settle a score with the jailor.

...

The creak of an unoiled door hinge got Nagora's attention. She put her blades back on. As she listened for the jailor, she backed into Sellannye's cell, holding the wax cylinder. The jailor was on his way down the steps on unsteady feet.

Celebrating Acindor's capture? Worsham, I wouldn't be surprised. You pay him lip service to join in his perverted games, but behind his back you've no more respect for him than I have. Or were you mourning, with a drink, the deaths of the twelve guards who rode out to join Acindor at the tent?

The jailor made it down the stairs. He took his time, protecting his fresh pitcher of beer as he descended. He was about to deposit it on the table out of habit when he must have realized the table was no longer in its usual place. Once he got his bearings, the jailor located the table and wobbled over to it. He deposited the pitcher with a crash and a splash. Then he picked it up again and slowly bent over the table.

Look at him, he's licking off what he spilled.

Nagora waited for the jailor to face in her direction. When he did, she pushed Sellannye's cell door open. She was a shadow in the shadows of the cell. Slowly she danced out of the shadows with hips swaying until she stood several strides from Worsham, revealing her body in profile. He peered at her over the rim of the pitcher as he drank from it. "My prince's jailor! What an honor it is to be in your presence," said Nagora.

Worsham almost fell back onto the table. The beer in his pitcher sloshed over its rim and ran down over his big hand as he tried his best to steady himself.

"The ... the ... Edana?"

"Surely you must remember me. You called me 'dragon lassie.'"

The jailor, in his stupor, tried to nod as his eyes grew even wider.

"Not so long ago you left me on that rock in the cave behind you so the sea would claim me."

The jailor smiled.

"My prince, your prince, told me that everything he knows about pleasing a woman, he's learned first-hand from you. And his only wish is that he be endowed with a weapon such as yours. That is why I've come to visit you, to examine your weapon so I may better grant my prince's wish."

The jailor's free hand reached for his crotch.

"That's what I want you to show me. I want to see your fine weapon."

The jailor made to untie his crotch piece, but in his haste spilled beer on himself. "It'll be easier if you put the pitcher down." He set it on the corner of the table, lifted his shirt, and then fumbled with the knot of his undergarment to get it undone.

Then he pulled it down to his knees along with his leggings. He straightened up despite the movement of his legs now being restricted at the knees.

Nagora approached, reached out, and touched the jailor's shirt.

"Remove this too so I can get the full measure of the man who bears a cock his prince so envies."

The jailor grabbed for the hem of his shirt and struggled to bring it up and over his head. As soon as he had it before his face, Nagora brought the wax cylinder up and held it between the thumb and index fingers of both hands. With care she broke it in two, revealing the poison tip of the thorn.

With the palm of her left hand she pushed on the jailor's chest as she pressed the tip of the thorn into his massive belly just below his navel. The pricking sensation was enough to cause the jailor to shuffle back against the edge of the table. Nagora had no problem pushing him back onto it.

Within moments, the jailor was unconscious. She pulled the jailor's boots and leggings off and then she finished pulling his shirt from around his arms and neck. His breathing rate had increased momentarily, but now it was steadying.

Then with all her might, Nagora pulled him by the wrists until they were level with the dog holes at the end of the table. His shins would be level with the dog holes at the other end.

Nagora set the hammer and iron dogs on the table next to the jailor. She shackled the jailor's right hand to a long length of chain, threaded the dog through a link, and hammered it into the holes at the table's corner. She then ran the chain once around the jailor's neck and brought it to the holes on the corner of the other side of the table. There, she again threaded a dog through a link and hammered it in place.

He'll barely be able to raise his head.

She let the jailor's left hand free.

Next, she shackled chains to his ankles and hammered the dogs to the corners at that end of the table.

Nagora had two dogs left. She nailed one into the edge of the table top between the jailor's lower legs. After pulling away the three-stranded rope that had held up the jailor's undergarment, she cut the knot from one of its ends to unravel the strands. Nagora cut away a strand and made a slip knot loop, which she slipped around the jailor's cock and balls. She pulled the slipknot tight and pulled the other end of the strand taut to the iron dog at the table's edge where she tied a double hitch knot.

Nagora picked up the remaining iron dog and shoved it in place between Worsham's legs so the ends came just above the slipknot on either side of the taut skin attached to the jailor's hairy jewels. With a dozen good whacks of the hammer she drove the dog to the tabletop, pinning Worsham's privates.

There's only one way you'll get your balls out of this.

Nagora crawled under the table with the hammer and whacked the tips of the last dog over so they lay flat against the underside of the thick table boards.

When Nagora stood again, she examined her handiwork. She cut the slipknot strand and pulled it free. This still won't hurt as much as the pain you inflicted on those innocent girls.

Nagora went back to get the knife and the key ring on the floor next to the plate. She flicked the pad of her thumb across the edge of the knife blade. Pointy, but not sharp, is it? Dull knives are difficult to cut with, aren't they?

When Nagora got back to the table, she moved the jailor's left hand so it rested palm up near his shoulder. She threaded his hand through the brass key ring and pulled it past his elbow. She placed three of his fingertips under the chain that ran from his neck to the dog on that side of the table. She raised the knife above her head and stabbed it with all her might into the palm of the jailor's left hand, but the blade must have struck a bone instead of the tabletop. Nagora pulled the knife to one side, tearing it from the bone. She raised it again, taking better aim to strike between bones, and stabbed once more with all her might, this time pinning the hand to the table.

Don't drop it or you'll never be free.

Nagora took her big blade from its sheath and hacked at each of the table legs near where they met the top.

Then she pushed the table over the top step of the cave entrance. She pushed harder. The leading legs broke, bringing the table's momentum forward fast enough to break the legs that followed.

The table slid down the stairs and into the water, floating the unconscious, spread-eagled jailor into his cavern of death.

Had you been awake that would have been a most painful ride. If you're lucky, you'll wake before high tide and be able to cut yourself free. Though you won't be quite the man you once were, will you?

Nagora went back to the hook where the key ring had been. She looked at the leather slippers that hung from the one next to it. What do I do with these? She was about to reach for the pair that belonged to her.

Again the door hinge above the stairs creaked. She stepped into Sellannye's cell.

"Worsham! You whoreson. We're coming to get a taste of some of what the prince didn't get tonight. Not exactly the same, but they'll do. Wake up, you horny bugger. We've brought our own ale too."

As two guards came down the stairs, Nagora kept to the shadow of the cell door, her eyes at its window. They had been celebrating too. She drew her big blade. She waited until they reached the bottom of the stairs.

"Worsham? Worsham? Where the fuck are you?" They looked around. "What happened to the fuckin' table?"

Nagora pushed the cell door open and spoke from the shadows. "Well lads, what are you waiting for to come and get a taste of what the prince didn't get tonight?"

They looked at each other, and one of them walked over to the cell. Nagora waited until he reached the doorframe to drive her big blade into his gut. Just as he bent over, she pulled it out, and swung the blade up, slicing his windpipe open diagonally until her blade hit his jawbone, throwing him back into the dungeon.

Nagora stepped out past him and faced the other guard who was unable to choose between dropping the pitcher of ale to reach for his sword or transferring the pitcher to his other hand and then drawing his sword.

I'll decide for you.

Nagora drove her big blade up into his chest from just below his ribcage. For a moment, she was what kept him standing as she stared into his wide-open, incredulous eyes. His mouth hung open. Blood gurgled onto his chin. She pushed back on her blade and then pulled it out of his chest. The dead guard collapsed backward against the stone floor.

A taste of Edana's blade.

The only sound in the dungeon now was her breathing. Nagora's chest was heaving and her breaths through her nose were coming fast and deep. Her heart pounded in her chest. It wasn't fear. Whatever it was, it made her want to kill again. It's my oath.

I will be your justice. I will be your vengeance. I will make them pay for the evil they've done to you. Hag, you're next.

The Hunt
Mâcîwin

Nagora ran up the spiral dungeon stairs to the door. She listened. Not a sound. Go. She opened it and stepped into the hall.

A lone taper on the wall across from the door lit the hallway. Another lit it further down in the direction of the prince's chamber. In between were shadows. In the other direction, she saw a corner. A dull glow came from around it. Nagora crossed the hall, moved along the wall to the corner, listened, and then peered around it.

A taper on the wall thirty paces away lit a door on the opposite wall. The door opened. She stepped back behind the corner and listened. I know that jabbering.

Chive.

The door closed. His muffled jabbering and shuffling came her way. Nagora took a quick glance down the hall in the other direction and kept her position against the wall near the corner. She held her breath.

As Chive shuffled past the corner, Nagora flashed her big blade. Chive let out a brief scream of surprise, ducked, and rolled to the opposite corner where he came back to his feet with a knife in hand.

"Where's Hag?" Nagora's question sounded more like a demand.

His eyes were open wide and his mouth hung open. He shook his head, and wasting no time, strode for the dungeon door. Nagora followed. He opened it and waved her in. She hesitated. Her breaths were still coming fast with her determination.

Chive grabbed Nagora's hand and pulled her in with him. He closed the door. Now they were both breathing hard.

He brushed back the hair from his face and looked at her. "I can't believe it. What do you think you're doing?"

"What I swore to do," hissed Nagora.

"You'll not get at Hag tonight. She's got a dozen guards with her right now. She's getting ready to leave for the Isle of Smoke with an armed escort, just about the last of the guards still alive here. They'll leave at first light, perhaps earlier if it's possible."

"Help me! Together we can take them and get her. You can get to her! All you have to do is put a knife in her heart. If you won't, I will!" Nagora's chest was heaving.

Raynhard shook his head and took hold of her wrist again. "No, Nagora. You don't understand. We have Acindor. That Hag is headed to Raganora will work to our advantage. We'll get her later. If something goes wrong tonight, all our years of planning could fall apart."

"No! I don't understand all the planning! I understand my oath to those girls! They suffered and died in this cursed dungeon!" When Nagora pointed to the cells below with her blade, Raynhard looked down. His jaw dropped. "I understand my promise to the girls! And I intend to keep it!" She yanked her wrist free of his grip.

"Perhaps we can get away with this." He pointed below to the two bodies on the floor. "And that you have freed the girls from those cells. I beg you, Nagora, as your king, for the sake of your father's freedom, and so you, your mother, and Sagora can be reunited with him to be a family again—stop. You've done more than enough tonight. Don't risk losing a better future for the people of this land. A future they deserve. A future you deserve. A future that holds unimaginable rewards for you."

Nagora stared into his eyes and raised her blade.

What makes you think I want to be your queen?

Raynhard backed down two steps without his eyes leaving her gaze.

Nagora continued to raise her blade until it was behind her and the tip found the entrance to the sheath. She let it slide in place and then flicked the retaining latch over the up-curved crossguard. Her breathing had slowed.

Raynhard swallowed and lowered his gaze. "Thank you, Nagora."

"For my da."

"For Yogari, yes. We do this for your father."

She took one step down.

Raynhard backed down the stairs, watching Nagora as she took one step at a time. When he reached the dungeon floor, he stepped over to the bodies and stood between them. Nagora had stopped on the third last step and was staring at Raynhard. She took her time coming down the last steps and kept her eyes on him all the while.

Why do I obey reason's call to duty when my heart desires vengeance? I don't like being torn from my oath to those girls.

"You're covered in blood. I don't like to see you this way, Nagora."

"You wanted a warrior. Now you have Edana. The color of blood becomes her, does it not?"

Nagora didn't wait for an answer. She ran to the sea cave steps. She ignored Raynhard's following footsteps and walked into the water.

As Nagora passed the jailor, she splashed water on his face. His eyes opened. He was in a daze. He said, "You … you did this."

"I did. I hope you'll remember me until the moment you die. Don't drop the knife. It's the only chance you have to free yourself. Remember that, as you watch the ceiling of this cave get closer and closer to you."

Behind the pillar, Nagora untied the air bladder, tugged on the rope, swam to where the ceiling of the cave met the water, and dove under.

"I was about to go in after you," said Lars as Nagora grabbed onto the curragh's edge.

"I know. I have kept you waiting. Brace with the oar. I'm coming aboard."

...

Again Lars gave Nagora his shirt. "Here's a blanket too. Hook says you won't be as cold with it on the way back. I've nuts and dried meat in my scrip. If you're hungry, let me know. And there's a waterskin too if you're thirsty."

"Hungry and thirsty. Hand them over. Do you know the way home?"

"Home is a long, long row from here. To the beach hut is a good row. We should be there before sunrise."

Nagora made herself comfortable in the bow of the curragh as she ate and drank. Her actions in the dungeon played out repeatedly as she tried to imagine other outcomes. If only I hadn't met Chive, perhaps I could have taken Hag too. Could I have taken her guards? Surprise would have been my only advantage. Against numbers, it's not always an advantage. I should have brought my bow. Tar piss! Raynhard's right. What I did, I did at great risk.

Nagora switched the focus of her thoughts to Lars, and soon, his long rhythmic pulls on the oars lulled her to sleep.

Lars's eyes were on hers. The flicker of light over his left shoulder caught Nagora's attention. "There," she pointed. Lars turned to look. "We're not far." She wiped a single tear from her cheek.

"You must be starving. I know I am," said Lars.

"You men are always hungry."

When the curragh touched bottom, Hook and Dangor were already alongside it to haul it further ashore. They helped

Nagora and Lars get out. "There's a warm meal awaiting you in the hut," said Dangor.

She smiled at him. "The best news I've heard so far on this new day. We'll do it honor. How goes Acindor?"

Dangor took her arm. "Last I saw him, he was still out. Sagora's keeping watch over him should he come to. He's dressed and in chains. He'll not be going anywhere on his own for a long time.

"Those poor girls you saved were not in good shape. Your mum and Geirador are bringing them to Srina's parents. They live the closest, on the outskirts of Yhorgal. They'll leave the parents jars of salve for the body wounds, but Tagnya's worried their spirits may never heal."

"At least they're away from the dungeon. Perhaps time and a new reign in the land will help," said Nagora.

"Aye, perhaps." Dangor raised his eyebrows and shrugged. "Well, let's take care of you two. Egg-drop soup and stone bread in the hut by the fire. Consider it your morning meal. After you've eaten, I'll give you no more than three counts to get some sleep. The lookouts above have your horses."

Nagora reached for her uncle's arm. "You didn't climb for eggs in the dark, did you?"

He shook his head and pointed.

Hook was smiling. "Nothing my hens like better than fish tails an' fish heads. Makes for tasty eggs."

Nagora returned his smile. "Thanks, Hook. Uncle's shore soup will be extra good."

Dangor shook her arm. "Egg-drop soup."

"If you insist." They all laughed.

"Uncle, I slept while Lars rowed. He'll appreciate shutting his eyes for a while, but not until he's eaten."

Lars patted his stomach. "If there's a fire and my stomach's been fed, I'll sleep for those three counts."

Dangor tapped Lars's shoulder. "Not to worry, the pot's full to the brim. Eat your fill and get some sleep."

Hook raised his hook. "I'll be on my way now. I'll rouse my sons when I gets home so they kin' go check our nets while I sleeps."

"Well-deserved sleep, Hook," said Dangor. "Thank you once again for your help. Thank Raddy again for taking such good care of those girls. Have a safe ride home."

Nagora went over to Hook and gave him a hug. "Thank Raddy again for rigging the ropes and bladders for me."

"I'll do that. Take care. You too, Lars. Glad we met."

Lars smiled at Hook. "Me too."

The Illusion
Mahtawinikewin

Nagora rode into camp with Lars and Dangor. Just about everyone was ready to ride out. Acindor was conscious. He was sitting on his horse with both hands shackled to the saddle and a black cloth bag covering his head. A warrior led his horse while another followed close behind.

Sagora rode over to greet her sister, uncle, and Lars. She motioned for them to follow so Acindor wouldn't hear.

"How is he?" asked Nagora.

"He regained consciousness after sunrise, complained of a terrible sore head. I gave him some willow tea to help ease the pain. He asked what had happened. He said he remembered nothing except that I had been standing above him to put out the candle lanterns.

"I told him it was too bad because it was a night I would never forget as he had made love not once, not twice, but three times. First he took my virginity and then each time afterward, he filled me with so much seed I cannot but be carrying his future heir to the throne."

"You think that helped relieve his pain?" asked Nagora grinning.

Sagora waved the question away. "Then he asked why he was in chains. I told him it was to ensure his protection from evil old Hag who's always tried to control his decisions. I told him if he wanted to become king, he would have to aid me in my quest to free the dragon and the last of the dragon riders from the Isle of Smoke. Only if he did this for me could I grant him access to the throne.

"He asked about my unicorn. I told him a unicorn only allows virgins and pregnant women to ride it.

"He asked about my troops. I told him I had one thousand I would lead to the Isle of Smoke to free the dragon. And I told him I would keep him chained and blinded during the day until we were at the battlefield on the plain before the Isle of Smoke. His bag will only be removed at nightfall inside his tent."

Nagora took all this in. "I want him to be traveling with my contingent. I'll take good care of him."

Sagora gave a thumbs-up. "I would rather you deal with him than me. You could learn something that'll be useful when it comes time to bargain with Raganora."

"That's what I'm hoping." And I want to keep him close to my blade.

Tagnya and Geirador approached on horseback.

Nagora turned Storm to face them. "Good morning, Mum, Geirador. Uncle told me where you took the girls. How did Srina's parents react?"

"They couldn't believe their eyes. Being woken up in the dark was both a frightening and happy moment. They send thanks to Edana, and they've taken in the other two girls. They promised to get word to Tagina's parents first thing today. As for Sellannye, they'll care for her until a relative is found or, if one is not found, take her in as their own.

"Daughter, I too want to thank you for you for freeing them. I can't get over how brave you have been," said Tagnya.

Nagora sighed. "May their healing begin."

Nagora looked to Geirador. "Any news from the prince's fortress?"

"At daybreak, Hag and two dozen riders left the fortress. Our guess is to the Isle of Smoke. We've no confirmation from Raynhard yet whether they've brought Edana's standard. If we don't hear from Raynhard within this count, we're to pull out as planned. Edana has two appearances to put in tonight." Geirador pointed to the twins. "Though, after last night, I won't be surprised if Edana's reputation precedes her appearance tonight."

"Our appearances will give life to the legend of Edana," said Sagora.

Gabe approached at a gallop. He reined his mount. "Ready to move out when you give the signal, Dangor. Congratulations, Edana." He looked from Nagora to Sagora. "You continue to be the most talked about topic among the warriors. They can't wait to see how this is all going to turn out."

Nagora looked at her sister, and they both smiled.

Sagora reached out to Nagora. "Little sister, I'll be waiting with Acindor to hand him over to you. When you've chosen two warriors from your contingent to watch over him, send mine back."

Nagora reached over to Lars. "Will you pick two for me?"
He flashed her a smile. "Right away."

Sagora was about to head for the front of her line when
Paruline approached with Raynhard on the back of her mount.

Raynhard dismounted and held the bridle of Paruline's
mount. "It took me a while to get away. I take it you saw Hag
leave at daybreak. The captain of the guard and his best men
are with her. They've got Edana's flag and two arrows to
bring to Queen Rag.

"Hag has been in quite a state since Edana secreted
Acindor away. That Edana alluded to him becoming king and
that Edana will carry his child, a future king too, has Hag pulling her hair. Hag is worried Edana will become queen. Not to
mention Edana's the Dragon Warrior Princess returned from
the sea. That has truly rattled her. And the quick death of the
twelve guards she sent to bring Acindor back to the fortress.

"Hag feels powerless against this Edana. Strange though,
she ordered the prince's chambers to be washed and made
clean like new again for his return.

"Hag took a satchel with vials and jars of ingredients I
know nothing about. She ordered me to burn whatever garments of hers that remained, along with her bedding, all her
herbs, and anything of hers remaining as soon as she left. Anything else that wouldn't burn was to be thrown into the
waters of the dungeon sea cave."

Raynhard paused and looked at Nagora.

She stared back at him with narrowed eyes. One day, I'll
get to Hag and I'll keep my oath to those girls.

"Since I found nothing of value that was worth saving, I
carried out her orders.

"The good news is that the other girls were set free before Hag left. Thank you, Nagora, for freeing those in the dungeon cells. In hindsight, it may not have been necessary to risk your life to do what you did. Nevertheless, it is done, and you've kept your promise to them.

"I made the rounds of the fortress. Most of those still there could do like Hag, pack up and leave. Those that stick around will be the few guards assigned to burial duty and a caretaker."

"Well Raynhard, is Chive no more?" asked Tagnya.

"I think so. It'll be reported that he was last seen leaving the fortress with his herb collection bag. He disappeared into the forest and was never seen again.

"Enough said, time we get moving."

"I'll get your mount," said Paruline.

"Thank you, Paruline.

"Tagnya, Dangor, if you will, I'll have a word with you."

Nagora looked away from Raynhard. "Sagora, take me to Acindor. Lars will find me." She kneed Storm and followed her sister.

Sagora stopped several riders away from Acindor. Does she have last minute instructions? "I've only ever called him 'Prince Acindor' or 'my prince' since he regained consciousness. The warriors guarding him address me as 'princess' or 'Princess Edana.'"

Nagora gave her sister a thumbs-up. "Good thinking. I'm glad you've warned me."

Lars pulled up next to them. "Edana, Tremon will lead Acindor's horse. Simana will follow."

Nagora nodded to both of them. "A warrior and an archer. Good choice, Lars. Please, tell them they have my complete trust. They're to call me 'princess' or 'Princess Edana.' If I want them to follow me off the trail with Acindor, I'll raise two fingers like this and point to my eyes. Other than that, they're to stay with the line. Oh! And tell them that if Acindor raises his hands to his left shoulder, it means he's thirsty. To the right shoulder, he's going to puke."

The warrior and the archer smiled after Lars had given them their orders. "Princess," they each said in turn.

You two are happy. Beats leading a mule any day. Poor warriors who got stuck with your beasts.

"Prince Acindor, since we got to know each other last night, do you mind if I call you Acindor?" asked Nagora.

"Do so."

Nagora detected a certain tone in Acindor's voice.

Is that boredom or anger? I bet he's pissed at himself for being taken.

"Good. Acindor, you can call me Edana and think of a name for your son."

The head under the bag jerked up, but Acindor did not say a word.

"We'll be riding quite a lot in the coming days. I hope you don't get saddle sores."

The contingents had split and headed off to stage their Edana appearances. Six days later, after their third appearance, they were to meet at the junction of the Windhaven Road that led to a lookout tower.

Nagora's contingent arrived first in the mid-afternoon sun. Dangor and a group of eight scouts set out ahead of the line so he could place his scouts along the path the warriors would take, making the loop that would create the illusion of a thousand crossing the hilltop into the forest.

At that spot, the road that crossed the hilltop led down into a valley and up the smaller, distant, neighboring hill on which a lookout tower sat. The tower had a view of what passed on the road above and what came and went on the road below, which was the road Hag would have taken on her way to the Isle of Smoke, the shortest way.

Just before Sagora's contingent arrived, Nagora surveyed the scene from Storm's back. *If they can count, this should make for a most important and most memorable report to Raganora.*

Well Storm, time for me to get my unicorn ready.

Sagora's contingent had just arrived. Sagora came alongside and dismounted. "Nagora, good to see you."

"Big sister! How did Edana's appearances go for you?"

"Right on time. No problems with the fire baskets. We've got our routine working smooth. No one followed us yet except for a few dogs we scared away."

"Aye, we had a dog problem too, but Aydan had it running home with its tail between its legs."

"Nagora, so far we've been lucky. What if it rains?"

"I asked the same question to Uncle. He said if it rains, we're to forget about even trying to use the fire baskets. Just plant Edana's standard. It'll be found. Anyway, it could rain inland where I show up, but not where you'll be near the coast. We must hope that what gets reported somehow takes into account the weather. Geirador didn't mention that?"

"I didn't think to ask either."

"Well, now you know."

Sagora pointed at the narwhal tusk. "Need help with that?"

"Sure, until I get the first buckle tied."

Sagora held it while Nagora fastened the buckles.

"There we go. Thanks."

Sagora pointed to the prince. "Acindor?"

"Been complaining since day one. Says his ass is sore. Can't wait to get off his mount and lie on his side."

"Let him complain."

"Damn right. If his ass bleeds, I'll have him tied with his belly against a mule's backside until he gets sore there too."

Sagora smiled at Nagora. "Edana, you're so cruel."

"I tell you, Sagora, if it was up to me, and I had my way with him, you wouldn't believe how cruel I can be. Anyway, today he'll be on the road below the hill with me, watching Edana's thousand warriors go by. Not all of them, but enough to make him believe so." Nagora handed Sagora the spear with Edana's emblem. "Hold the flag."

After applying her red paint, she climbed onto her unicorn. "Aydan, go with Sagora. Send him back to me when we're done."

"Nagora, be careful on the road."

"If Acindor tries anything, he gets an arrow in his back. And if he survives that, I'll finish him off." Nagora reached back and tapped the handle of her big blade.

Nagora led her warriors across the road as soon as Dangor gave the signal. Once on the other side of the road, she turned down the hill on the side the lookouts could see. She took up position about three hundred strides below from where the warriors crossed.

Tremon led Acindor to Nagora and took up position on the side of the road. Simana, with her bow strung and an arrow nocked, kept to the other side of the road.

Nagora removed the bag from Acindor's head as she urged her warriors on. After two hundred or so had gone by, Nagora put his hood back on. He would have to listen to the remaining warriors ride by.

"Acindor, one thousand warriors with bows, spears, swords, and supplies to last thirty days. Will you help me convince your mother to free the dragon? Doing so would ensure that you take the throne with an heir to a line of kings. That line will stretch from you to the far future of this land. Think about it.

"Will your mother dare put up a fight against such a force?

"Who will win the battle on the plain?

"A dragon for a kingdom. Simple. Though your mother, the queen, may choose to keep the dragon. If she were to do that, that would mean your death and the death of your bastard son on the day of his birth. That, I guarantee you.

"Think of it. What will you say to your mother to convince her?"

Acindor did not speak a single word in response.

When their show of force was over and the last of the troops had made their way across the hill and ridden into the forest, Dangor led his scouts ahead. Not long afterward, they arrived at a fork in the trail.

Nagora would lead her contingent to the left. Dangor would scout ahead with four scouts.

Sagora would take the fork to the right. Geirador would scout ahead for her with his four scouts.

The Secret
Ka kaskamoci kanaweyihtamihk
pîkiskwewin

Four days later, after two more successful Edana appearances, Nagora's contingent broke camp in pouring rain. It was the first rain since arriving in the Land of the Danu, and it came down like it meant to drown them.

Cold, wet, and shivering in the night, Nagora planted her sixth Edana flag a hundred strides from a hut near a smithy's shop. A pale yellow glow came from the hut's window. It was enough to make her want to be inside near the flame and the fireplace that produced the smoke.

That night, her bedroll under a tarp was her only choice.

The rain had not let up all night. They had no choice but to rise and ride. It would be a long, slow slog through forest trails to make it to the forest hills on the edge of the plain opposite the Isle of Smoke. They had two days to make it there, one day to prepare, and on the fourth day the battle would begin if negotiations failed.

So much for a rain of fire arrows in a downpour like this one. Often when it rains like this, it settles in for days of endless rain. I hope this will clear.

To make matters worse, Dangor's scouts reported the horses would be knee-deep in mud before long if they continued on their planned path.

"We'll detour up over higher rocky ground. We might have to lead the horses on foot if conditions are too slippery. It'll take us a while longer, but at least we won't be up to our arses in mud," said Dangor.

Nagora looked out from under the hood of her waxed woolen rain cape. "Fine, Uncle. Lead the way."

Dangor had been right. Despite the downpour, the warriors' spirits were up. They had come prepared for wet weather, and they were on the move shrouded in the cold, gray soup that fell upon them as they led their mounts over the wet, slate-strewn terrain.

On they went until the hillside became a ridge, causing them to march on ever more carefully. Finally, the ridge brought them to a forest trail. The leafy trees amplified the pouring rain which tore leaves and threw them to the ground.

Ahead was a huge old oak tree. Dangor was there tending a good fire. Nagora never ceased to be amazed that he could always find a way to start a fire, even in conditions like this.

It pays to carry fire starter in your scrip. Uncle prefers milkweed silk.

Dangor approached Nagora. "We'll have respite from the rain here if we can rig a few tarps from the branches. We'll brew hot forest tea to wash down our rations. That'll give us a lift. One of the scouts spotted a deer. I hope she gets it. If she does, we'll have venison tonight."

In no time, warriors rigged tarps with ropes thrown over branches. They lit another fire and brewed tea under the rain-buffeted tarps.

Everyone is out of the rain, at least for a while.

Tremon removed the hood that covered Acindor's head and held a hot cup to the prince's lips for him to drink. From where he was, he could not see Nagora and did not try to look around. Rather, he focused on the hot drink.

Nagora turned in the opposite direction and stood on tiptoe to scan the trees ahead. Something moved. The hunter?

"See her yet, Nagora?" asked Lars.

"I saw movement then it stopped. She's probably stopped to rest. Look. There." Nagora pointed.

The branches swayed and then the scout staggered clear with a deer across her shoulders.

Nagora raised her fist. Others turned to see and cheered until the hunter dropped her prize on the ground before Nagora and said, "The king's deer, killed on the king's land to feed the king's warriors."

Lars had looked to see where Acindor was. He was satisfied he wasn't nearby, so he translated the hunter's words for Nagora. "Trowan, she's one of Romanika's archer's. They often hunt together."

Nagora smiled. "When this land truly becomes Raynhard's, may none of his subjects go hungry for fear of killing a deer that belongs to the king." Nagora gave Trowan her cup. "Thank you. We'll feast tonight thanks to your skill."

Trowan had already gutted the deer. Two warriors carried it away, tied it onto one of the pack mules, and covered it with a tarp.

The line was moving again, and so was the rain because the wind had started to blow.

It could be a sign that it's going to clear. If it veers, we'll be in luck. If it stays, we'll be in for a long, cold, wet night.

Nagora looked back at the line behind her.

They're all thinking the same thing.

The wind howled and slung the rain at their backs. Leaves stripped from the flailing branches of trees cartwheeled past them. Just when it looked like the forest would be ripped up like a huge rug and shaken to get the dirt out, the wind lightened and veered slowly. The rain all but stopped except for all the drops being blown from the leaves on the trees. The sky had become a lighter shade of gray.

It'll clear overnight.

They were making good time now. Dangor would only call a halt with enough light left to set up camp.

We're making up for the detour.

Ahead at a clearing, Dangor waited on his horse. They were about to head into a valley. He pointed to two mountains in the distance. "Nagora, from the one on your left, if it's a clear day, you can see all the way to the Isle of Smoke and the plain that lies before it. We'll be skirting that mountain's ridge line. It extends to the forests hills that surround the plain on the tip of the coast."

"When will we be at the mountain?" Nagora asked.

"If we can break camp by sunrise tomorrow, we should be there by noon day."

"Where will we camp?"

"On the other side of this valley. Depending on how things went with Sagora, she should be camped on the other side of the ridge or closer to the mountain where we're heading. If they've gone ahead of us, we'll pick up their trail for sure tomorrow."

"Or we could be ahead of them," said Nagora

Her uncle nodded. "That's a definite possibility."

What must have been a peaceful brook in drier times, meandering and gurgling along the valley floor, was now a raging river of roiling mud with broken branches and trees. The scouts had found a suitable place to cross just above a cataract affording a good view of the swift, oncoming water. They had strung ropes across upstream to snag sizable debris coming down river that could be a danger to the riders and their mounts as they crossed. Riders kept an adequate distance from each other so as to maneuver out of harm's way should it become necessary.

They made the crossing without incident, though Nagora imagined one. How would you like to go for a swim Acindor? Would you survive in this muddy rush of water? I bet you can't swim.

It's not time to lose our card in this game.

Farther up the mountainside, the scouts had found a decently level, narrow strip of ground for the contingent to set up camp. The rushing waters in the valley below were a distant murmur.

By nightfall, the spit-roasted venison was all but gone. Warriors around the fires were picking the bones clean before tossing them into the fire. Extra warriors on the night watch tended the improvised racks upon which soggy cloaks and pieces of clothing had been strung to dry near the fires.

Acindor sat at the fire near his tent. One of his legs was chained to a tree. Tremon and Simana sat at their own fire a dozen strides away.

Nagora sat cross-legged before Acindor.

"Edana, your troops are mercenaries, aren't they?" asked Acindor.

"They are. I handpicked each one of them in the Land of Skulls. Godomor the Terrible allowed me to choose from his fiercest and most skillful warriors. They can't wait to drink the blood from the skulls of those they'll slay on the battlefield."

Acindor's lips twisted.

"How will you pay them?"

"I've paid them already." Nagora reached into her scrip. She turned her back to Acindor to put on the human hand bone bracelet. "I saved their king from a plot to overthrow him. Remember this?" She held up her right arm. Acindor tried to conceal his reaction. He had trouble maintaining eye contact.

"Rhysonnger, Vorpinger's brother, purchased a poison from Hag, through you, to put in candles offered as a deadly gift to Godomor. They would burn poison fumes that would have eventually killed him. Rhysonnger paid you with his own niece's flesh, eleven-year-old Sellannye, a poor, abused, motherless child to be abused even more by you. She is free now, no longer locked in your dungeon. I freed her. And the other two, also."

The anger in her voice was rising.

"I split Vorpinger's skull with an axe. I brought his brother before Godomor to confess his plot and now Rhysonnger is buried up to his neck in dirt, staring into his dead brother's eyes."

"All that I did because the sea would not take me, Edana, the Dragon Warrior Princess. Hag was wrong. And she knows it. She knows I'm stronger than her." Nagora pressed her fist to Acindor's chest. "And Hag knows I'll free the dragon and destroy her."

Acindor spit on the chain his leg was shackled to. "Not if she destroys the dragon first. Then you'll never destroy her. You don't know the power she has. You think she is an old witch. Well, she's not. She's an ancient witch. She's ancient and powerful. Her power is her beauty. I know it. I've seen it. I've tasted it. When the last dragon dies, she'll have her power of eternal beauty forever. She'll be invincible."

Nagora grabbed a stick from Acindor's small pile of firewood and pointed it at him. "You believe that. You believe Hag, you who have yet to watch yourself fuck a virgin for the very first time. You try. You fail. Your failure enrages you."

Acindor blinked and looked away. "My failure enrages me because I've watched myself fuck Hag. Not the Hag that you see. But Hag, the beautiful. When I fuck with her it's unlike anything you can imagine. My cock grows so big and hard when she rides me to my ecstasy inside her. If it were you, my cock would tear you open."

Nagora snapped the stick. "What potion does Hag give you that convinces you of that?"

"None."

"Then she takes a potion that allows her to convince you."

Acindor stared at Nagora. "It's not a potion. You don't see, do you, Edana? She gets her power from the same place as you."

"From the dragon?"

"From dragon eggs."

Nagora pointed the broken stick at him. "How can that be?"

"When she drinks the liquid of a dragon's egg, she becomes the beauty she once was long ago, with all the irresistible charm you can only imagine, but I have tasted. It's but a moment's glimpse of what is promised her if she succeeds in destroying the last dragon. And I want her that way for me alone because she showed me what I can be."

Nagora leaned forward and rested an elbow on her knee. "But that can happen only if you sire a son from a virgin. Your son resides in me."

Acindor rolled his eyes. "I don't know that. You say I spilled my seed inside you three times. I've no memory of that. I do have memory of every time I experienced ecstasy with Hag. But with you—no."

"So you would side with evil to satisfy the desires of your flesh?"

Acindor's voice became a sneer. "For that, and for this kingdom that will be mine."

Nagora pointed a finger at him. "But only if you sire a son with me. You see, here is your chance to side with good. Convince your mother to hand over the reins of power to you. If you can do that and then, as your first act as a benevolent monarch, release the dragon and its rider from the Isle of

Smoke, you would stand a chance to earn the first seeds of loyalty from a people you could govern justly." Now she pointed both fingers at him. "And they would grow to love you and your son—the future heir to your throne."

Acindor stuck his chin out. "That could only happen with the birth of a son I sire. As far as I'm concerned, I'm not the father of the child you say you carry."

She looked Acindor in the eye and stuck her chin out. "I'm Edana. I have power over light and fire. I have that power until the day I give birth to the son of a king who is just and good and full of love for his people and the land they live in. On the day I give birth to that future king, I will lose my power over light and fire. But that future king will inherit it to do good and fight against evil."

Acindor leaned back and bowed his head. "And if my mother should not relinquish her throne to me and decide to meet you in battle, what will happen?"

Nagora waited for Acindor to look up at her. "I'll rain fire down on her and her troops. My warriors from the Land of Skulls will slay every one of them, hack their heads from their shoulders, drink their blood from their skulls, and tie the empty skulls to their saddles. Then they'll ride home with the skulls and nail them atop the walls of the fortifications of their towns."

Acindor crossed his arms. "And what of my son you carry in your womb?"

Her voice was a sneer. "He'll burn in my womb, not worthy to inherit my powers."

"And what of me?"

She answered through clenched teeth. "Before the nightfall of the day of the ultimatum I give your mother, you will be drawn and quartered on the battlefield. Then I'll cut into your chest and rip your heart out and stuff it into your mouth. Next, I'll chop your head off and kick it to the middle of the battle-field for the carrion birds to peck at until all that remains are the scattered pieces of your skull bones."

Acindor brought his two fists together and struck them to his forehead.

Dangor was leaning against a nearby tree as Nagora left the prince to go find her bedroll.

He's heard everything I've said, and yet he smiles.

As she walked past him, he whispered, "Good night, Edana. Sleep well." She smiled and went on her way.

The Key
Âpâpiskahikan

The next morning after Nagora's contingent broke camp, just before they pulled the black hood over his head, the look on Acindor's face told her he had not slept that night. A dream had troubled her sleep. Nagora had fallen asleep holding her amulet pressed to her lips with one hand and her father's knife at her heart in her other hand. The strange eye had appeared again. It spoke to her in what Godomor had confirmed was the language of the dragon, the same as the Language of The People, the First People of The Land. *"Nagora, Yogari nitaweyitam kîya ôma nâtamâkêwin pakitinowewin Danuka. Miska apachichikana âpâpiskaham âsokan kanaweyimowewina Danuka mihcet awâsisak.* Nagora, Yogari needs your help to free Danuka. Find tools so he can unlock the bridge to protect Danuka's children."

I understand those words so well, but I don't know if I can make sense of them. In the past, when the eye appeared and spoke to her, it was to reassure her. Only once before had it told her to do something. That led to her becoming Edana. In this dream she had, for the first time, clearly heard the part before "ka". It was clearly "Danu" with "ka." A complete name?

The eye spoke Da's name and mine too. "Danu." Land of the Danu. Land of the Dragon. The people here are known as the People of the Dragon. Could this dragon's name be Danuka? People have children. Children are the future of the land. If Danuka can be free, then it can protect the children for the future of the people of the land. Does that make sense? Is that the message the eye is telling me?

"Find tools ... unlock the bridge." How do we unlock the bridge? To lock a door, we have a lock on it. To make the lock work, we need a key. The key is a tool. The eye said "tools." More than one? How many? Many keys?

There's something obvious I'm missing. Leave it be for now. It'll come.

Nagora's contingent climbed the mountain diagonally. When they made it to the ridge trail, the scouts reported they found no tracks to show anyone had gone by that way. Dangor sent a scout back along the ridge trail in the direction Sagora and her contingent would come. "I want to know if they're all right or not. Or if they've been delayed, how long they'll be in coming."

The going was faster along the ridge trail that took them down the side of one mountain and up another. By noon they had reached its top and, true to Dangor's word, the Isle of Smoke was visible.

Dangor pointed to the plain below. "See there. It looks like battle preparations. They're creating a two-flanked wedge with two trenches that converge, leaving themselves two retreat routes: one to the Isle of Smoke, the other back inland along the main road."

Nagora looked to her uncle. "So they could either retreat to the fortress on the Isle of Smoke to starve to death, or head to the castle at Windhaven where we would have to starve them out as well."

Dangor shook his head. "You know that's not our intention. We'll free Yogari and the dragon. That operation will be underway well before the battle on the plain starts."

"I know, Uncle. I was just thinking about the old battle siege stories you had told me about."

Dangor sighed. "I know. It's not how I like to fight. It takes a well provisioned force to fight a siege, let alone sit one out in a fortress."

He looked along the ridge trail they were on. "We'll break here for a bite to eat. Most likely the scout should return before we're back on the move again."

Nagora nodded and sat, taking in the detail of the Isle of Smoke in the far distance. It was so much closer than the time Moreena had taken her to the mountain cliff where she could see it in the distance. That time, if she had held an acorn on the tip of her thumb on her outstretched arm, the isle was smaller than the acorn.

Now it fits in the palm of my hand. The arc of the bridge is like a bent twig with tiny ants moving along its length. The fortress on the other side looks like rough-hewn blocks of wood stuck together on the muddy mountainside. Only a few trees are visible on either side of the island. A tiny plume of smoke is rising from the volcano's mouth. Were it to erupt now, most of the lava would flow onto the sea side of the island, away from the fortress and the bridge. Then again, like Uncle would say—Who knows how or when it'll blow?

Da, as long as it doesn't blow before we get you away from it.

Dangor pointed along the ridge they were on. "This ridge trail brings us to the forested hills above the plain. First, we'll come to a stone bluff where we pick up the trail into the forest. Raynhard's people should be at the bluff to meet us. From the bluff, they'll take the Isle of Smoke raiders to the boat at a secret harbor they call Keyhole Harbor. Others will take Edana's warriors to their campsites in the hills.

"Before that, though, we'll have a view of the battlefield. We'll be facing the point of that wedge we see now. We should get a report from one of Raynhard's spies before we make final plans for our attack."

Dangor looked in the opposite direction and pointed. Geirador and the scout he had sent approached. "Looks like we'll find out what happened to Sagora's contingent."

Geirador wasn't too pleased. "We got mired in mud. It'll take the others another day to get here. They sent me to report. I met this fellow," he indicated Maylor, the scout, "on his way to find us."

"We almost did too. We didn't take a chance and stuck to the high, rocky ground. Slow going, but at least we were moving. Other than that, is everything okay?" asked Dangor.

Geirador nodded. "I'll move on with you. Maylor, you can report to Lars."

...

At the bluff, Raynhard's people were waiting. Raynhard had told Dangor that six men who had originally served with King Bernhard's guard were to meet them, and he would know at least one of them. Two of them approached.

Could they be members of The Guard I met last year?

"Dangor?" asked one of the men.

Her uncle squinted as he bit his lower lip and nodded. "Aye. You I remember. Kurt, right?"

"Kurt it is, Dangor." He wore a welcome smile.

Dangor pointed at him. "We met on the very first day I set foot in Windhaven with this lass's da, Yogari. This is ... "

"Edana," said Kurt as he bent his two middle fingers into his palm, splayed the other two and his thumb, brought his hand to his heart, and gave her the dragon-chord salute. He pointed to his companion. "This is Edward. Welcome, Edana."

"Please, call me Nagora."

Kurt smiled and winked at her.

Dangor placed a hand on his friend's shoulder. "You must know of Geirador?"

"Know of him, yes, by reputation. Glad to meet you."

They all shook hands.

Dangor wagged a finger. "Edward, now I remember. It was your daughter that Tagnyoriva gave her doll to."

The Rider's wife Moreena told me about. More confirmation.

"That is so. My granddaughter still plays with it."

Dangor smiled. "You're a happy grandfather! Good for you. How have you been?"

Edward's chest expanded as he took in a great breath. "Well, we've managed a living for ourselves far from the evil influence of Queen Rag. Raynhard sought us out, and we've promised to do all we can to help his cause. Thank you for bringing this force. Now I think we stand a damn good fighting chance," said Edward.

Nagora searched Edward's face. He was confident. What does he know that we don't?

Dangor's brow furrowed. "Only half of us are here. The other contingent will get here tomorrow. They got mired in mud. Geirador brought us the news."

"With the rains we've had, I'm not surprised. We wondered if anyone of you would show up today. We were expecting only a scout," said Edward.

"Well, we're here, and there's work to be done. Which of you is to report?" asked Dangor.

Before he answered, Kurt pointed to the woman and two men who were approaching.

"Sorry, we're late." Lars looked to Romanika and Tankar. "We were making sure everyone was clear on why we stopped," said Lars.

Dangor reached a hand up to Lars's shoulder. "This is Lars. He'll translate as you report. Kurt, Edward, meet commanders Romanika and Tankar. They lead our contingent from the Land of Skulls."

Kurt and Edward shook hands with Lars and the commanders. "Welcome to our soon-to-be-fought battle. We're truly glad to have your support," said Kurt.

After Lars translated the commanders smiled and replied, "Our warriors look forward to the battle."

Kurt cleared his throat. "My job to report. Garrisons from all outlying towns and villages have been called into the Isle of Smoke. Those that have answered the call have been returning with what remains of the weapons and uniforms of those who have deserted. Most of those desertions have occurred in the garrisons nearest the towns and villages where Edana appeared."

"Good," said Dangor, as he tapped Nagora's shoulder.

"It gets better, Dangor. Most of those deserters have taken their weapons to join up with the cells of our rebel force. Members of The Guard have been training the fighters from those cells in secret and will be leading them and the deserters who have joined them."

The faces of Coyle, Brin, Tavi, and their captain, Ardal, surfaced from Nagora's memory of her encounter with The Guard almost two years ago. Counting the faceless ones she had not seen because of the dark, that meant a possible dozen rebel contingents.

Dangor spoke her unvoiced question. "Kurt, that would make for a rebel force of how many?"

"Minimum two hundred. Half of those will carry bows. The others, swords and spears."

Dangor's smile broadened, and so did Nagora's. That's double what Raynhard had told us at the meeting.

Romanika and Tankar nodded to Lars and smiled briefly.

Dangor was about to say something, but Kurt's raised finger stopped him.

"And Dangor, we've just gotten news that Stone Standers with slings are on their way here. They're traveling light and fast in groups of ten. In all, three hundred of them, we've been told. Their commander, by the name of Grimrod, will meet here with Raynhard to discuss how they can best be used in Edana's battle plan."

Now Dangor's smile split his face in two. "Kurt, that's great news! Now we've got a force of six hundred armed with weapons!"

Tankar and Romanika jabbed Lars's shoulders with clenched fists, obviously pleased with the information their smiling translator gave them.

This news warmed Nagora's heart. *The Stone Standers are true to their word, and Grim's leading them. Now I see why Edward is so confident that we stand a damn good fighting chance.*

Kurt continued, "Edana's call to come witness the freeing of the dragon has worked. There are more and more people on the roads headed this way to see Edana on her unicorn and the dragon fly free from the Isle of Smoke. If there's a battle, we've no way of telling how many among them may be tempted to join in. That could be a hindrance more than a help."

Romanika and Tankar looked at each other. The information did not please them.

Nagora's dream of Danuka's eye was still fresh in her mind and was begging her to make sense of it. Later, I could learn something from this report.

"And the activity on the plain?" asked Dangor.

Kurt pointed. "An arrowhead trench pointed our way. As you can see at the far end, most of the troops have set up camp. They've built up log walls three logs high and are digging a ditch on the outside, all along the length of the log walls. Dirt from the ditch is thrown up against the logs.

"Seems like the idea is to split the attacking force in two," Kurt used his hands to illustrate as he spoke, "so it has to attack on two fronts. The ditches and log walls would be to slow down attackers on horse. It'll take good riders on good horses to clear the ditch and the log wall. They'll have to ride well past the point of the wedge to do so."

"Troop count?" asked Dangor.

Kurt scratched his chin. "With the latest arrivals this morning, we counted eight hundred, give or take a handful."

Romanika and Tankar gave their full attention as Lars translated.

"Archers?"

"At least three hundred."

"Any mercenaries among the eight hundred?"

"None."

"All conscripts, trained by the mercenaries?" asked Dangor.

Tankar smirked at this piece of information and shook his head.

"Except for a handful of King Bernhard's original force."

"Who's in command of Rag's troops?"

"Grallimdor, a man from Windhaven. He used to manage the harbor. He was a favorite of the mercenaries because he was one who acted most like them, even learned their language, and prayed to their god. He's a skilled swordsman and an able rider."

Dangor bit on his lip as he listened. "How many horses?"

"Seventy so far."

Dangor's eyes widened. "That's more than we estimated."

"Thirty-six in the fortress, and the rest are at the camp stables on the plain. However, it looks like another temporary stable is being set up to accommodate as many horses. The horses from the fortress will most likely end up there. That would make sense if they plan to set up defenses on the bridge to protect access to it and the fortress beyond. By tomorrow noon, that should become clear."

Romanika and Tankar looked to where Lars was pointing as he translated, nodding as they took in the information.

With this added information, Nagora tried to make sense of her dream. Protect access. Unlock the bridge? How is that going to protect the children? What am I missing?

Kurt took a stick and drew a rough map in the dirt at his feet to show the isle and the fortress. "The lookout tower above the fortress got washed down the slope two days ago. Looks like one of the fortress's back walls is under stress with the mud and stone piled up against it. What with all the trees stripped from the slopes, there's nothing left to hold back the rocks and mud."

"Will that wall hold?" asked Dangor.

"Not if there's another downpour like the last one. That was a lot of rain for one day. It's making digging the ditches below the log walls a thankless job. Throwing mud and water is not an easy task. They will not finish the job."

Tankar scanned the sky in all directions as he listened to the running translation. Is he trying to predict the coming weather? He's looking for signs, that's for sure. The day of the battle is too far off to make a reliable prediction.

Dangor pointed to the plain below. "An awful lot of people are working down there. How long have they been working on the ditches?"

"This is the eighth day. The very next day after Hag's arrival, work started and riders went out with orders for outlying garrisons to head for the Isle of Smoke. You're right about a lot of people working down there. They've forced many children to work there, at least two hundred."

A grim look took hold of Romanika's face as she shook her head. Tankar spit.

Nagora clenched her teeth. Unlock the bridge to protect those children? That can't be. "Uncle, what'll we do? Fight against innocent children? Raganora must surely intend on keeping them behind those log walls with her troops to make Edana think twice about raining fire arrows down on her troops."

"Nagora, we'll have to wait for Raynhard to arrive. We'll discuss a new strategy to counter Raganora using children to shield her troops."

Tankar pulled a hand through his hair until it came to rest at the back of his neck. He bit at his lower lip. Is he searching for alternatives?

Dangor looked back to Kurt. "Anything from inside the fortress?"

"Nothing. Supplies have been trickling in daily to the camp on the plain." Kurt pointed. "Basically, what it'll take to feed their force, but nothing for a prolonged battle or siege."

"Keyhole Harbor?"

"The Sea Wolf and crew are ready."

"Kurt, if you were in Queen Rag's position, what would you do?" Dangor's eyes were on Kurt's face.

He stared back at Dangor. "I guess you haven't heard. We know what she's going to do. Raynhard must have gotten word of it days ago. Raganora's been spreading a message of her own since Edana started appearing with her unicorn standard and inviting all to come see the dragon set free."

Nagora crossed her arms as she looked at Kurt. "What message is that?"

Kurt held her gaze in his. "'Come witness the execution of the dragon on the Isle of Smoke Bridge on the feast of Maxxa.'"

A deep chill swept through Nagora's body.

Dangor made a fist. "Damn, she knows we have her son and she has no intention of negotiating to free the dragon in exchange for him. For some reason, she must think it's to her advantage. But what advantage?"

Nagora bit her lower lip in thought. "If we're to believe Acindor, Hag'll get what she wants. What'll Hag give Raganora in return? She's already rendered her services. How has she convinced Raganora that she'll be able to maintain her hold on power by killing the dragon and allowing her son to die? Do you think Raganora would let her own son die?"

Kurt snorted. "Small price to pay to stay in power. Acindor has never proved he's fit to rule. Everyone knows the man can't stand on his own middle leg. How's he going to control the kingdom?"

Romanika nudged Tankar, grinned, and shook her head.

Kurt continued, "Hag's been his bloody nursemaid all these years and has kept him out of Rag's way by trying to find him a virgin bride. You don't make a name for yourself as king if all you're known for is kidnapping and terrorizing young girls throughout the land in search of a virgin wife."

"What'll we do? I wish Raynhard were here," said Dangor.

Nagora looked at her uncle. "I say we don't take a chance. We move to free Yogari and the dragon as soon as we can. We mustn't wait. Once we get inside Queen Rag's fortress, we'll know what's up. From there we'll make our move. Uncle, let's face it. If she's going to kill the dragon, she's also going to kill Da. He's the only one who can control the dragon, and he's the one who fought her lover and threw him to his death from that bridge. She's going to kill Danuka and Yogari."

Dangor's eyes opened wide. Then he squinted at Nagora. "Wait. What did you say? What was that name you said?"

"Danuka?"

"Where did you learn of that name?"

The two commanders kept their eyes on Nagora and their ears bent to Lars, obviously not wanting to miss a word.

"Last night, in a dream. I've never told you about this because, on occasions in the past, I thought I was not myself, and that I was imagining things. A strange eye appears and speaks to me, usually to reassure me. For the first time, last night, I understood its name. It spoke it clearly in my dream—Danuka."

Her uncle held both her arms and looked her in the eye. "Do you realize what has happened?"

Nagora shook her head. "What do you mean?"

"Your amulet's been revealing its power to you. 'Danu,' you already know, means 'dragon.' 'Ka' means 'Mother.' 'Dragon Mother.' Danuka's been speaking to you. What did she say to you in the dream?"

She repeated the words. "'Nagora, Yogari needs your help to free Danuka. Find tools so he can unlock the bridge to protect Danuka's children.' I've been trying to figure out what she means. Tools to unlock the bridge? Are those keys? Protect Danuka's children? Is she referring to the children on the plain scattered among Rag's troops behind that ditch? Or the people of the Land of the Danu?"

"Geirador." Dangor took hold of his arm. "Didn't you do some work for Yogari? Something that had to do with building the bridge? Make a key of sorts? Would you know where that is?"

"Aye, I did some work for him. He did call it a key, but I never knew why. It's always been in the same place, right smack in the middle of the bridge. It's locked in a stone there."

Nagora reached for her head. "I don't understand."

"Okay, you see, it's a big metal pin about the length of your lower leg and as big around as your ankle." Geirador used his hands to indicate the size and cylinder shape. "The handle part of the key, as Yogari calls it, is a metal ring half as thick as the pin and it's fitted into an oblong hole at the top of the pin. The big ring can be made to pivot up into an upright position. When the ring's not up, it's lying down, kept out of the way, and recessed on that stone on the bridge. The ring can be lifted up when needed.

"I once saw your father attach pulleys to it when they were using teams of mules to haul big logs across the bridge.

"To be honest, I never knew why he called it a key except that the handle part, when upright above the big pin, looks like a key's handle you can turn."

Dangor had been listening attentively. "Geirador, you did say it's attached to a stone 'right smack in the middle of the bridge'?"

"Aye, that's the keystone of the bridge." A big smile spread on Geirador's face.

Nagora reached for Geirador's arm. "What about the keystone?"

"Tell her," said Dangor.

"The keystone holds the bridge together. Remove the bridge's keystone and it'll fall apart."

Nagora pulled on Geirador's arm. "Sorry, I don't understand how that can be."

"It's not easy to explain. Try to picture what I tell you."

Geirador took a long breath as he appeared to order his thoughts.

One of Romanika's eyes squinted as her mouth hung open in a twisted smile as she focused on what Lars was translating.

Again Geirador's þig hands went into motion as he explained. "The Isle of Smoke Bridge is a stone arch structure, curved like a strung bow. When building such an arch, all the big stones are cut and fitted together on a temporary wooden support frame."

Nagora nodded. "Like on top of the face side of a strung bow?"

"That's it, Nagora. When the wooden frame is removed, the keystone in the middle of the arch holds the bridge together as the weight of all the other stones from both ends, which make up the arch, come to rest on it."

She had to ask. "Can the keystone be removed?"

"Possibly, if it was designed to be removed. Yogari never mentioned that."

Nagora's hands were moving faster than she could speak. "It must be removable. Why else would Danuka have asked for my help? Da must know of Raganora's plan and he knows a way out, but he needs my help, our help, to unlock the bridge, to destroy it. We need to find tools for him. But what kind of tools? If we knew how the keystone is locked in place, we would know what we're looking for," said Nagora.

Again Geirador took a deep breath. "I'll tell you how I understand it from what your da told me about it, when he asked me to make the metal pins that would lock the keystone in place."

Nagora touched his arm. "Please, Geirador. Not too fast. I want to be sure to understand this."

Tankar and Romanika were nodding.

"Imagine you're looking at the middle row of stones that forms the arch of the bridge, and that you're looking at it from its side," said Geirador.

"As if I were looking at a strung bow from the side as held to shoot an arrow skyward?" asked Nagora.

"Aye. Now move in closer so you can see three stones, the keystone and the stones on each side of it in the center row. Imagine that you can look through these stones as you would through clear blocks of ice."

"I see them," said Nagora.

"The big pin that goes through the keystone from top to bottom would be the trunk of a tree. The pins, which lock the keystone to the stones on each of its four sides, would be the branches that grow up and out from the tree trunk."

Her eyes, as well as those of the commanders, were riveted on Geirador's fingers, illustrating his words. "I see the tree with branches spread from inside the keystone up and out into the stones on its sides."

"Good. Now imagine grabbing the handle on the top of the tree trunk to pull the keystone up and out," said Geirador.

Nagora shook her head. "It can't be done. The branches have it locked in place to the stones next to it."

"Aye, and at the bottom of the tree trunk the roots also spread out to hold the keystone in place. Actually, a big fluted end on the big pin, flush against the keystone."

Nagora began to nod and gesture with her hands. "Okay, now I see it. All the pins are separate pieces. The only pin that has something attached is the big pin and that's the ring handle at the top.

"So the separate pins of the branches are first inserted into the side stones and kept in position ready to slide into the aligned holes of the keystone when lowered in place."

"Very good, Nagora. That's it."

"Okay, how do keys work?" Nagora answered her own question. "They're inserted into the keyhole of a lock and then turned to unlock the lock. Geirador, what do we need to turn the handle on top of the keystone?"

The commanders' and Lars's eyes shifted to Geirador.

He blinked before answering. "I would use a stout iron pry bar, at least as long as you are tall. Stick it through the handle on the top of the big pin, push or pull it in either direction to make the big pin turn. It would take two people to turn it."

"Okay. That's one tool. Danuka said to 'find tools.' That means at least one more. What are we looking for?" asked Nagora. She had trouble keeping her feet still. The answer was at hand. She could feel it.

"I've been thinking about the big pin," said Dangor.

All eyes turned to her uncle.

"Its fluted end on the bottom of the keystone plugs the hole there. The ring handle at the top is set in an oblong hole in the big pin, allowing the handle to move up and down. If the big pin were hammered down, the fluted end at the bottom would no longer plug the hole there."

Nagora held her hands together. "The key would be completely inserted and ready to turn." Her excitement mounted. "What would that do? What happens when the hole on the bottom is unplugged?"

"Whatever was held in by the plug comes out," said Dangor.

"Okay. So what comes out and what happens? Is the keystone unlocked? Can the keystone now be pulled out?" asked Nagora.

Geirador snapped his big fingers. "I think I understand Yogari's design now."

All eyes were back on the big blacksmith.

"What comes out makes way for the branch pins to slide deeper into the keystone, and so—out of the stones at its sides. When that happens, the keystone has been unlocked—ready to be lifted out. I'm guessing it's fine beach sand that was used to keep the branch pins in position in the side stones to lock the keystone in place. Water would also be needed to wash the sand out.

"And why the bridge was built on a temporary wooden frame now makes sense. To build it wide enough to accommodate two teams of horses crossing it side by side, each stone had to be cut at the proper angle and laid on the frame so the force of its weight pushed not only back to the land, but in two other directions."

Geirador made a fist with one hand and placed it against the corner made by the sides of his thumb, open palm, and pointer finger. He pivoted the knuckles of his fist against the side of his hand and finger. "One that pushes toward the center of the bridge's roadway along its length." Then he pivoted his fist toward his thumb. "And the other that pushes toward the keystone at its middle.

"With the keystone lifted out, the stones that were shoulder to the keystone twist in the direction they are pushing and topple inward enough to allow the bridge to collapse on itself." He lowered his outstretched fingers so he could pivot the knuckles of his fist onto the knuckles of his other hand, and then let them fall down and away from each other.

Six heads were nodding and Nagora was smiling. "And it all makes sense to me too! There we go! We have our tools! A heavy pry bar, a heavy hammer or the broadside of a big axe, and water.

"But I still don't get the part about protecting Danuka's children," said Nagora.

Romanika lifted a finger and nodded once. She too wants to understand.

Dangor raised his hand. "If Raganora is going to execute the dragon on the bridge, the only way she'll be able to do that is to get it to the bridge and chain it there on the handle of the keystone. Kurt, do you know if there's a ballista at the fortress?"

Tankar's eyes widened.

Kurt held up a finger. "They only have one left that's operational, to our knowledge." He looked to Edward, who was nodding. "They have about ten or twelve bolts left. They would probably use one of those big, barbed bolts to kill the dragon, like they did when they hunted down all the other dragons."

"That means the ballista would have to be set up on one end of the bridge or the other," said Dangor.

"I'm guessing they'll set it up on the mainland side so those come to witness the execution can see the bolt being fired at the dragon," said Geirador.

Edward and Tankar were nodding.

"And witness Raganora give the command," said Nagora. "They would have to set up on the mainland side."

Dangor touched Nagora's arm. "Aye. But these are all guesses. Will Rag actually do it that way?"

Edward said, "Here's my opinion, to try to answer Nagora's question about protecting the children: If you can give Yogari what he needs to unlock the bridge, as you say, that will allow him to free the dragon at the same time. If that happens, just ask these three who saw Yogari fly over Windhaven on the first dragon he tamed." Edward had pointed to Kurt, Dangor, and himself.

He continued, "I think you would get the same reaction on the plain. People would be in awe. There would be hope again that things in the land will change for the better. I'm willing to bet most of Rag's troops would drop their weapons on the spot."

"And we wouldn't have to risk killing innocent children in battle," said Nagora. "So do we stick to Edana's planned appearance on the plain on the Feast of Maxxa?"

Romanika bared her teeth in a tight smile as she nodded repeatedly.

Dangor was biting his lower lip as he nodded. "It'll be a further demonstration of Edana's power. As Edward says, it could play in the balance to influence Rag's troops to throw down their arms and desert her on the spot, before we even engage in battle. Especially, if Yogari flies Danuka free."

Dangor looked to Kurt. "You'll need a signal from us at the fortress to let you know if we're moving to free Yogari and Danuka. At the same time, it'll be a signal for a diversion. How about a fire arrow shot out of the fortress, skyward toward the mainland?"

"That would do," said Kurt. "What do you suggest as a diversion?"

"Attack at the far corner of the wedge. It's closest to the outside stables that have been set up, and it's closest to the bridge. Hit the stable tents with fire arrows. Smoke and fire and spooked horses will stir things up for sure.

"Have a lookout watch for a rider on the dragon's back flying away from the fortress or the bridge. Once Yogari and Danuka are free, don't worry about us. We'll make it out the way we're going in."

Edward stuck his hand out. "In that case, I suggest that your raiders going to the Isle of Smoke head for the Sea Wolf now to leave on this night's tide. The sooner you get there, the sooner you'll gather the information you'll need to plan your moves. It's your call. Talk with your people first.

Soon as you decide, let me know. I'll lead you there. Kurt will wait here for Raynhard and the other contingent, if you decide to go."

"Give us a count or two to discuss and decide," said Dangor.

Kurt and Edward went to join the other four men who had accompanied them.

After discussing the situation with Romanika and Tankar, all agreed the raiders should head for the Sea Wolf as soon as possible with Edward.

To that end, Lars would go with the commanders, ensuring those who had volunteered to join the raiding party would get their weapons and rations ready.

Then they were to seek replacement volunteers for those from Sagora's contingent who had not arrived yet.

Once the raiders were ready, all were to meet with Dangor and Edward before leaving, so Kurt and Geirador could witness the formal decision and report to Raynhard on how it was reached.

Lars left with the two commanders.

Dangor turned to Geirador. "I've things to discuss with Nagora before we all meet to formalize our decision. It won't take long."

"I'll go brew us some tea in the meantime," said Geirador.

Dangor gave him a nod. "We'll go find you when we're done."

What he's about to tell me is weighing on him. I think I can guess what.

As Dangor led Nagora a few paces away, he bowed his head and brushed a finger across an eyebrow. "Lass, this isn't easy for me to say. I have to say it though. And in the light of what we've just learned and the situation we find ourselves in, I have to tell you I don't agree with it." He looked her in the eye.

"This must have to do with what Raynhard told you and Mum the day after we captured the prince." Anger surfaced in her heart.

Her uncle nodded and kept his eyes on hers. "Aye. I'll give it to you straight. Raynhard doesn't want you to be part of the raiding party to the Isle of Smoke."

I knew it, Raynhard. You betrayed me. She clenched her teeth to hold back the anger. Stay calm. You're not mad at Uncle. "His reasons?"

"Your actions inside the prince's fortress. He thinks you'll act on your own and not follow plans and put the whole operation at risk. He said you weren't yourself at the prince's fortress." Dangor looked away.

"Do you agree with him?" She kept her voice calm.

His eyes sought hers. "I've already told you, no."

"Does Mum?" I want to know.

Dangor pursed his lips and shook his head once. "I won't speak for her. She was quite baffled with what Raynhard told us."

Do I dare ask what Ryanhard's exact words were? "Uncle, I don't know what he told you exactly. I just want to say this: He asked me to take on the role of Edana. I accepted with all that entails."

Nagora reached for the dagger at her belt. "You told me Da had left his knife to be given to his child who he hoped would be loyal to The Cause also. Raynhard gave it to me. I want to give Da his knife so he'll know I'm his daughter and loyal to The Cause, because freeing Da has become my cause. Raynhard wants to take that away from me." She put the knife back in its sheath.

"As for my actions in the prince's fortress, they were motivated by an oath I had sworn to a girl I witnessed die because of the abuse Acindor and his jailor had inflicted on her. I swore the same oath to the other girls who suffered there. Uncle, I kept part of my oath.

"Now Raynhard wants to put an end to my role? He doesn't realize all I've done for him and for his cause.

"If I'm to be one of the raiders, under your command, I promise you I will obey your orders. Have no fear, Uncle. I'll not put our enterprise at risk. You have my word."

"Nagora, I trust you. I want you at my side on the Isle of Smoke. I want to help you free Yogari and protect Danuka's children, as Danuka wants you to."

Nagora hugged him. Raynhard, you've lost my trust.

"Let's go see if Geirador has that tea boiling," said Dangor.

Lars returned with the two warrior volunteers and Aydan.

Dangor watched the big red hound head for Nagora.

"Don't worry, Uncle. Aydan's only come to say good-bye."

While she scratched Aydan's chin at her hip, she listened to the introductions.

"Dangor, Nagora, you've already met the archers: Trowan, Derk, and Jared." Lars pointed to them.

Dangor smiled and nodded. "When I showed them the map of the Isle of Smoke and its fortress layout. Tsimor was there too." He shook hands with the four, as did Nagora.

"And today, these warriors volunteered to join us: Tommassen and Kymasen," said Lars.

"From Tankar's unit?" asked Dangor.

"Yes," said Lars.

Dangor and Nagora reached out to shake their hands. "Glad to have you with us. Lars, tell the volunteers I'll be showing them a plan of the fortress when we get there."

Their handshakes were strong and confident. Trowan, who had killed the deer on that rainy day, wore a big smile. She's fearless. And so are the others, I'm sure.

The warriors had packed two pack mules with weapons, ropes, fire arrows, and extra rations. Lars had also brought two of the biggest axes he had been able to find, thanks to Tankar. He was showing them to Dangor and Geirador, and judging by Geirador's smile, he approved.

Dangor suggested they have a piece of hardwood and, if they could find one, a long metal rod. Geirador suggested he ask Edward, who was approaching with Kurt.

"Have you decided?" asked Kurt.

"Aye, we'll be leaving with Edward, just as he suggested. Now that you're here, Kurt, we'll make it official. First, I have a question for Edward.

"Would you have a long metal rod or a pry bar you could lend us?"

"I think I have just the thing you'll need at my place. Soon as we get there, I'll show it to you."

"Good.

"Well, Geirador, Kurt, let's make this official," said Dangor as he put an arm around Nagora and pointed to each volunteer in turn, and then to Nagora. "These are the raiders I'll take with me to the Isle of Smoke to free Yogari and Danuka: Trowan, Derk, Jared, Tsimor, Tommassen, Kymasen, Lars, and Nagora. We leave in a count. Inform

Raynhard, Gabe, Tagnya, and Sagora of my decision, our decision, and how we came to it. Give them a true account of all
we discussed and agreed upon."

He let go of Nagora and embraced Geirador. "We'll see
you soon to celebrate a great victory." He shook Kurt's hand.
"Thank you, Kurt."

Nagora thanked him also.

Then she embraced Geirador. "Tell Mum and my big sister
I've gone to get Da, and I won't come back without him. Hug
Pare for me."

Lars shook Geirador's hand and Kurt's.

"Uncle, will you allow me a moment with my prisoner?"

Dangor gave her a nod.

"Lars, who will you send Aydan to?"

"Romanika."

Nagora bent to bring her face to Aydan's. "Be good to her,
you big bad boy. I'll see you in a few days."

Then she ran off in Acindor's direction.

Nagora found Acindor just off the trail, sitting with his
back and head resting against a tree. The black cloth bag still
covered his head. Tremon was standing next to him with his
hands one on top of the other on the pommel of his big sword.

Simana sat cross-legged on the ground on the other side of
Acindor. Her bow and quiver were next to her. She was filing
the tip of an arrow. She stood when Nagora approached.
"Edana," she said.

"Simana." Nagora gave them a nod and wasted no time
taking the bag off Acindor's head.

She stared at him, and he stared back.

"I'm going to free the dragon. I'll deal with you after. I can't wait." In her mind though, Edana dragged him over to the edge of the stone bluff, stood him there naked with his hands tied behind his back, and said to him: I want to hear you scream louder than the girls ever screamed in your dungeon.

His back would be to the plain below. Edana would grab his cock in one hand while she pointed the tip of her big blade at his neck to force him back closer to the edge until all that was keeping him from falling over was her hold on him. Edana would release the blade's pressure at his neck so Acindor could look her in the eyes. "Scream," she would order as she would bring her blade down in one swift motion to cut him free.

"You'll never do it, Edana. You don't know who you're up against. The dragon will die, and you'll taste Hag's incredible power. You'll wish you had never come this way with your mercenary warriors. All your warriors will die. You'll die before you can ever deal with me. I wouldn't be surprised if Hag has her way, and she offers you to me. Then you'll taste how I rip you apart. Edana, you'll scream like no woman has ever screamed before."

The bastard! Does he read my mind? Nagora slapped Acindor's face with as much force as she could and threw the cloth bag at him.

Nagora left before Edana did what she wanted to do.

Stick to the plan.

Acindor spit and then laughed.

The Wolf
Mahihkan

The waiting raiders mounted as Nagora approached. Lars held Storm's reins. She took them from him without a word and swung up into her saddle. She leaned over on the horse's neck, away from Lars, hugged Storm, and patted his neck until her own heartbeat slowed. The mid-afternoon sun on her back helped calm her.

Edward arrived on his horse.

Dangor waved Edward alongside. "Keyhole Harbor is where you and your family have been living all these years?"

"We have, far and out of the way from everyone. Hardly anyone knows of Keyhole Harbor unless they've been guided there by sea by someone who knows exactly what to look for. By land it's the same thing, and if you did see it from land, you wouldn't believe it's a harbor unless you saw a boat anchored there. Anyone just happening by wouldn't even notice it.

"Same with our home. We can see anyone coming long before they spot us. Even then, they would have to have a keen
eye or a good nose to find us. We don't exactly have a beaten
path to our door. You'll see what I mean when we get there."

When the raiders came to the coastal trail, they picked up
their pace. Nagora inhaled the sea breeze. The scents from the
nearby forest mingled with the breeze. The smell cleansed her
mind.

Almost six counts later, the coastal trail ended in a meadow half surrounded by forest, and the other half with rocky
outcrops of jagged stone.

Edward drew to a halt. "Any sign of a lodge nearby?
Where would you look to find a harbor?"

His questions drew blank stares. Nagora's eyes searched,
but could see nothing that drew her attention.

"Follow me," said Edward.

He led them past one of the rocky outcrops and on through
a maze of more stone guardians, silent sentinels, watchers that
would never speak. The ground was of stone chips and short
bushes. A careful scout would have to know what to look for
to find the trail.

Edward dismounted and led them on foot. When he
stopped, he asked, "Do you see the boat?" Hmm. I would
have to be looking down. Nagora moved past Edward and
climbed the stone outcrop that would give her a view seaward.
When she turned to head back the way she had come, her
right eye glimpsed a boat's stern. She stopped and turned toward it, staring down into a hole that gave her a limited view

of a boat. For all the viewer knew, it could be beached at the water's edge.

The raiders took turns having a look.

Edward then took them further along an invisible path to a cleft in the rock. "Through here, one can climb down to the harbor." They went a short ways and then they had a clear view of the harbor. It was a steep climb, but the steps carved in the stone made it an easy one.

"Easy, but steep. Tough coming up. Careful going down.

"Come. I'll take you to my home. Most of the crew'll be there."

The raiders walked back along the invisible path to get their mounts. Edward then led them back along the stone chip trail, past the cleft, on over a ledge, and down to another meadow. A garden and a lodge came into view. It was made of stone and curved into one of the bigger rocky outcrops, the back of which gave onto the meadow they had come to at the coastal trail's end. It reminded Nagora of the home she once shared with her uncle.

Two men, approaching on foot, greeted them. They called her uncle's name. Dangor laughed and raised a hand in recognition.

"Mikersen and Pickersen, you old sea dogs! Wouldn't I know that I would find you two here."

They laughed as they approached to embrace Dangor. Dangor started the introductions. "Tagnya's and Yogari's girl, right?" Mikersen asked. "She's got Tagnya's eyes and nose, and Yogari's chin. I can see that even with the red paint."

"Good eye as ever, Mikersen."

"Heard you were going to be part of this fight, Dangor. We're glad to see you and be able to help out. As well as the rest of the crew."

"Is that Yogari's boat in the harbor?"

"Aye. Everything below decks and the water line is new. As well as the sail. We salvaged what we could from his old boat. We figure he'll be proud of the job we've done."

Dangor finished introducing the warriors.

"Only nine of you going in? Sure you don't want extra help? Some of the crew would sure like to be involved."

"We're counting on you to be on the water. We don't know if the dragon can fly. We figure it can still glide, and Yogari could take it down to a waiting boat. While you're waiting, you could catch a good many fish. That dragon'll be hungry. Not to mention Yogari."

Mikersen scratched at his bearded chin. "Hmm, if that dragon's going to be landing on our boat, we would have to un-step the mast. That dragon has surely grown. It will be big and unable to land on the Sea Wolf. Conditions on the water could become unfavorable."

Mikersen held up a finger. "Look Dangor, if that becomes necessary, at worst, Yogari could land it on the water and we could tie lines onto it. The dragons used to fish in those waters, and they were known to set down on calm waters."

Dangor nodded in agreement. "You've got good points. It was young when taken into captivity. It's an adult now. Don't know if it has grown to its full size for lack of good food and exercise. Knowing Yogari, he's been doing his best to keep it healthy."

"We'll prepare for a water landing," said Mikersen. "I'll have crew members take down the supplies you'll be bringing. It'll make your climb down to the boat easier. There's a corral over there for your horses. If you come back this way, they'll be here for you; if not, we'll find you. Raynhard's planning on winning this one."

"We're going to do our best to help make it happen," said Dangor.

Nagora spent time with Storm after unsaddling him. "I'll be gone for a few days. When I come back, we'll ride just for the pleasure of it. We'll bring Lars with us. We'll be happy and enjoy the days we ride together, won't we?" She let Storm nuzzle her as she combed her fingers through his mane.

Inside Edward's lodge, a woman, who Nagora guessed to be Edward's wife, was busy with her two daughters and her son, preparing the evening's meal. They weren't wasting time.

The woman brought mugs and a big pitcher of ale to the table. "We've been expecting company. How many, we weren't sure. We planned to feed a dozen or more. There's never been so much excitement since we moved here, believe me! We're happy to help fight for The Cause. The country will take shape again in King Raynhard's hands. How we dearly miss his da! You'll never know."

The woman paused with both hands on her hips, head cocked to one side, staring at Nagora. "You weren't here a moment ago when Edward introduced the others. You must be Tagnyoriva's daughter, right?"

"My name's Nagora."

"I'm Edina. You're not much younger than your mother was when she first set foot in this land. She gave my daughter a doll, and now my granddaughter plays with it." She smiled at Nagora. "Tagnyoriva's girl." She shook her head. "I was hoping to see your mother today."

Nagora smiled at Edina. "She's on her way to the forest above the plain with the rest of our force."

"Now don't be telling me what you're doing here. I know it's a secret, and I would rather know about it only after it's all done and over with."

"When you do finally hear talk of all this, you'll be able to tell those who speak about it that you met Edana in person, and that she's fiercer than they could ever imagine," said Nagora.

"Your red paint does give a fierce look. Will I see your unicorn?"

"Someday, perhaps. Not today. Not tomorrow. If you're at the plain before the Isle of Smoke on the day after tomorrow, you may catch a glimpse of Edana and her unicorn."

A legend already. Edana and her unicorn. I can hardly believe what I've become.

"You must be hungry. This morning's catch should satisfy you. We made fish-bake pies."

"They smell great from here," said Dangor. "We'll do them honor. Believe me."

Lars translated what Edina and Dangor had said. He and the other warrior volunteers were all smiles as they rubbed their bellies.

Just as they finished their tasty meal, Mikersen came through the door. "I suggest you make it down to the boat before sunset. It's a dangerous climb down in the dark if you've never been down it at least several times in daylight.

"Once we get settled in down there, we can discuss our plans. Then get some sleep before we leave with the tide."

All nodded in agreement and stood. "Edward and Edina, thank you for your generous hospitality," said Dangor.

Edina gave a dragon-chord salute. "Edana, you take care now. We're counting on you." Edina had a tear in her eye as she said those words.

Nagora returned her salute with a smile.

Edward walked with the raiders to the cleft in the rock that led to the way down to Keyhole Harbor. He shook their hands. "Careful as you go down. Dangor, I had one of Mikersen's men bring down the pry bar you asked about."

"Thanks, Edward. We truly appreciate that," said Dangor.

"Best of luck to you. See you soon." Edward saluted them.

The remaining daylight, the carved footholds in the rock, and the strategically pegged handholds helped in their descent. Halfway down, Nagora looked up and then back down. I'm glad we took Mikersen's advice, finding these in the dark would have been very slow going.

When they reached the bottom and set foot on the dock, three two-fisher curraghs sat side by side, tied to the dock. They could easily fit on the deck of the Sea Wolf, which was tied at the end of the T-shaped dock. Dangor tapped her shoulder. "We're about to set foot on the Sea Wolf. How do you feel, Nagora?"

"Somehow, closer to Da."

Lars stood beside Nagora, his eyes taking in the Sea Wolf.

Nagora took his arm. "Well, does it look like the whaler you worked on?"

"This boat is built for speed. Like a whaler it's pointed at both ends and carries a single mast, but taller than a whaler's. A whaler is much wider with lower sides, making it more stable for the catch we haul on board, but slower over the water. This boat is about as long as a whaler, eight or nine of my arm spans and just under three wide. A whaler is closer to five wide."

Lars pointed to the Sea Wolf. "See the low narrow deck shelter. It straddles the mast fore and aft. On a whaler it's only forward of the mast to the bow, wider, higher, and flatter, a platform to throw harpoons from.

"Oh! And we have a masthead nest for the archer with his bladder bow."

"Bladder bow?" Nagora squeezed his arm.

"The archer has a heavy barbed arrow tied with twine to a coil of rope with a big sealskin air bladder attached to its other end, lying on the deck. We rely on the archer to pin the bladder to a whale so we can more easily follow it when it swims below the surface. The more bladders pinned to a whale, the sooner we can tire it out and get closer to throw our harpoons, especially in stormy weather."

Nagora let his arm go. "Sounds like that could be a dangerous job."

Lars grinned. "It is. It usually falls to the lightest crew member. But he has to be strong enough to pull that bow, and fearless to do it from up top in bad or good weather."

They walked to the Sea Wolf. My da's boat! Finally, I get to see you.

The Island
Ministik

Nagora stepped aboard the Sea Wolf. She ran her hands along its coaming, touched the mast, a rope, and a pulley, and then peeked over the bow to look up at the carved wolf head. Its bared teeth, ready to bite into oncoming waves with its tongue lolling from the right side of its jaw, told her it would give the Wolf an impression of speed when under full sail.

Keyhole Harbor was basically a hole in the cliff wall with a single narrow opening onto the sea, like a deep bowl that had cracked and had a triangular piece missing from its bottom up to its top edge, open to the sky.

Another boat the size of the Sea Wolf would fit. A boat that makes it in here before a bad storm has nothing to worry about.

Mikersen showed the raiders where they could bed down. He pointed to tarps they could sleep under on the open deck in case of rain or sea spray. Or they could manage cramped quarters inside the small deck shelter. "If you wish, we can let you sleep until we get to our destination."

Will I be able to sleep? Will the others? "They'll decide." We'll see how we each deal with the mounting tension.

Mikersen showed Nagora and Dangor over to the deck shelter. "Let's go over the plans for when we reach our destination."

"It'll be easier now. Conditions later could make it more difficult," said Pickersen.

Two of the Sea Wolf's crew had set the map and two lanterns on top of the low deck shelter roof aft of the mast. The sun was setting, and the rosy color of Keyhole Harbor was changing to black. Other lanterns lit the length of the deck.

The raiders gathered around the shelter roof. The chart showed the tip of the Land of the Danu and the Isle of Smoke. Pickersen pointed to a hole on the coast. "Keyhole Harbor." He let his finger travel over the map on the angular course the Wolf would take. His finger stopped. "The Isle of Smoke. We leave on the tide. A gentle breeze should bring us off the backside of the Isle of Smoke at least three counts before daylight. We're expecting good conditions. The tide will be out when we get there. We'll drop two anchors and let ourselves slip as close to shore as we dare on the two rodes. By sunrise, you'll land on the beach. It'll be rocky, wet, and covered with slimy seaweed. Who's the climber in your group?"

Nagora raised her hand. "I."

Lars, who was translating for the others, raised his hand. "I'll climb too."

Nagora smiled at him. "Looks like we are two."

"Once you set your ropes, up everybody goes. My crew will tie on your supplies and you'll haul them up," said Mikersen. "Then we'll wait and see what Yogari decides. We'll wait for you people to come back down."

Dangor touched a finger to the Isle of Smoke on the chart. "We'll be on the island for three days. The latest we'll leave is sunrise on the fourth day. If we don't show, you leave."

"That's right. Unless you get a message to us before then. Questions?" asked Pickersen.

There were none.

Pickersen rolled up the chart. "In six counts, we sail. If you want sleep, now's the time."

Nagora put on the sheepskin hat Paruline had made for her, and then she pulled her black cape over her sheepskin vest. She found a spot on deck and curled up under her cape. Most everyone else on the Wolf did likewise, except for the two crew on watch. One stood at the bow, the other at the stern.

Lars lay down opposite Nagora. He smiled and looked into her eyes.

"You look happy," she said.

"It feels like home to be back on boat," said Lars as he closed his eyes.

Nagora closed her eyes on Lars's sleeping face.

The sound of oars pushing off against the narrow rock walls of the harbor's entrance, mingled with sharp orders yelled to crew members, woke Nagora from her deep sleep. She didn't move until the crew had maneuvered the Sea Wolf to the straighter and wider part of the entrance. Here the crew set the oars in position in the water and pulled in silent unison to bring the Wolf out onto the sea's gentle swell.

They picked up their cadence and the Sea Wolf came alive as it snuck further and further away from the coastal cliffs.

Nagora listened to the Wolf groan as its long underbelly flexed, the boat rising and falling on the sea swells below the starlit sky.

Mikersen called out an order. Some of the crew shipped their oars. He shouted another command and the Sea Wolf's sail climbed the mast, its top boom sliding up along the oiled surface.

The Wolf's groans grew louder as its sail filled and the stays and the sheets drew taut.

Mikersen called out another order, and the crew shipped the remaining oars, dripping the sea's cold salty water on deck.

Nagora stood and spread her legs more than if on land. The Sea Wolf undulated under her as it raced over swells turning into waves. When sure of her balance, she wrapped her cape around her and made her way to the stern.

Pickersen was just taking the helm from Mikersen. "Well Nagora, what's it feel like?"

She breathed in the salty sea air. "It's everything Uncle has ever told me about it and more, because now I know it's my da's boat. The Sea Wolf is truly alive."

"Secrets kept from you, lass, for your own safety. At least Dangor told you about the Wolf, and like you say, she's alive. And if we take good care of her, she'll take us wherever we want to go."

Dangor approached, reached out to Nagora, and placed something in her hand. "Your mother asked me to give you this. She says you'll know what to do with it."

Nagora moved her fingers over it. It was her mother's arm bracelet with the diving dolphins. She swallowed. Mum, you thought of me. This gift is precious. She threw back her cape and pulled up the sleeve of the right arm of her woolen shirt. She slipped the bracelet up her arm until it came to rest snug around her upper arm, a good hand's width above her elbow.

Mikersen and Pickersen watched. "Time for her first lesson at the helm?" Mikersen asked Pickersen.

"I think so. Wind's favorable. We're on a broad reach. Our course is set. We've got stars to guide us. We can put Edana at the helm."

Pickersen pulled Nagora closer to him so he was standing behind her. He backed up along the tiller and placed her hand on it where his had been. "You hold on here, arm out ahead of you so you can keep it against your hip. Spread your legs so you can control how far you push or pull the tiller. Right now, you hardly have to stay on course. It'll feel strange to you the first few times. But you'll get used to it. I'm right behind you, so don't worry. Now you can feel this big stick push against your hip and pull away all on its own. What you want to do is control that a little at a time."

"I don't know what I'm doing because I don't know where I'm going," said Nagora as her hand gripped the fine hemp-rope knotwork, wrapped around the tiller handle.

"That's right. Now I'll give you a star to steer the Wolf by. It'll keep us on the course we want to go." Pickersen pointed, "There, ahead, just above the masthead. Do you see that group of stars? Imagine your mother, lying on her side propped up on one elbow and with one knee up."

"Aye, I see it."

"That group of stars bares a woman's name. Your da likes to call her the Woman Watching at her Window. He says she's watching over the Sea Wolf. Your job at the helm is to keep the mast of the Wolf pointed at her. Remember, to stay on course you push or pull the tiller just enough to make the mast point at her. Understand?"

"Understood." Her uncle had told the story many times, but had called those stars The Woman Waiting. The star stories were all making sense now. Mum, your wait will be over soon. I'll bring Da home to you.

Pickersen must have let go his grip on the helm, for now she continually fought with it in response to the wind and the waves.

"Relax. You're at the Wolf's helm now. She's a big vessel. The sea and the wind push her around easily. You only have the tiller connected to her small rudder to push or pull her from the action of the sea and the wind, so she won't react as quickly as you would want. It'll take you a while to learn the feel of the Sea Wolf on the sea as she rides down and climbs up the swells of the waves. You'll figure out at which moment it's best for you to push or pull the tiller.

"The person at the helm does a lot of things at once: steers the vessel, keeps an eye on the sail and the wind direction, and continually scans the horizon all around so as not to be caught unaware of sudden changes in the weather."

I'm trying to relax. Not easy to control this magnificent beast. But what's it like when conditions get wetter, wilder, and colder?

Okay, now scan all around the horizon. Wow! The river of diamonds the Sea Wolf left in its wake as it bounded onward over the waves was a ribbon of stars on the sea. How beautiful! Soon, the Wolf resisted where it was headed.

"Find your star."

"I'm trying to." She pulled on the helm as they rode down a wave and pushed on the helm as they climbed the next swell. Finally, she had the mast's tip find its place in the crook of the Waiting Woman's knee as they came over a big swell.

Pickersen asked, "How does it feel?"

"It feels like I'll need a lot more practice. Though, it feels like the Sea Wolf would take me anywhere I want to go."

"Same spirit as your mother when she learned. I'll take over now. Look at the horizon to starboard. See if you can spot something."

Nagora leaned against the starboard rail as she held on and looked. "Are those the coastal cliffs poking a line of jagged shadows into the sky?"

"That's right. Can you spot anything else?"

Nagora looked again, lower on the horizon. "I see a group of yellow and orange stars right over there." Nagora pointed.

"Not the color of other stars, right?"

"That's right. If they aren't stars, what do you guess them to be?" asked Pickersen.

"Fires?"

"Whose fires would they be and where would they be?"

"Our force's fires on the backside of the hill, above the plain at the Isle of Smoke?"

"That's right. I want you to keep your eyes on the horizon for the lights at the fortress of the Isle of Smoke. They won't be visible for long. Let me know as soon as you see them, then start counting anchors. Let me know the count when you no longer see them."

Nagora did as told and went to stand next to her uncle, who was also watching the horizon.

"Lights!" Nagora yelled. She counted. "Five anchors!" They had just passed the strait that separated the Isle of Smoke from the mainland. Soon they would be behind the island and heading for their landing spot below the cliffs. They had at least six counts until daybreak. They would be in position with plenty of time to spare.

Nagora searched the sky to find the Dragon Tamer. Da, I'm coming. Soon you'll be free. Soon you'll be with me.

Mikersen shouted an order, and Pickersen brought the Sea Wolf on a new course, with the wind on their port quarter. In the distance, the faint plume of smoke, which continually rose from the ancient volcano of the Isle of Smoke, snaked up against the starlit background. As they neared the island's coast, the wind had become a gentle breeze, pushing them along to their destination in the dark. The Isle of Smoke was a growing shadow on the foreground of the sky's starlit tapestry.

Slowly, the Sea Wolf made its approach.

Mikersen called out an order, and rowers slipped their oars into the water. Other crew brought the sail down and furled it.

"Do you think we have a chance making it up the cliff before sunrise and then on to the fortress?" asked Dangor.

"It wouldn't be worth chancing it. It's dangerous enough in daylight. Wait for early dawn. You'll have the solid footing of the beach for your gear. You can either descend to the fortress in the shadows of dawn, or wait for the sun to rise over the rim to have it at your back as you descend. Personally, I would go early," said Mikersen.

"Thank you for your thoughts." Dangor turned to his team. "I want to be at the base of the cliff as soon as the tide permits, even if we're up to our knees in water, that'll be fine.

"We'll climb as soon as there's a glimmer of sun on the horizon. We should have all our gear up there before the sun crosses the lip of the horizon. We'll have just enough light to get moving and hopefully enough darkness to make it down to the fortress unseen."

Mikersen yelled an order. An anchor dropped into the water. Oars pulled against the gentle swells. Mikersen yelled the order again and another anchor dropped into the water. The oars on the other side of the Wolf pulled. Then all the oars pulled twice in unison. Mikersen called out an order. The rowers raised their oars.

"Dangor, our anchors are set. We can pay out on our rodes and get the Wolf as close to shore as we dare. Once you and your raiders have left the cliff, we'll row back out into deeper water, drop a hook, and stand by there. If you need anything, give us a shout."

Mikersen's crew started to pay out the anchor rodes.

The bow of the Wolf slipped closer to the cliff. Beyond the stern, the tiniest crack of orange light was pushing over the horizon.

One of Mikersen's crew was calling out the depth soundings as they floated their way closer to shore. When he called stop, crew members belayed the anchor rodes. The Wolf pulled the rodes taut as it rose and fell in the sea's easy swell. One of the crew measured the depth with an oar—less than an oar's length.

The crew members allowed the anchor rodes to slip ever so slightly from their belaying posts. "Stop!" yelled the sounder again. "You'll have water up to your waist here, and to your knees or above at the cliff's base."

The sliver of orange had grown to a ribbon's width. Nagora, Lars, and Dangor were the first to wade ashore with ropes and grappling hooks. As soon as they made it to the base of the cliff, Lars threw a grappling hook.

Good throw, Lars! That's my man. That's almost two boat lengths to the top. Would the others have been able to throw the hook so high?

Already, Lars was swinging a second hook in lazy circles at his side. His bent knees straightened as he released the rope. Its hook sailed upward, pulling the leading end of the rope over the top. Gingerly, Lars pulled the rope. The grin on his face told Nagora it too had found an anchor hold. Lars put all his weight on the rope before releasing it to pick up a third hook.

He stepped aside to find sure footing among the slippery rocks before attempting the throw. When Lars signaled the hook was holding, Dangor and Nagora each grabbed a rope and began to climb. Before starting his climb, Lars watched until the climbers were almost halfway up, a little over half a full count.

The cliff face was straight up, but its jagged projections gave ample footholds for their climb.

Lars caught up to and passed Nagora and her uncle. He reset the hook of his rope before helping Nagora over the top. Dangor was not too far behind, giving them time to reposition Nagora's hook.

They helped Dangor over the top. His hook did not have to be reset.

The crew from the Wolf rowed the other raiders to the cliff's base in curraghs filled with their gear. Within two more counts, all the raiders had reached the top.

Below, crew members tied raid supplies to the ropes, and the raiders began to haul them up. The leading edge of the sun's disk was pushing above the horizon, just as they finished pulling up the last bundle of gear.

The Fortress
Sohkîsihcikewin

The raiders divided the ropes, extra bows, and bundles of arrows and fire arrows among themselves. Lars had the pry bar and axes. As soon as they loaded their packs on their backs, they set off along the volcano's lower rim, following it to the spot on the slope above the fortress where they would tie off a rope to control their descent to the fortress wall.

When the group arrived at that spot, they were in dawn's dim, rusty darkness. They had no time to waste. Lars tied one of the rope coils around a huge rock and then tied the other coils of rope to it, one after the other. While he did that Nagora, Dangor, and the others surveyed the fortress for signs of movement.

Two lights burned, one in the lower courtyard near the fortress stables, and the other near a guard tower on the wall above the stable courtyard. No movement was visible within the perimeter of those lights. The guards on duty could be anywhere in the shadows of the fortress walls.

Beyond the fortress, in the dimmest early light of the morning, a smoky mist, oozing down from the forest hills, enveloped a good part of the plain.

Under the cover of the remaining darkness, the raiders prepared to descend the steep, muddy slope to the fortress wall. Nagora took it in. Did most of the water drain from the mud and stony debris? Had the sunlight of the past day dried it out? We're about to find out.

Dangor leaned close to her and Lars. "Nagora, you go first. The others will follow. Lars and I will be last. Watch the fortress for movement. If you see something, whistle once. We'll all freeze. Whistle twice when we can continue."

"Got it."

As Lars translated the orders, Nagora sidestepped down the slope at a decent pace, her hold on the rope affording her good control. The muddy crumble of earth and rock fell aside without too much noise. Most of the way down, her footing was solid, as opposed to sinking in mud.

Soon Nagora would be on the spine of the debris slide caused by the heavy rain. More of the solid debris, of stones and rock chunks, had settled here, leaving the mud and rain water to run off on each side.

Ahead, the drift of debris reached up the fortress wall to within a body length of its top.

When Nagora reached the debris peak at the wall, she looked up. With someone's help, it'll be easy to make it to the top.

Moments later, the others joined her.

Lars removed his big sword's scabbard from over his shoulder. He held one end out to Tommassen. Nagora stepped on with her hands resting on the wall, and they hoisted her. Soon she was peering over the wall and around its perimeter as far as she could see. The other side of the heavy, timber wall against which the debris slide had piled up was braced up with four long, heavy timbers set at an angle, resting at the base of the opposite wall of the livestock yard.

Not a guard in sight. Nagora pulled herself up and over the wall onto its perimeter walkway. She double checked for guards. All was quiet. She leaned over the wall and signaled to Lars, who threw over a rope which she tied to the walkway where she stood. All climbed up in no time.

The archers and Nagora strung their bows and nocked their arrows. Two warriors drew their blades.

Dangor pointed to the two guard towers at the corners of the opposite wall. Tommassen and Kymasen, with blades in hand, left in each direction to secure the towers. The archers covered them. With the all-clear signal, everyone met at the opposite wall.

Dangor held open a hand-drawn map of the fortress. "This is the section of the fortress where they keep the livestock." He pointed. "A chicken coop in that corner. A pigsty in the other corner. Opposite us, in the middle, the stable for the cows and sheep."

"Judging by the supports they've roughly thrown in to bolster the seaward wall, they decided it was a good idea to move the four-legged animals out. Looks like they won't use this yard until the debris is cleared and that wall is shored up," said Lars.

"So we're probably safe in this part of the fortress," said Nagora.

"As long as no guards are assigned duty here," said Dangor.

Dangor continued going over the map, pointing to each element for everyone's benefit. "If we were standing with our backs to the wall we came over, that would be the back wall. Here, where we are, is the front wall. Side walls, left and right. Guard towers, left and right.

"Looking over the front wall, we have the courtyard. Starting with the closest door to our right is the entrance that leads to the kitchen, up five steps inside and straight ahead.

"Important for you, Nagora. Just inside the entrance to your left, near the floor just before going up the steps, is a small, sliding, vented door, leading to the wooden duct system. The ducts bring heat from the volcano's vent house to the chambers in this part of the fortress. They're big enough for you to crawl along. Along the top of the floor-level duct are vertical ducts. They bring warm air up to louvered vents on the chamber walls. You could listen from those places."

"So I'll have to sneak in there?" asked Nagora.

Dangor nodded. "We'll get to that later."

"At the top of the entrance steps to your left is a hallway with access to various chambers: two for guests, a dining hall, and Raganora's throne room. Above the throne room are Rag's chambers, accessed by the staircase here, near the other end of the hallway.

"Back in the courtyard is the main entrance to the queen's throne room. Steps take you up to a landing that meets the hallway. Straight ahead are the doors to the throne room.

"On the other side of the courtyard are entrances to a workshop, kitchen, eating area for the troops, the jail, and barracks.

"On the front wall of the courtyard is the gate to the main fortress yard. To your right is the vent house, with the cage that's now used to lower food and water to your da. To your left at the other end, horse stables and smithy.

"On the main wall of the fortress are four towers, one at each corner and one on either side of the main gate. Beyond the gate, the road veers left, then right, to the bridge."

Lars nodded and reached for the map so he could go over it with the archers, Trowan, Derk, and Jared. Tommassen and Kymasen also leaned in to have a look.

When Lars gave it back to Dangor, he folded it and put it away. "Lars, Nagora and I are going below. We're taking Jared with us. I want you in the tower to your left to keep watch and signal if someone comes into the courtyard. Have the other two archers ready to fire on them if they look like they've spotted us and are coming to engage us.

"We're going to look for eggs in the coop to bring to the kitchen."

Lars gave Dangor a thumbs-up, gave his orders to the archers, and headed to the tower.

Dangor, Nagora, and Jared made their way to the tower on the right. The ladder beneath the trap door brought them down to the stockyard level. The gate to the yard was ajar. Dangor placed Jared there as a lookout. In the chicken coop, her uncle found a candle lantern and lit it. He chuckled when the remaining hens woke up and cackled.

Nagora spotted a basket made of woven saplings. She put straw in the basket and set about rummaging for eggs. She found nine and showed her uncle.

"Great. Now give me your bow and quiver. Pull your big blade from its sheath, and then pull the hood of your sweater and cloak over your head."

Nagora set the basket on the ground and did as Dangor had ordered.

"The entrance door to the kitchen should be unlocked. Hobble over to it, bent over with the basket on your left arm. Under your cloak, have your blade ready. Open the door. If someone's there, keep your head lowered and cough as you hand them the eggs. It'll be up to you to play it from there. Only if the coast is clear do you slide the vent door open. Then bring the basket back out and set it on the doorstep entrance. That way, we'll know you're headed into the duct. Don't forget to close the vent door behind you.

"Remember, find out as much as you can about the situation. We'll do our best out here. Be very careful when coming back. We'll have an eye on that door watching for you. We've got you covered. The rest of the time you're on your own. Are you ready?"

"I'm ready." She picked up the basket and hobbled out of the stockyard toward the entrance to the kitchen.

Nagora opened the door and shuffled into the entrance that led to the kitchen. Not a sound came from the kitchen.

Quiet. Probably not for long.

She found the vented trap door to the duct at the base of the wall to her left.

She set the basket on the step outside next to the entrance door.

Just as Nagora bent to push aside the trap door, a pot clattered to the floor, and a cat complained. Her heart beat fast as she leaned against the wall. The cat was rubbing up against her, purring.

You little bugger! I almost shit myself.

She picked up the cat, opened the door a crack, and let it go out.

Nagora quickly pushed aside the trap door and crawled into the duct space. She used her elbows to pull herself along until her feet were in. The toe of her right boot found the sliding vent frame and slid it closed. She crawled ahead in total darkness. The duct went right, rose on an incline, turned left, and leveled out.

Because of the warm air in the duct, she left her cape in the corner. She was in a space between the hallway to her left and the chambers to her right. This air duct must be on a slight incline toward the vent house. Makes sense. Warm air rises.

Soft light filtered down ahead of her. Nagora crawled ahead more cautiously. She came to a place in the duct where it opened onto a vertical shaft above that led to the louvered vent opening of a candlelit room. The louvers opened upward to draw warm air up into the room.

She sat and peered up through the open louvers into the room. The dim ceiling beams of the room were visible. A low rasping chant came from the room. It was Hag's voice. I'm sure it's her. This is Hag's chamber.

For a moment her heartbeat raced as her mind made plans. Stop! I promised Uncle. Focus on the task.

The heat in the duct was comfortable. In colder weather, they must open vent traps at the other end to allow more heat in.

Nagora passed two more vertical shaft openings, with neither light nor sound coming from them. At the next one she came to, she could stand in the narrow wall space and edge her way along it for several paces.

Must be a bigger chamber. The queen's throne room.

Light from the windows on the other side of that room trickled in through open louvers at six places and on two different levels in the wall space just above her. The lower-level louvers were just above Nagora's head.

She braced herself in the space and climbed to the first set. The louvers' openings afforded her a view of the high ceiling and the windows high on the outer wall of the throne room.

She moved the louver so it opened on Queen Rag's empty throne room. The large, fur-cushioned, wooden throne sat up on a dais. Two long tables stood on each side of it. No other furniture was visible.

Subjects would either stand or kneel before her and state their business.

She repositioned the louver and came back down to a standing position.

Move on to the vent house.

...

Nagora knelt to return to the duct crawlspace. The air became warmer as she moved on. Then warm air blasted upward past her face and above her head.

She reached up, following the warm air flow into an overhead shaft that angled off to her right. As she moved her head back to the left side of the crawlspace, daylight lit the top of the slanted vent shaft. The light must come from a vertical shaft above.

Along the two opposite corners of the shaft, ropes ran their way through a series of metal eyebolts. She reached up and found the ropes at the top of her vent crawlspace.

Could they be the same rope set in a loop? If I pull one, it closes the chimney vent trap to keep the heat in. If I pull the other one, the chimney vent trap opens. I could climb the angled shaft, and the vertical one. It most likely gives access to the vent-house roof. I'll do that later. First I want to see what lies ahead.

Nagora crawled along through the warmer air in the duct.

Finally, she came to a rectangular funnel opening at the end and peered down over the opening. Warped, rough-hewn planks rested on an iron grid. In the crack between two planks, she glimpsed a pale, reddish glow in the depths below. Directly over the volcano vent shaft where Da is held prisoner? Must be.

Wow! Before Raganora built the fortress, the vent-hole opening here must have been as big as the vent house. Could dragons have flown down the vent shaft before the time of the fortress? If there's a cave below where Da and Danuka are, there could be other caves.

Da must know.

Ahead of Nagora, three doors hung from horizontal hinges. If she stood on the planks and pushed against one of them, it would swing outward.

This is where they control the heat entering the vent system. Simple, yet effective. Dare I get close to the doors for a peek through the cracks?

Nagora lay on her side, brought her knees up, and pulled her legs up and out over the opening. She lowered herself onto the planks, maintaining her hold and testing how solid her footing was.

Nagora chose a plank that was less warped than the others and put her full weight on it. She leaned forward to the crack between two of the hanging doors.

There, before her, about twenty paces away and bathed in the shaft of morning light, was a winch mechanism—a big geared wheel that would turn the oak-planked barrel cylinder attached to it. A chain was wrapped around the cylinder.

It must hold the cage that can be lowered to the cave where Da is in the vent-hole shaft.

Above, heavily framed beams skirted the opening to the sky. A much lighter wooden railing sat on top of those beams.

The viewing gallery?

Nagora imagined Queen Rag saying, "Come see the last dragon," to her guests, back in the early days when the dragon could fit in the cage.

Huge iron eyebolts had been screwed in place on the beams above and on the timbers of two walls.

To slip chains through to hold the dragon?

Nagora listened and looked. No voices. No sound of movement. She crouched and pushed on the hanging door panel before her to peer toward the fortress yard. The huge doors of the vent house that gave onto the fortress yard were closed.

She turned her head and peered to her right. She counted six heavy, wrought-iron rings hanging from the stout pintles that had been screwed or driven into the timber walls, three at knee-level height and three at shoulder height spaced three strides apart.

With the tips of her fingers, Nagora let the hanging door panel return to its vertical position. She stood up and leaned back into the crawlspace. She crawled back to the angled shaft.

Nagora tested both ropes. One became taut right away. The other became taut also, but could still be pulled. When she released it, the rope slid back through her fingers to its first position. With the help of the first rope, she climbed the angled shaft and then up the vertical shaft to the edge of its opening.

The ropes controlled a trap door panel which, now, was open.

In cold weather it must help control how much heat flows through the vents.

Nagora crept up to the top of the vertical shaft and took a quick peek over the edge. She was in the duct chimney, about sixty paces away from the vent house. The chimney was about two body lengths above the viewing gallery of the vent-house roof. To her left lay the courtyard.

She brought her head down and waited a few moments before taking another peek. This time she looked toward the main fortress yard. Chains, lying on the ground, led to big iron rings fastened to the timber walls of the fortress. A section of the main gate was visible, and over it, a part of the Isle of Smoke Bridge.

Nagora ducked down again before taking a final look in the opposite direction. I'm about thirty paces from the wall of Rag's throne room.

Guards from Raganora's courtyard wall can easily see this chimney and the viewing gallery below the roof of the vent house. The viewing gallery is not a good place to be unless we take care of the guards from the wall. There will be guards posted up there anyway.

No. I'll stick to watching from behind the hanging doors.

She lowered herself all the way back down to the duct's crawlspace.

Nagora focused on the muffled voices coming from the other side of the wall. Carefully, she sat up and turned to face the wall so she could stand and peek through the louvers. Four spear-carrying guards filed into the throne room and flanked the throne. As Queen Raganora entered, she was talking to a soldier she addressed as Grallimdor.

The commander of her troops?

Not too far behind them, Hag followed, clutching her staff with its amber eye held in place by the open mouths of three silver snakes. Nagora's whole body tensed as her oath to the girls in the dungeon sea cave surfaced. Stick to the plan.

Queen Rag sat on her throne, facing Grallimdor who stood at attention, while Hag shuffled to the space to the left of the throne.

"Tell me, Grallimdor, you are sure everything is ready and we can go through with this?" asked Raganora.

"Yes, your Majesty. The ballista is ready to be moved into position. More than enough stout chains and iron rings have been fastened to the fortress yard walls to hold the beast. I assure you, we'll have it under complete control. If the Rider can't control it to get it into the shackles and chains to keep it calm, it will cost him and the dragon their lives."

"Tell me, when will you raise the cage?"

"At midday. Do you wish to watch?"

"No. I'll be on the other side of the bridge in my tent by then. But I need you to reassure me. Do you truly know what you are doing, Grallimdor?"

He straightened as his chest expanded. "The ballista will," Grallimdor paused, "at all times, be aimed at the dragon ready to kill it, either at your signal or should we judge it has become too dangerous to control.

"From the moment the dragon comes off the cage, and out of the shaft in the vent house, the ballista will be aimed at it. As we bring it, chained, into the fortress yard, the ballista will be aimed at it, right up until we lead it across to the other side of the yard. There the dragon will be chained to all the iron rings we've affixed around the main fortress yard perimeter. We'll have it under control."

We'll see about that. Nagora made her hand into a fist.

"By the end of this day, the chains from the key at the middle of the bridge will be linked to the chains holding the dragon in the fortress yard. Tomorrow morning, as we move the dragon to the bridge, we'll have the dragon follow the ready-to-fire ballista across the bridge. You see, the dragon would have to pull loose from the timber walls of the fortress and the stone bridge. Before it could ever do that, we would fire the ballista's great arrow to kill it."

"From what I've heard, we'll have many in attendance to witness the executions," said Raganora.

Grallimdor nodded. "Yes. Even until after dusk yesterday, people were making their way here on the main road. Then they set up camp along to the forest edge of the plain. More will most likely arrive today. The common folk have been heeding your call."

Raganora tilted her head. "You think so? What if they heed Edana's call and not mine? Will they join Edana's force in battle? That is what I would like to know."

"Not if they wish to keep their lives. Most will not even be armed. A noisy rabble at most." Grallimdor waved his hand in dismissal. "It will soon be quieted with a well-placed volley of arrows."

"Will our defenses on the plain hold?"

"Our defenses give us the advantage of having Edana's force split in two to attack us on two fronts. If, at any time, her force breaches our defenses, they will be falling into a trap, surrounded and eliminated."

Raganora cleared her throat. "Tomorrow, Edana will cower when the last dragon in the land is killed before her very eyes. It will dash all hopes the people had of a return to what their land once was.

"The dragon rider killed my true husband. My husband killed all the dragons, except that one. The Rider and the dragon have suffered in that hole for years. Tomorrow, I will order them killed. They will not, under any circumstances, be set free alive."

Nagora's fist had opened and now her hand gripped the handle of her big skystone blade. She gritted her teeth. I could hack through the louvers and attack you, Raganora, but I won't. I'll stick to the plan.

Grallimdor had been nodding. "What will be your signal tomorrow to carry out their execution?"

Raganora brought a hand to her throat. "I will be wearing a red scarf at my neck. At midday, when I untie it and let it fall to the ground, kill the dragon first, then the Rider. Leave their bodies to hang from the bridge, one on either side, until they rot and the crows pick their bones clean."

Raganora turned her gaze to Hag. "My dear Hag, you will finally get your reward with the dragon's death."

Hag's eyes opened wide, and her yellow teeth showed as she sucked in a great breath past her crooked smile.

Raganora shrugged and seemed to force a smile. "I know you truly did your best to help my son become a man. I don't hold you responsible for the outcome. I know that I held you to that condition all these years, but now, given the situation, the time is right to waive that condition. Better late than never, as the saying goes."

Now Hag held her staff with both hands as her tongue snaked out of her mouth and licked her lips.

"Thus, my dear Hag, when the deed is done, we will part ways. You may return to your chamber to await the moment of the dragon's death, out of harm's way."

"Thank you." The words came out of Hag's mouth in a rasping hiss as she bowed to Raganora before shuffling away.

Raganora motioned Grallimdor to her side and placed a hand on his arm. "My dear Commander, you may dismiss the guards. I have a personal matter to discuss with you in private."

Raganora stared at Hag until she hobbled away with the help of her amber stone-headed staff. The guards followed her out.

When they were alone, Raganora spoke in a hushed voice. "I can't believe the tale of this Edana. She is supposedly the virgin with the powers of a dragon that my sniveling lout of a son let the sea take away, but she returned and took my son away to be her mate so she can bear him a son, the future heir to his throne. What woman in her right mind would want to mate with him? I'm his mother and I can't even love him as a son. She can have him for all I care. Let's face it. He hasn't the brains to rule a chicken coop. How could she even think or believe he could rule a kingdom?"

"Raganora, my dearest, fear not. I've already told you, the captain I sent to Yhorgal conducted the investigation Acindor should have conducted in the first place. The one taken away by the sea was raised by a curragh maker. Her body and that of another girl executed by your Acindor were found floating on the sea further down the coast. Descriptions of the bodies leave no doubt. And the poor curragh maker drowned himself out of grief."

"I know. But what of the captain's investigation into the tower lookouts' report of sighting a thousand warriors cheered on by Edana on her unicorn with my son at her side?"

"That too, is nothing but a rebel ploy to create an illusion of more warriors riding by than actually did. Mind you, her unicorn's hooves of fire at night are quite impressive, I'll give her that. It certainly has motivated the common folk to come witness the event here on the plain. They are going to be surprised to see the dragon killed instead of freed.

"We have no fear of her raining fire arrows on our troops with the children there. I think Edana will be quite disheartened tomorrow, won't she, Raganora? You will win the day."

Not if I stop you.

Then Raganora whispered. Nagora strained to hear her.

"Tonight, when the dragon and the Rider are chained to the far corner of the fortress yard, four of your men are to come get Hag. They have to convince her they are bringing her to my tent on the plain to meet with me in secret. But to do so, she must hide in a vegetable bag in a handcart that will bring her across to my tent, then back here after our meeting. Instead, your men will leave her in the bag, place her in the cage, and lower her to the cave where the dragon was held. She'll rot there, and I'll be rid of her useless magic."

Grallimdor spread his arms. "You are too generous with your witch. I'll see to it myself."

Raganora held up a hand. "Oh! Just in case something should go terribly wrong, our boat is ready. Is it not?"

"My boat, our boat, is ready in Windhaven Harbor, should we need it."

"And the dragon's gold?"

"All hidden on board. We are ready for every eventuality."

"Rumandor will be in charge of things this side of the bridge. How many men will he need?" asked the queen.

"Ten men in all to take the dragon from the hole, chain it, and subdue it. They will help control the dragon as it follows the ballista to the bridge tomorrow morning. I'll need every other man available on the plain, even though the ballista will most likely be the deciding factor in the battle tomorrow, if there is one. After it has fired on the dragon from its position at the bridge entrance on the other side, the ballista can be easily swiveled into position to fire on the enemy. "Should things not go our way, at worst, we ride to Windhaven to our boat."

"If it comes to that, I want this fortress torched."

"Whatever you order. Is there anything else?"

"No, I think we've got it all covered."

Oh no, you don't.

"We'll prepare to raise the dragon now. As soon as you, your servants, and cooks have crossed to the other side of the bridge, we'll raise the cage."

Raganora held out a hand for him to kiss. "We'll not be long."

Then she stood to leave the throne room. A few paces from her throne, she paused and looked slowly around the room at the tapestries, the high windows, her throne, and finally, at Grallimdor. "Courage." Raganora's word was barely audible. She continued out of the chamber.

Nagora crouched down and slipped into the duct to make her way to the vent house.

The Cage
Kipahitokamik

As Nagora approached the end of the duct at the vent house, the place was abuzz with activity. The rattle of chains being rigged by soldiers echoed along the duct.

She was content to lie at the lip of the rectangular funnel and listen to the preparations being made. It was no time to risk being seen peeking through the crack of the hanging door panels.

The work came to a stop, and the soldiers quieted down. Grallimdor spoke, "Well, Rumandor, what's the situation?"

"Sir, we've got six iron rings on the ceiling perimeter beams and six on the back wall. We've got two sets of three chains that run from the wall rings to the perimeter beam rings. The three hanging ends of the first set run to a big shackle for one of the dragon's legs. Same with the other set for its other leg.

"We'll lower the two big shackles to the top of the cage where the dragon will perch. It'll be the Rider's job to fit the shackles around the dragon's legs and hammer the shackle pins in place to lock them.

"In that bucket there, we've got a smaller chain with a shackle and its pin for one of the Rider's legs. On the other end of his chain is the link he'll attach to one of the dragon's leg shackles. Only when that's done will we raise the cage higher.

"Right after lunch we'll tie that bucket, along with the other one containing your instructions to the Rider, to the inside of the cage before we lower it to the Rider."

"You make sure nothing falls out of those buckets," said Grallimdor.

"Don't worry, sir. We'll tie them securely."

"Basically you'll have control of the dragon's legs once the shackles are on?"

"That's right, sir. All done with chains and rings you see here on this wall, and then to the rings on the walls of the fortress yard. We can lock the chains to any of the rings with chain-link pins."

"That's good. Now, how do you get the dragon out of the hole?" asked Grallimdor.

"Once the shackles are on, we raise the cage as high as we can and attach a new chain to the cage. We tie it off to the big beam we've laid across the perimeter beams at the ceiling. Once that is fastened securely, we release the crank mechanism. The new chain on the cage takes the strain. That allows us to remove the original cage chain. We undo the whole crank assembly and set it aside so as to clear the vent hole.

"We've tied three ladders together with crossbeams. We'll lower the ladder assembly into the hole and hope the Rider can coax the dragon to climb the ladder, like a caged bird climbs the inside of its cage."

"Oh! That's what it is! Good thinking. Remains to be seen if it works. And will the ballista be in position?" asked Grallimdor.

"Yes, sir! With a bolt ready to fire on order."

"Rumandor, we've decided that tomorrow you'll have the dragon follow the ballista to the bridge. It'll be easier that way. Then we'll set the ballista up at the bridge's entrance on the other side so we can use it in battle on the plain should we need to."

"Good thinking, sir! You're right. It'll make our job easier."

"Will you and your men eat before raising the dragon?" asked Grallimdor.

"Yes, sir. That's our plan, since after that, we'll most likely be eating rations the next few days."

"Enjoy your meal."

Nagora waited a moment and listened. Grallimdor must've left.

"All right men. Leave everything as is. We'll go eat and finish this right after."

Rumandor's men dropped the chains and kicked them aside as they followed him out of the vent house.

Nagora swung her legs over onto the planks and took up position behind the third hanging door panel. She crouched and pushed it open a crack. She couldn't see a soldier in sight. One of the big vent-house doors was ajar.

She looked at the crank mechanism over the hole. Next to the knee-high stone ring that skirted the hole stood the two buckets Rumandor had described.

The coast was still clear. Nagora ran over to the buckets, took the one that did not have a chain in it and ran behind the big wheel.

I can get a message to Da.

A round loaf of bread had been pushed down on top of a big chunk of dry cheese that sat on top of the instructions. Nagora removed them, unfolded the piece of paper and read the instructions. She pulled her father's knife and sheath from her belt and placed it in the bucket. She covered it with the folded instructions and the cheese before pressing the round loaf back in place.

She peered around the big wheel. The way was clear. She returned the bucket where she had found it and ran back to slip behind the hanging door panel.

Nagora was getting hungry too. She crawled back to the angled shaft where she had left her water gourd and scrip. She ate some dried fruit, nuts, and two rock-hard, oat and currant biscuits. These she washed down with water from her gourd. Nagora took her time, and while she ate, she ordered the valuable information she would convey to her uncle and the others.

Then Nagora crawled back to the vent house.

Behind the hanging door panel, the clicking of gears and the winding of chain being tightened on the oak-planked cylinder resonated.

"Bring it up as high as it goes." It was Rumandor's voice.

"We're almost there, sir." The gears clicked slower now, and the men, who must have been turning the wheel to crank the gears, groaned as they strained in their efforts to raise the cage.

"Good enough. Lock it in position. Now can one of you swing in there?"

"I'll go, sir."

"When you're in, I'll hand you these two buckets. The first one is heavy. Make sure the chain inside it is tied to the bucket handle with the rope. Then hang the bucket from one of the cage bars and tie the rope to it.

"Do the same with the second bucket. Tie that bucket to the bar."

The iron cage creaked and grated. The sound must have been caused by the soldier's weight as he swung into its opening.

A few moments later Rumandor ordered, "Steady! Good. Hold it there. Don't drop it. It's heavy. Tie another bend around the bar to make it doubly secure. Now, do the same with this one."

Several moments later the volunteer called, "All's secure, sir. I'm coming out."

"Give him a hand."

Then a soldier said, "Ready to lower away, sir."

"Good. Hold on a moment, I'll confirm with the commander just in case the queen has changed her mind."

Rumandor left.

"Reckon we'll be able to get the bloody beast up here? From what I've heard, it has doubled in size since it was sent down there with the Rider. It don't fit in the cage no more," said one of Rumandor's men.

"Well, if the Rider hasn't doubled in size, we should be able to bring up the dragon. It'll be slow going. Extra hands on the wheel will get it up. My worry is the chain. It hasn't always been oiled proper over the years. Rust and all. You never know how bad it's eaten into the chain, do you?" asked another.

"Think it could break?"

"Guess we'll find out soon enough." He laughed.

"Aye and if it does, we'll have nothing to show to Edana. What'll happen, do you think?"

"Maybe she'll cook our goose with the flamin' hooves of her horny pony," said the joker.

"Ha! Do you believe all that?"

"Well, there've been all those reports, including the first one when she seduced the prince. They all say they saw Edana on her unicorn with flamin' hooves. I won't be one to call them liars. Anyways, we'll probably see her tomorrow, won't we? According to what she says, at least."

"Well, if she comes after me for not freein' the dragon, she'll be mistaken because today I'm doin' everything in my power to get it out of this hole. What happens to it up here isn't any of my doin'."

"I'm with you on that."

Rumandor had returned. "All right men. Queen's headed across the bridge directly. She won't be stopping by to see the dragon. We can lower away. Controlled and easy, men. I don't want the contents of the buckets lost on the way down."

"Yes, sir! Controlled and easy it is."

The quick click-click-click sound of the crank's gears, being repeatedly released and locked with the control arm of the crank, echoed in the vent house. Slowly, a half-dozen links at a time, the cage chain unraveled from the oak cylinder of the crank mechanism.

What had Uncle said? A rope of more than three hundred strides in length would be needed to reach the cave where Da is held. That's a long way down.

"We're there!" yelled one of the soldiers. It was a full count later.

Rumandor spoke. "We'll give him time to get to the buckets, read the instructions, and think about them. I would like to have been a bat in that cave to see his reaction to Edana's message we sent down a few days ago. Keep your eyes on that cage. Let me know what happens."

"Yes, sir. Will do."

Nagora crept closer to peek through crack separating the panels.

The soldiers knelt on the stone floor next to the knee-high stone perimeter where they could lean over the edge and peer down at the cage.

Someone paced the length of the vent house back and forth. He must be Rumandor.

"He's hooked the cage, sir. Pulling it in. Looks like he's got it tied off. He's jumped in. Checking the buckets. He's untying one, the message bucket. He's gone back into the cave with it.

"He'll be awhile, sir. He'll probably eat the cheese and then study the instructions. Sir, do you think he'll talk over the instructions with the dragon?" asked the joker.

"How would I know? Who knows? All these years in that hole, I would have thrown myself down it before talking to some beast."

Like the soldiers, Nagora waited. No use being impatient for their reports. Whatever time it takes, it takes. Da has waited all this time.

She tried to picture him in the cave now. She took her amulet and pressed it to her lips.

Da, have you found your knife yet? Perhaps you're reading the instructions or you're hungry and eating the bread and cheese. What do you look like? Are you weak and frail? You mustn't be too weak, you hooked the cage and pulled it to the cave entrance and tied it off. That takes strength. What does the inside of your cave look like? I'll probably never know until you tell me. Will you be able to control the dragon? Will I see it fly? Will it breathe fire? Will it frighten me?

Many more questions crossed her mind as she waited. It was like she was back on her beach at the sandy spit, sitting on the edge of the high-water mark and watching the tide go out. Many times, she had spent long counts, watching the waves recede until they reached their lowest level. Those were times when so many unanswered questions about the sea had crossed her mind. Each time was different. And each time, the sea left different gifts upon the sandy shore.

On one day, a big storm's wild sea had surged well above the usual high-water mark. Its still snarling waves had receded and revealed a whole new landscape in place of her once familiar beach.

Its landmark dunes, tall marram-grass knolls above the high-water mark, and the half buried, sun-dried skeletons of evergreen trees from faraway-eroded cliffs had all gone.

How could the sea have taken it all away from me and left me with a flat expanse of wet sand, strewn with dead jellyfish, crab carcasses, and clam shells?

The screaming gulls that fought each other for the broken crab carcasses didn't give her an answer.

I feel like that day. My world is about to change again.

"Rider's in the cage! He's looking up!

"Seems to be examining the chain in the bucket. He's gone back into the cave. He's released the cage. Cage is swinging free, sir! He's jumped out, grabbed onto the bottom edge of the cage. It's tilted. He's pushing off the vent shaft wall with his feet. Again! He's doing it again. Again! He's making it swing out more and more.

"Son of a bitch! Look at that. Can you believe that?"

"What is it, man? Report!" demanded Rumandor.

"Sir! It's the dragon. It jumped out of the cave, spread its wings, and landed on the top edge of the cage. It's got its neck around the cage's chain and its wings wrapped over and around the sides of the cage. Everything is swinging. Can't see the Rider. Dragon has its tail curled up. When the cage gets too close to the shaft wall, it steadies the cage with its tail."

"Do you see the Rider?"

"No, sir! Not yet! Dragon is adjusting its hold on the cage. It's shifting its weight on top of the cage.

"There's the Rider now! Sir, he's still hanging on from where he was. He's swinging his body and moving to his right to the other side of the cage. Now he's swinging more. Swung his right hand up to the side bar of the cage entrance. He's pulling himself up. He's got one knee inside. Now both. He's standing in the cage, sir.

"He seems to be moving around the cage, checking the dragon's weight distribution. Dragon's not moving, sir. Quiet and under control.

"Sir, the Rider's giving the thumbs-up. Do we bring them up?"

"Of course we bring them up, but not all the way up."

"Yes, sir."

Nagora kept her eye at the crack. Two men grunted and strained at the big wheel. "Sir, we're going to need more help. You were right. It's a heavy load. Pull rope on the four pegs around the wheel would help. Four men on the rope and two at the wheel should do it."

"You, men! Bring the rope."

The men stepped quickly into place. They would be pulling across the vent-house floor and would surely end up just to the right of the hanging door panels.

"Ready, men?"

"Yes, sir!"

"Start pulling."

Now six men were grunting, but this time the big wheel was turning because the gears sang their click-click-click song as the cage chain wound back around the solid oak-plank cylinder.

"Stop!" Rumandor ordered. "Take a look. What's the situation?"

Nagora kept peeking through the space between two of the hanging doors. The soldiers took several well-earned, deep breaths as one from the wheel went to his knees on the floor to bend over the stone-rimmed lip of the hole. She stepped back.

"Lookin' good, sir! Cage is barely swingin'."

"Good. Continue."

The click-click-click song continued, and Rumandor regularly ordered a stop.

Nagora guessed he counted the number of chain turns on the cylinder so the soldiers could check on their progress and the situation with the dragon and the Rider.

"Sir! I request archers on the gallery above the hole. Next time I go look over the edge, I don't want that dragon to take a bite out of me or burn off my face."

"Fair enough. Six men to stand with bows strung and arrows nocked on the perimeter hole of the vent-house viewing gallery. In the meantime, we'll raise the cage some more. You won't look over until the archers are in position."

"Yes, sir!"

"Pull!"

When Rumandor ordered the next stop, Nagora clenched her fists and took a deep breath.

"Prepare to fire on my order."

A long moment passed before the soldier spoke. "Sir, the Rider requests to speak to you."

Rumandor stepped to the edge of the hole and went to his knees.

"I'm in charge here. What do you want?"

If only I could hear Da's voice, but I can't.

"I can't give you that. You could use it as a weapon."

What is Da asking for?

"Sir! Beggin' your pardon, the Rider has a point. Dragon's been in that hole all these years and there's no telling how it'll behave. The man wants to have the best chance he can to control it. He's going to be chained to the dragon anyway. Just that could get him killed. Our archers'll have him in their sights anyway. He won't be able to swing that to do any harm before taking a few arrows, will he?"

Rumandor seemed to weigh his soldier's words, and Yogari's.

"You there! On the pegs on the wall behind you, above the vent doors. Bring that grid-cleaning hook. Tie a rope to the handle loop and then lower it to the Rider."

I know what they're talking about. I saw it on pegs there. It was a wrought iron bar at least as long as she was tall. One flattened end was shaped into a point for about two hand lengths and then bent to make a corner hook. A big loop, she could put both her arms through, was on the other end.

It must be to clean off debris that gets attached to the grid under the planks.

"Easy does it. Not too fast."

"Sir! He wants the rope too."

"Give him the rope too."

"He's tying the hook to one side of the cage. Sir! He's got the chain from the bucket out. He's fastening the shackle to his left ankle with the hammer.

"Thumbs-up, sir. Do we send down the dragon's shackles?"

"Not yet. The chains will be too short to work with. We'll bring the cage up more, then lower the big shackles.

"Pull!"

The gears clicked.

"Stop! Lower the shackles for the dragon. One at a time. Left leg first.

"Lower away, nice and easy. Slowly, slowly. Don't move. We're right above the dragon's back. I don't know how we can get it past the back of the wing.

"You'll have to help us from down there."

"Look at that, sir. He's got the rope coiled over one shoulder. The iron hook's hanging down behind him as he climbs the corner of the cage. He's at the top. He's using the hook to poke the dragon's right wing. The dragon moved its wing. It doesn't look happy. Now he's got space to walk on top of the cage. He's reaching up with the hook. He can almost touch the shackle. If we lower it some more he'll be able to push it so it slides over the left side of the dragon's back. Lower. Lower. Some more. There. He wants us to lower it more. Stop.

"He's using the hook to get the dragon to bring its wing back. He stepped onto the wing. The dragon has lifted its wing and pulled it over its back, and the Rider's riding the wing. He's hooked the chain. Now he's got a hold of it and has stepped onto the dragon's back.

"The Rider slid down the chain to the top of the cage. He's goading the dragon to get it to stand. I can't see from here, but I'm guessing he's fastening the shackle to the dragon's leg. He's hammering.

"Dragon's not too happy. The Rider's talking to it, patting it. He's disappeared again.

"Rider's standing. He's fashioning a harness with the rope we let him have. He's using the hook again to coax the dragon to stand and lift its left wing. He's disappeared under the wing. He's at the dragon's head. He's talking to it, patting it. He's placed the rope over the dragon's snout.

"That's what he fashioned, a bridle. He's making adjustments to it. Looks like the dragon has cut the rope to the length the Rider wants. The Rider's tying it and checking the adjustments of the bridle. He's fixed it so a loop goes from one side of the dragon's snout out, over the back of its neck, and back up to the other side of its snout.

"He's thrown the remaining length of rope around the dragon's neck. He's gauging how much he has and where it rests on the dragon's neck.

"He's making knots in the rope. Looks like two sizable loops. He's tossed the rope back over the dragon's neck. Now he's tied it at the front and is bringing the loose ends back to the loops that are resting just above the wings. He's tied those ends to the loops on each side. He seems satisfied with his work.

"The Rider's got the dragon raising him onto its back with its wing. He's grabbed hold of the rope and is sitting on the dragon's back, just above its wings. He's adjusting the rope, positioning the loops. He's placed a foot in each loop and has grabbed onto the bridle rein loop.

"He's made a rope saddle of sorts to keep himself in position when sitting on the dragon's back.

"He's signaling for the other shackle.

"Good. Lower ... lower ... lower some more.

"Steady! Lower ... lower ... lower. A little more ... lower. Stop. He's got it under control. Lower some more ... more ... more. Stop.

"He's let himself slide down the dragon's back behind its left wing by hanging onto one of the saddle loops. He's standing on top of the cage and goading the dragon with his hook to get it to stand. It's standing and raising both wings. The Rider's able to duck down and come around from the front to the right side where the shackle hangs.

"He needs more length on the shackle chain. Lower ... lower ... a little more. Stop.

"Now he's crouched over and attaching the shackle. He's standing, talking to the dragon, patting it, now goading it to stand taller. Dragon's doing it.

"Rider's crouched again. Now, he has plenty of room to tie on the shackle. He's hammering the shackle pin in place. Looks like he's done. He's patting the dragon and talking to it. He's ducked under its wing, gone around the front, and come up behind the left wing. He's hooked the rope saddle and is pulling himself up onto the dragon's back. He's sitting just like he was before.

"Sir, we're ready to raise a final time."

Nagora peeked through the crack. Rumandor knelt on the floor and leaned over the stone rim. "Rider! We're going to raise the cage now as far as we can for the final time.

"Then we'll lower the chain from the crossbeam above. You'll fasten it to the cage. The cage's weight will then hang from the crossbeam. We'll remove the crank to have clear access to lower ladders to the cage. Then you'll coax the dragon to climb the ladder out of the hole."

Rumandor pulled back from the edge of the hole and stood. "Report, man!"

"Sir, we've got a thumbs-up. The Rider's sitting on the dragon, reins in one hand and patting it with the other."

"Ready, men? This is the last pull—on three. One, two, three!"

The soldiers grunted. The gears clicked. The cage did not have far to travel.

"Stop! Lower the crossbeam chain," Rumandor ordered.

The reporting soldier directed the ones above. "Lower ... lower ... some more ... more. Stop. He has the chain. Now he wants more length. Lower ... lower. Stop.

"He's fastening the link unions and hooks. He's double checking each one as he goes. Looks like he's done, sir."

"I want to see your commander's face."

That's Da speaking! The first time I hear his voice. A lump came to Nagora's throat.

"Sir, the Rider."

"I heard him." Rumandor went to his knees again.

Nagora listened to every word Yogari spoke. "Before you take the tension off the crank, I want you to take up the slack in the leg chains and make sure they're secured above. Then, go slow when you release the tension. If I yell 'stop,' do so immediately. If you want me to keep this dragon under control, you'll have to do as I say. Is that understood?"

"Yes!" said Rumandor. "Men, a slow and steady controlled release. On three. First we take up the slack on the leg chains. Understood above? Verify those chains are secured, and the crossbeam chain."

The leg chains rattled as the soldiers took up the slack.

"Leg chains secured, sir!

"Crossbeam chain secured, sir!"

"Men, I repeat: slow and steady controlled release. On three—One, two, three!"

A soldier pulled the release gear. The gear engaged so that with each pull of the lever, the cage would descend one gear notch at a time.

"Sir, release is complete. Full weight of the cage is on the crossbeam chain."

"Disengage the release gear. Haul all the chain over to the other side of the hole. When you clear the crank of its chain, go ahead with dismantling the crank assembly."

Nagora kept her eye at the crack between two of the hanging doors.

The crank's cylinder spun freely as the soldiers pulled the cage chain from it and fed it into a box that rested on a small cart on the other side of the vent hole.

Next, the soldiers removed the big wheel and crank gears from the oak cylinder center shaft. Ropes, thrown over the center crossbeam and tied to the big oak cylinder, allowed the soldiers to lift it from its two stone supports that stood opposite each other on the rim of the vent hole.

Other ropes, tied to the oak cylinder, allowed the soldiers to pull it over to the side of the vent hole to be lowered to the floor. From there, the soldiers rolled it out of the way and wedged it up against the wall, just to the right of the hanging door panels. Nagora stood behind the panels ready to glimpse Yogari.

Three stout ladders, set apart from each other by the width of a single ladder, had skinned, arm-thick saplings lashed across them to create the wider ladder for the dragon to climb. Five men brought the ladder into place with the help of more men on the vent-house roof viewing gallery. They helped raise and then lower it into the vent hole. Once in the hole, soldiers tied the ladder to chains that circled the outer stone rim of the vent hole.

When it was in place, Yogari spoke again: "I want a length of solid rope. I'm going to try to haul the bottom of the ladder closer to the cage chain and lash it in place. I want to get a slight angle on this ladder. It's not going to be easy to coax the dragon up because its legs are shackled to these chains. You people have to make damn sure the chains stay behind its wings and out of the way so they don't become tangled and trip us on the way up. My best chance will be if I can stay on the dragon's back. It'll be a tight squeeze for us. I doubt I would be able to coax it out from above.

"Keep the chains loose enough so the dragon can move freely, yet not get tangled. We're going to come up slow, one big rung at a time. There had better not be anyone in the room above because we're going to be a tight fit. Your men on the vent-house roof viewing gallery will be fine.

"Once we're out of the hole, I will dismount and check that the dragon hasn't injured itself on the climb out. After, we'll make our way to the fortress yard. Don't worry, we won't try to fly away. This dragon hasn't taken flight in all its years of captivity. If it tried to fly, it wouldn't get very far. It would be like a young bird needing to learn how to fly all over again.

"I warn you, one arrow or one spear prick is all it will take for me to completely lose control of the dragon. I suggest your men keep their screams to themselves. Anyone issuing orders, please do so in a calm, controlled voice.

"One more thing, I am shackled to its left leg. That's where I'll stay. If you take me away, I cannot promise you will have control over the dragon. Even if you think the chains holding it will keep it under control, you will be in for a surprise.

"Have I made myself clear?"

After a long moment of silence, Rumandor answered. "Yes. Clear. Allow me to transmit your message to the remaining fortress troops. When I return you can come up.

"Give him the rope he asks for." Rumandor left for the fortress yard and hollered for an immediate assembly of the fortress troops.

As he addressed the troops, it sounded like someone delivering orders from a higher authority. It was the impression Yogari had conveyed—skilled, knowledgeable, firm, and in control.

When Rumandor returned, a soldier reported, "Sir! The Rider has lashed the ladder to the cage. It's now at a slight incline. I don't know if it'll stay that way during their ascent."

"Clear the room.

"You! On the roof. I want a running account of their progress. I'll be standing at the gates to this room, speak so I can hear you. If the Rider orders you to shut up, do so. Understood?"

"Yes, sir!"

The Rider
Otêhtapiw

Nagora pressed her face to the widest crack between the hanging door panels. Her eyes were riveted on the stone rim of the vent hole, waiting to see Danuka's head appear. Yogari's voice coaxed the dragon into position. She understood the language he spoke, the language of The People. He used words and expressions that sounded so familiar to her. "*Pêyâhtak sîmâk, Danuka*—Easy now, Danuka." "*Wîcikiya*—Together with you." "*Kinanâskomitin, Danuka*—Thank you, Danuka." "*Môsak*—Always." And "*Miywâtisiw Okâwîmâw*—Good Mother." So it's true, Danuka is a female. Da your tone is confident, calm, and reassuring, not only for Danuka, but for me too.

So this is the power my amulet has been revealing—the power of the language of The People—the power to speak to Danuka, like Da. I too am a Dragon Talker. I have that power.

For the first time, a low, sad moan rose from the vent hole. It was Danuka.

Nagora shivered. When she was young, at Geirador's, in the corral an old mare had lain down to die. Geirador knew not of what, except she was old and had worked hard all her life and was moaning in pain in those last moments. Danuka's moan resembled that.

The tops of the ladders sunk below the stone rim of the vent hole and the chains lashed to the ladders became taut.

Danuka's weight must be on the ladder.

Yogari's voice was calm and encouraging.

The dragon's moan shortened and came in quick, successive pulses.

The face of the soldier above, holding one of the shackle chains, showed he was in awe of what he saw. A shade of terror crept across the same soldier's face as his lips twitched. He backed away, pulling the chain with him.

Nagora's eyes traveled down the chain just in time to see Danuka's massive head appear over the rim of the vent hole. It resembled that of a horse, yet more than three times the size of the biggest horse she had ever seen. Its nostrils flared as the head hooked itself over the stone rim. The bridle rope Yogari had tied in place was pulled back to the base of Danuka's eyes by the tension on the reins as Yogari held on. The dragon bared her teeth in the effort she was making to hold on and pull forward. Her teeth were like those of a cat, except for those between the upper and lower fangs. They were serrated and so sharp and deadly they could bite a man in half.

The skin on the lips, snout and the forehead was scaly like that of a snake.

The skin around the dragon's mouth and nostrils was a glistening dark red of ripe choke cherries. This red color carried back among dark, shimmering, blue scales. Her eyes were red and bulged out like a frog's eyes and were at least as big as Nagora's two fists held together. They were in continuous motion, taking in the surroundings. For a moment they caught Nagora's eyes and looked inside her. The nostrils flared, and the eyes moved away.

The dragon's moaning had become quicker and shorter as it redoubled its efforts to pull itself up and forward. Its neck reared up behind its head with the effort of the pulling.

Behind the red ears, the scales on her neck were bigger than those on her head. They bristled with an added shade of green that turned bright copper, depending on how they caught the light from the hole in the roof above.

The massive head rose from the floor, its long neck arched over in Nagora's direction. The head came down, almost hit the floor, but stopped just short. The dragon's huge right eye stared into Nagora's wide open right eye. Nagora's momentary terror turned to calm. *Danuka recognizes me.*

The dragon turned her head and looked back to her right. Nagora's eyes followed. What she guessed was a part of Danuka's wing came up from the vent hole. The big, single claw from the massive joint of the unfolded wing opened and then clamped down on the stone rim of the vent hole.

The dragon's huge head swung back, her eyes on Nagora's eyes. *She smiled at me! I'm sure of it.* Danuka's head turned to the left and looked back. She was watching her other wing claw come up.

Yogari said, "*Miywâtisiw Okâwîmâw*—Good Mother," and "*Nipêpîm, Danuka*—My baby, Danuka."

The dragon's head swung back part way. She rested her right cheek on the floor and moaned with effort. Her neck arched higher as it broadened and rose further out of the vent hole.

The rein on the dragon's right side rippled. Then a hand wrapped around the rein, flicked it, and another ripple traveled along the rein. Slowly, she rose some more. The hand became a forearm, then an elbow, and the top of a head.

Da's looking down, watching Danuka climb.

The dragon climbed higher. Yogari was now in view. His face was framed in a black beard with streaks of white that ran down the corners of his mouth to his chin. He wore his hair pulled back and tied into a single long braid at the back. It swung from side to side as he hung onto the reins and looked down over his shoulder from one side, and then the other, all the while talking to Danuka. He wore a sheepskin vest that hung from his broad, sweat-covered shoulders.

Yogari's right side, from the waist down, came into view as the dragon rose more. His right foot was in the stirrup loop he had tied, and his knee was bent so it was at waist level. In this way, he straddled Danuka's back. The iron hook hung from the loop of his leg shackle chain. It ran over his left shoulder and down across his back to his right hip.

He continually patted the dragon's neck. As she stopped her efforts, Yogari took his bearings as he was now above the level of the rim of the vent hole.

The first place his eyes went to was Nagora's eye at the crack between the panels. He stared at her and smiled. Oh! Da! I want to run to you.

Then Yogari cast his eyes around the room and up to the soldiers.

He leaned over and rested his left cheek against Danuka's neck while he patted her. "*Âmi-tasi, nimâmâ*—We are almost there, my mother." Again he looked directly into Nagora's eye. "*Kîyânaw kaskitâw*—We can do it."

Yes, Da, we can.

Yogari stood in the rope loop stirrups and looked down at the ladder beneath the dragon. He spoke to Danuka. He had her turn her head and neck and brought them past the hanging door panels to face the vent-house entrance gate.

The dragon rose some more; obviously she had brought her right leg up another rung. She reached out the claw of her right wing and dragged it further along the rim of the vent hole.

This time her left leg brought her further out of the vent hole. Next came Danuka's left wing. She let go the grasp her left wing claw had on the vent-hole rim and raised her wing up to the ceiling. She then brought the closed claw forward toward her head. With this movement, the dragon had pulled her left wing from the vent hole.

All Nagora could see now were the fine, textured scales on the topside and leading edge of Danuka's wing. It looked strong yet flexible. Here, in the wing, the red was like her snout and mouth.

The dragon's efforts under Yogari's patient coaxing made her moan louder.

She pulled herself forward with her giant wing claws, clamped to the ceiling beams.

Danuka shifted all of a sudden. Part of her great left wing came pressing against the hanging panel doors. Nagora scurried back into the vent shaft in case the door panels would not resist the pressure.

The panel doors swung and the vent house shook. The dragon moved forward. Her wing brushed against the panels. Yogari's voice remained calm. "There. We are out. We made it, Mother. You are happy. Control your tail, Danuka."

Nagora returned to the crack between the panels. She brought her eye to it. At the same moment, Yogari's smiling face peeked over the fold in the wing. He was staring at her eye.

He was standing next to Danuka.

Yogari ducked back under the wing. The door panel pulled open. A hand reached in at the level of her knee. Nagora bent and grasped her father's hand. He gave her hand a squeeze then let go, and the panel closed.

A chain dragged on the floor and Yogari spoke to Rumandor. "Before I take the dragon into the fortress yard, I want you to know that she is very hungry. If you want me to be able to control her so she won't be a danger to you or your men, you'll have to feed her, and soon. A dozen freshly killed hens would be a good start. They won't have to be plucked or gutted. That should give you time to find a sheep or goat or a calf.

"I doubt one of your troopers will volunteer to be the meal. If the dragon isn't fed soon, then I fear one of you will soon be her meal and more than one of you will die from the hunt."

Rumandor yelled: "Round up all the hens in the coop. Go to the plain. Bring back a calf and a pig. Make that two calves and a pig. Tell them why. If they don't deliver within three counts, I can't promise there'll be a dragon to show tomorrow."

"Thank you. We'll stay right here until the hens arrive," said Yogari.

Danuka is so big. She was squatting on her talons, belly on the floor of the vent house. Her back almost touched the ceiling. If she stood, she would touch the ceiling and could break through it if she so decided.

How could she have grown so much on such little food? And how could Da be in such good shape? He's not fat, nor skin and bones like someone who's been starving. His muscles are like ropes and he's very limber.

The chain dragged on the floor again and Yogari spoke to Danuka.

He's checking her over for injuries sustained on the climb out of the hole.

The dragon moved now and then, shifting her position at Yogari's request. The huge wings deployed as much as they could in the vent-house space. Nagora caught glimpses of Yogari moving under and along the parts of the right wing. He ran his hands along the trailing edge of the wing, then reaching to feel the topside and underside of the wing.

Yogari came alongside Danuka's lower back and ran his hands along the ridge of the backbone scales. All the while he talked to her. "You will be fine, Mother. Do not worry."

As he spoke these words, he paused in his inspection and found Nagora with his gaze. He smiled at her.

This man has so much confidence. He's my da. I know I'll do whatever he asks of me.

Yogari continued running his hand along the ridge of the her tail. Now his back was to Nagora and from the way he stretched to feel as far along the tail as possible, he was at the limit his chain would allow.

He made his way back, picking up his chain as he went. He coaxed the dragon's wing up higher, blocking Nagora's view of the ceiling vent hole and the soldiers above.

He's coming around to this side. If he can get Danuka to position her left wing to block the view from the vent-house gate, he could come to me.

Again the chain dragged slowly. Nagora glimpsed Yogari from the waist down. He wore leather hide pants sewn together with strips of leather lanyards. His boots were also fashioned from leather hide and were held in place with strips of leather that crisscrossed from the ankles to the knees.

Da has made good use of the hides of the animal carcasses sent down to feed him and the dragon.

After completing his inspection of the leading edge of the wing, Yogari had the dragon lift her wing so he could step behind it. Then he had Danuka bring the leading edge down to the floor so the trailing edge stood up like a fan for his inspection. He started at the wing's junction to the body and worked his way back along the edge.

Da is making his way back to me. The hanging door panels can't be seen from the vent-hole gallery, nor the entrance gate. In a moment I'll be able to meet Da in the shadow of Danuka's wing.

Nagora crouched and pushed on the panel before her.

She duck-walked into the shadow, let the panel close behind her, and stood waiting, listening as the dragging chain came closer. Danuka started to moan again, but did not move.

The dragging chain stopped. Yogari stood before her, a shadow within a shadow. She reached out her hand.

It came to rest on his chest that breathed and held a heart that beat strong and steady. A hand covered hers and before she knew it, another hand pulled her into her da's embrace. Now his two hands held her close, his cheek next to hers. "My child, my daughter, you've come," he whispered in her ear.

"Aye. I'm your daughter, Nagora. We've come to free you and Danuka."

"Nagora! Nagora! My Nagora!" He released her from his embrace, reached to her face with his hands. His right hand caressed her features. His face was close to hers.

He's trying to see me in the dark.

"My daughter."

Nagora breathed in her father's scent. It was unique. A spicy sweetness, mixed with the smell of leather and something else that could only be the smell of Danuka. The combination was intoxicating. Somehow it made her not want to let go of her father. I've dreamed about this day for so long. She pulled Yogari to her, buried her face against his chest, and breathed in the heady scent. As she inhaled deeper, he kissed her forehead. "My child."

"My da." Nagora fought back her tears of happiness. Focus on your mission. Stay in control. She exhaled, and then took a normal breath. "Da, there are two of us. You have twin daughters. Sagora is your other daughter."

Yogari held her hands. "Twice gifted. How can I ever thank your mother? How is my Tagnya?"

"She's fine. She's nearby."

"How did you get here?"

"By sea on the Wolf. We climbed the cliff. Uncle Dangor is leading us. There are nine of us. We're here to free you and Danuka.

"Da, two nights ago, Danuka spoke to me in a dream. She told me to find tools to help you unlock the bridge. You must have a plan. What tools do you need? How can we best help you?"

"Nagora, Danuka spoke to you and you understood?"

"Aye, Da, clearly."

"You must be wearing the amulet I gave your mother."

"I am."

"Three times gifted—by the stars!" Yogari pulled her close again. "My daughter, Nagora, you are a Dragon Talker. Danuka kept her promise. I have a plan. Do you know what Raganora has in store for me?"

"I heard it all this morning."

"So you know. If you can get a big axe to me on the bridge, take out the ballista, and give me cover fire with bows, I'll be fine."

"That we should be able to do. There'll only be ten men controlling your move to the bridge from this side. We'll be able to take them, and, we'll get more help from our warriors on the mainland to take out the ballista."

"With my brother leading you, I know you will."

"Are you sure you don't need nothing else?"

"I have this iron hook. With a heavy axe, I should be good.

"Nagora, we have little time. I have so many questions!"

"Rider!"

Rumandor's yell made them freeze for a moment.

"Stick to the plan. Get me a big axe."

Yogari let go of her. He hauled on the chain and yelled, "Have the hens arrived?"

"They have. Where are you?"

"Checking the dragon's wings for cuts it could have gotten from the climb out of the hole."

Nagora pulled back the panel and crouched through the opening. Her heart was pounding in her chest as if she had just run the length of her beach. *Da, I could never have imagined meeting you this way.* Her heartbeat slowed. She swallowed. The scent that seemed to have enveloped her while under Danuka's wing dissipated. *Could it be that Danuka's scent was taking control of me? Making me not want to let go of Da? Why?*

The answer will come. Right now you have a task. Focus on that. The axe. A big axe. Where did I see a big axe? Bigger than those Lars brought. I know I saw one here today. Where?

Her mind raced back to their climb over the fortress wall in dawn's early light. *There it is!* It rested on one of the huge beams that wedged diagonally from a post at the base of the inner stockyard wall to the sagging crossbeams of the debris-laden outer wall. The posts that held those diagonal beams in place had been sharpened with an axe and most likely driven into the ground with the broad side of the same axe.

If it's still there, that'll be the one.

Light filled the crack between the panels behind Nagora. She put her eyes to the crack. Yogari had coaxed Danuka to fold her left wing closed against her body. She also folded her right wing.

Yogari was moving toward Danuka's head. In one hand, he held his shackle chain that he pulled along as he walked forward, and in the other, the iron hook.

"We've got the dozen hens you requested. Doesn't seem like much for a beast that size," said Rumandor.

"They'll calm her hunger until tonight."

"The cows and pigs should arrive within a count or two. How do you want the hens?"

"I will come forward as far as I can on my chain. Place two hens at a time in a bucket. Set the bucket down where I can reach it with the hook. I'll feed the dragon."

"You heard the man. Do it," Rumandor ordered a soldier.

Yogari retrieved the bucket the soldier had set on the ground just outside the big open doors of the vent house. Then he went to Danuka's head. He spoke gently to her. She opened her great mouth. Yogari placed the two hens in, feathers and all. She did not close her mouth until Yogari spoke. When he did, the two hens disappeared in two movements of her jaws.

Yogari returned to the bucket for two more hens.

When Yogari returned the final empty bucket, he spoke to Rumandor. "I've kept my word. I want to remind you of my warning earlier. Your men can have their bows strung and arrows nocked, but I prefer they not be drawn. As for that ballista, I hope you know how to use it. Have you inspected it? Have you fired it recently? It's a dangerous machine. I know what it can do. I destroyed two just like it many years ago. I hope you won't give me cause to destroy this one too."

"Enough talk, Rider! We're going to move you out into the fortress yard."

"Fair enough. Let's get on with it."

"Archers above! Arrows nocked! Not pulled. I repeat: not pulled. Have them ready to pull, aim, and fire at the Rider. Understood?"

"Yes, sir."

Beyond Rumandor in the fortress yard, Nagora glimpsed part of the ballista and the soldiers who would maneuver it. Other soldiers were taking up the chains to control Danuka.

"Rider, bring the dragon forward."

"As soon as we're clear of the vent house, I'm going onto the dragon's back. It'll be easier for me to control her. Don't be surprised if she spreads her wings. Even if she could fly, the way you've got her chained, she wouldn't be able to go anywhere. Relay that to the guards in the yard."

Nagora sat on the planks with her knees drawn up so she could have a better view where the hanging door opened wider.

Da has Danuka under control, that's for sure. As long as some stupid soldier doesn't panic, Da will be able to bring Danuka safely to the other end of the yard. Uncle and the others will have a partial view of Da on Danuka's back.

Yogari picked up his shackle chain and talked Danuka into moving forward.

The big chains rumbled through the iron hoops around the vent-house perimeter beams and walls. Danuka cleared the vent house. She spread and lowered her left wing. Yogari stepped on it and the dragon raised her wing. He grabbed the bridle rein and rope saddle. He stuck a foot into the loop and pulled his other leg over the base of her broad neck. He patted her neck and talked to her as she brought one leg forward and then the other.

Danuka's steps sent tremors that rippled through the vent-house floor and Nagora's backside.

The dragon's long tail came sliding back into the vent house as it uncurled from her right side. It touched the hanging door Nagora sat behind. She held her breath. The tail followed, and Danuka stood to her full height as she straightened her two stout legs. Her tail helped her keep her balance. Yogari swayed from side to side with each of Danuka's steps. Wow! What is it like to be sitting where Da is?

He can see over the fortress walls. Did the people on the mainland glimpse Danuka's head? He is so at ease, like I am on Storm's back.

Wow! By my stars! The dragon slowly raised her wing talons. They both went up along each side of Yogari, two body lengths higher than him. Some soldiers screamed and dropped chains. Rumandor yelled at them to keep calm and hold their positions. As the dragon spread the taloned joints away from Yogari, her wings unfolded until they looked like sails on a boat. They were so big that their tips reached to each side of the fortress-yard walls. Ever so slowly, she flapped her wings back and forth like cormorants do when drying their wings. Where the sunlight caught Danuka's scales, iridescent waves of reddish blue to coppery green rippled over the backs of her wings. And then, the taloned joints of the wings tilted forward.

Soldiers ran to the other end of the yard and took up the chains there.

The dragon stopped moving forward and flapped her wings up and down. If Da let her, Danuka could lift off the ground. After a dozen flaps of her wings, she brought them back down and folded them in at her sides with her talons projecting ahead of her.

"By my stars! Man, did you see that?" The voice came from above. An archer seeking confirmation of what he had just witnessed? You better believe it.

Yogari looked around the yard and along the walls at the troops assembled there.

He's waiting for them to regain their composure.

He patted Danuka's neck and talked to her. Again, the dragon continued her slow advance to the wall at the other end of the yard. And from what Nagora could see, the soldiers were doing their best to control the chains and their fear.

Nagora let the hanging door panel swing back to vertical.

Why didn't Da just unleash Danuka's strength in an attack on the fortress troops?

There are ten of Rumandor's men and about twenty others. Thirty in all. He could have asked for us to attack the troops. We would have to take out the ballista first. Such an attack, combined with the fear Danuka would strike in the troops, would make getting control of the fortress easy. Yogari and Danuka would be free.

I guess he fears that ballista at close range. Maybe he doesn't want to risk losing control of the bridge. They'll be giving it to him, putting him where he wants to be. Why destroy the bridge in the first place? How's that going to protect Danuka's children? And why had he planned and designed a keystone that could be removed to destroy the bridge? He did that all those years ago. It must be a Dragon Talker's secret we don't know about. He can't know the future. Or can he? No one knows the future. A chill ran through her.

That's what too much thinking does.

Nagora pushed the hanging door panel. The big ballista was now in the middle of the fortress yard, pointed at Danuka. Its big bow string was cocked and its bolt in place. Six armed men stood by the ballista, along with three archers on each side.

Beyond, Yogari had dismounted and was sitting cross-legged on the ground in front of Danuka. The chains that held her close to the wall did not leave her much room to move. She was on her belly on the ground with her tail wrapped around her.

It will be a long night.

Nagora let the panel close before standing.

Just then, the sound of approaching footsteps and Rumandor's voice filled the air. "This shouldn't take too long, lads. When you're done this, you'll get a double ration of ale."

Nagora froze where she was behind the panel. Then with care, she positioned herself to take a peek at what was going on. A soldier's backside came into view as she put her eye to the crack.

He was attaching a loop of rope around the center shaft of the oak-planked cylinder that had been wedged against the nearby wall. He brought the rope up, as did the soldier on the other end of the cylinder, and then together they pulled, rolling the cylinder over to the stone rim of the vent-hole shaft.

"That's it, lads." Rumandor was standing nearby.

Nagora pulled her eye away from the crack and eased herself back into the duct.

Rumandor spoke again. "It won't take you long to reassemble the crank and gear wheel. Getting the ladder out of the hole will be the tough part. Once reassembled, we reattach the cage chain, wind it on the cylinder, take up the tension so we can remove the overhead chain to the beam, and we'll be ready for our passenger.

"Hag'll be a light load, lads. Easy to lower once we get her into the cage."

This just confirms the death sentence. Rag won't send Da and Danuka back down there with Hag. Okay, Queen Raganora, you're in for the fight of your life.

"Sir, Hag'll be fuming when we take her. She'll be spitting poison. Sir, we fear her as much as we fear that dragon out there."

"Fear not, lads. Once the captain tricks Hag into hiding in a vegetable sack and we stick her in the cage, and then we lower it, the cage's chain will be at its end before she fights her way out. She'll have no choice but to step into the dragon's cave below. Our job will be done."

"Sounds like a plan, sir! Hag can't weigh more than a dozen cats in a wet sack. Mind you, she'll squirm like that many when we try to put her in the cage." Another soldier laughed.

I've heard enough. Time to head back to report to the others.

The Dream
Pawâtamowin

On her crawl back through the vent, Nagora took her scrip and her waterskin and moved along. Hag's chanting accompanied the dull candlelight glow that seeped from the louvers of her chamber. Again, a chill ran up Nagora's spine. Glad I won't have to deal with you. Then she pushed that feeling to the back of her mind.

All was quiet at the kitchen. Nagora slid the duct vent door open and crawled out. She went to the outer door to gauge the situation. All the eyes of those above the walls were on Danuka. The gate to the livestock yard was open a crack. It was only thirty strides away.

She donned her cape, drew the hood over her head, and limped over to the livestock yard gate. If anyone sees me, I hope they think I'm from the kitchen going about my business. She took her time crossing to the gate and did not stop to look back once.

...

Inside the yard, Nagora ran to where she had seen the big axe. With its head on the ground, the end of its handle came up to her chest. She grabbed hold of it and gauged the heft of the big double-bladed head. The axe was designed to split wood with ease, and its weight was ideal for driving fence posts into the ground with the broadside of its head.

This should do for Da.

She made her way to the tower ladder.

On her climb, Lars greeted her. Nagora took hold of his arm. "I have to meet with all of you."

Lars pointed. "They're all at the other tower."

"They've been watching Danuka?"

Lars had a childish grin on his face. "We've seen Danuka and want to see more of her."

They snuck over to the other tower. Dangor had his head poked out of the tower entrance across the way, waiting for them to hurry over. They did so in a crouched run along the walkway.

Dangor's face was happy. His eyes shone like a little boy's. "We saw Yogari! My brother is looking good. We saw Danuka spread her wings. She's huge! Now she's out of sight."

"We'll not see her until they move her and Da to the bridge tomorrow. They are tied to the wall at the other end of the fortress. Danuka is squatting on the ground with not much loose in the chains that hold her," said Nagora.

Dangor held Nagora's shoulders. "You've seen Yogari up close?"

"I touched him and talked to him. He held me in his arms for a few moments. He's so glad we're here."

Then Nagora filled them in on everything she had seen earlier as she listened in on Queen Rag's conversation with Grallimdor and everything she and Yogari had spoken about.

Lars touched her arm. "Did he say why he wanted the big axe?"

"No. He didn't have time. If you ask me, he knows what he's doing. It must be to cut the shackle chains. And if we guessed right, to help unlock the keystone.

"Uncle, he's so confident and in control! Did you see soldiers with drawn bows around the courtyard?"

"No. They had them strung with arrows nocked, but not one with an arrow drawn."

"That was one of Da's conditions. They've listened to him and given him everything he's asked for."

Lars's eyes were open wide. "I would too if I knew he were the only one able to control that dragon. The size of Danuka!"

"Uncle, Da controls Danuka so easily. He's amazing. Danuka's amazing. When she flapped her wings in the yard, I swear, if Da hadn't controlled her, she would have lifted off the ground!"

"Lass, that's our Yogari. Your da is a true Dragon Talker and Dragon Rider. It won't surprise me if he flies Danuka to-morrow. In the meantime, let's keep our heads closer to the ground. The battle isn't won yet."

"I know. Have you planned how we pick off the ten that'll remain here?"

"We've come up with some ideas.

"This officer, Rumandor, tell us about him."

"He's an old soldier. Probably not effective on the battle-field as a fighter; though he's good with his men. If you have a job that needs to be done, call on Rumandor and his men. They'll get it done. He set up everything to get Danuka out of the hole—the chains, the anchor pins, and the rings around the fortress yard. It's probably him and his gang that shored up the back wall here."

"Okay. Here's our thinking. The bridge is a long, wide arc, like a strung bow is part of a circle. If you stand at either end of the bridge and look to its middle, you can't see clear over to the other side. But you can see to the middle of the bridge. And the bridge's side walls give cover from the waist down to those standing on the bridge. Remember, it's wide enough for four riders to cross it comfortably side by side."

"That's right," Nagora said.

Dangor continued, "Even on horseback, you can't see to the other side. Rumandor has ten men. They'll be busy con-trolling the chains that hold Danuka until she's tied to the key in the middle of the bridge. Is he going to follow them to the bridge to supervise, or watch from the nearest tower at the fortress?"

"Either way, will they stay at the bridge once they've locked Danuka's chains in place, or return here? We're guess-ing they'll come back so as not to be hit by anything that comes flying at Danuka and misses her. They'll return before execution time.

"That's when we'll make our move to take them, getting their uniforms so that our movements to the bridge don't ap-pear suspicious."

"So Uncle, then how do we position ourselves to protect Da?"

"Once we get Rumandor and his men locked up in the fortress jail, we move, in uniform, to the bridge with two carts."

He pointed to Nagora. "You mentioned the handcart they plan on moving Hag with. It should be available. And we spotted a mule pulling an empty one across the bridge, going for the animals to feed Danuka. We're hoping it will stay here when it returns.

"We fill the handcart with tools Yogari could need and a variety of weapons to choose from for his own use."

As Lars translated, the raiders nodded.

"It'll be a challenge to get the bigger cart into position on the bridge between Danuka and the ballista. It'll carry our bows and arrows, and fire arrows. Once we tip it over on its side, we'll be able to shoot at the ballista from behind it.

"We'll let Yogari choose who he wants to help him free Danuka from the chains.

"The others will give them cover. We hope to find a big table or two to help give us cover. If we do, we'll bring them over on the big cart."

Nagora held out two fingers. "There are two in the queen's throne room."

Dangor nodded. "And we'll have to move into position fast and signal the start of our attack so the planned diversion on the mainland can start at the same time. Let's hope warrior archers can move into position to help us."

Trowan smiled and spoke to Lars. "She says they'll be in position."

Dangor returned her smile and continued. "Tomorrow, as soon as Danuka is outside the fortress, we begin our hunt for what we need on the bridge. We'll assemble what we find in the corner of the courtyard near the barracks entrance. After that, it will be a watch-and-wait situation that'll tell us how to move on Rumandor and his men. Questions?"

Lars finished translating, and the warriors had no questions.

"If you think of something, anything you have a question about, or a suggestion, let me know. Until then, we keep watch and take turns getting rest. Lars, can you take care of setting up watch duty?"

"Sure."

Tommassen, who had been keeping watch at the tower window, called for Nagora to come. He pointed.

She peered out the window, then leaned out the door. "Uncle, a mule's pulling a cart across the bridge. It could be the calves and pigs Da ordered for Danuka."

Dangor looked up from where he sat. "I doubt they'll be brought into the fortress yard right away."

"The cart's behind the wall now. I think you're right. Two calves and a small pig were in it for sure.

"The tower guard is out. He's lowered a basket with a rope over the wall. He's bringing it back up. Looks like it could be written orders. He's taking something to the next tower. Moving carefully along, he's keeping an eye on Danuka.

"The cart driver is on the mule's back. Looks like we'll have our cart. He didn't wait for an answer. I wonder what's in the orders."

"Perhaps we'll be able to find out from Rumandor tomorrow when we take him," said Dangor. "For now, I suggest we eat, and then get some sleep." All agreed and dug into their rations.

While they ate, Lars announced the watch order. It was a rotating watch of six counts for each pair he named, except for Nagora who he paired with Dangor and himself. They would take first night watch.

After their light meal, they split into two groups, each taking a tower.

While Nagora, Dangor, and Lars curled up under their cloaks, Tommassen stood at the tower window, taking first watch with Trowan who would be watching from the other tower. As she closed her eyes, Nagora pictured Lars going to take watch at that tower when they'd wake up.

Dangor woke Nagora from a dream. In it, Hag was spitting words in her face: "Again I kill the mother's children." She tried to banish Hag's words as she blinked her eyes open.

"The sun hasn't set yet?" she asked.

"Just about to. Lars has already left for the other tower. He kissed you before I woke you."

As the sun slipped behind the distant hills above the plain, nightfall crept down over the fortress. The fortress was quiet despite the tension of the day's events.

Nagora stood and did her best to shake the dream from her mind.

Hag had poisoned Mum's unborn children. Is she going to poison Sagora and me? Not if she's in the cave in that vent hole. She'll be headed there soon. Good riddance.

Nagora crouched and made her way to the other tower. Its window afforded a more general view of the queen's courtyard, main fortress yard, vent-house roof, and bridge in the distance.

Lars hugged Nagora as he let her take the tower window position. "I'm going back to the other tower, in case something comes up and I have to convey Dangor's orders to the others." No wonder Gabe chose you as his second. When on task you're always thinking and prepared.

Fires in the camp on the plain were coming to life like captured fireflies.

Torches were being lit along the top of the fortress yard wall and on its inner walls. The fortress's famous prisoner was now on display aboveground.

Below in the courtyard, the gate opened. The wheels of an empty cart bump over the courtyard's cobblestones. Someone held a lantern, leading the way.

Probably Grallimdor.

Four guards followed, hauling a small cart.

Will Grallimdor's honeyed words persuade Hag? I could be there listening. I prefer watching from here.

The small procession stopped at the door that led to the inside corridor where, directly opposite, stood the doors to Queen Raganora's throne room. Turning right, down the corridor, led to Hag's chambers, and further on to another interior door to the kitchens.

Grallimdor went inside with his lantern. The soldiers waited alongside the cart.

Darkness had enveloped the courtyard except for the torchlight that streamed in from the fortress yard's inner gate the guards had left ajar.

...

The door at the top of the entrance steps opened, bringing with it light from the lantern Grallimdor carried. Hag held onto his other hand. In her right hand, she held her snake-headed staff.

I doubt she'll relinquish that.

Grallimdor led her to the back of the cart.

A soldier approached and held out a sack. He gave Hag the choice to step into it or have it pulled over her head. Either way she would have to cover her head. She stepped into the sack.

Grallimdor encouraged her, even suggesting she keep her staff, but bring the snake-head end into the sack next to her feet. She complied and crouched to allow the drawstring of the sack to be drawn closed over her head. No sooner was it closed, it opened again.

From where Nagora listened, Grallimdor's voice was a whisper. "What did I tell you? You can open it at will, but you must stay inside until you get to the queen's tent. Keep your staff under you."

The other soldiers approached and gently placed the sacked Hag feet first into the cart's bed of straw.

The soldiers carefully wheeled the cart about and headed out of the courtyard, following Grallimdor.

To a surprise you won't be too happy about.

The courtyard gate closed. Nagora waited and listened. For what, she wasn't sure. Danuka's moan sounded. It was a low and almost plaintive sound. It brought the guards on the fortress yard walls to attention. Danuka moaned again, not as loud, but as long. She moaned a third time, just audible from the tower. The dim light from the roof opening of the vent house died.

No screams came from the vent hole.

Had transferring Hag from the cart to the cage been uneventful?

Or did Hag accept it as her fate? That chill down my back again. Why? I can put her out of my mind now. Eventually, forever.

On the distant dark plain, dancing flames caught Nagora's eye.

Parallel flames danced in the dark, stopped, and spun in a circle.

Edana dances on her unicorn for the last time.

Voices, barely audible, rolled up to the fortress from the plain.

Witnesses proclaiming Edana's appearance? Most likely.

The flames of the dance of Edana's unicorn grew dim and faded into the night. Hundreds of fires from the forest hills above the plain came to life.

What thoughts are running through the minds of Queen Rag's troops? How many will desert under the cover of darkness? What are the children thinking?

The rest of Nagora's watch was uneventful. She made it to the tower where Lars was. "I'm tired, Lars." She held him for a moment.

"It's been a long day for you. A long-awaited day. Tomorrow will be even longer. Try to get some sleep. I'll bed down in the other tower."

Before he left the tower, she had already curled up under her cloak.

Lars drew it up closer to her head to cover her neck. "Sleep well," he whispered. She fell into sleep's restful arms as soon as he left.

The Chains
Sakâpihkan

At sunrise, all in the fortress were awake. The fortress yard was alive with activity. Orders were being yelled. Chains were rattling as soldiers threaded them into position. Armed soldiers were hustling to their posts. A pig squealed for a last time as it was butchered to feed Danuka. Or did Danuka eat it alive? A heavy, smoky mist bathed the plain and the forest hills surrounding it.

Before the sun burns this off, it will be close to noon.

Dangor stood next to Nagora. "Looks like they'll be moving Danuka right after she's eaten."

"I think Rumandor wants as few problems as possible. Soon we'll oblige him, won't we, Uncle?"

"That's right."

Nagora kept her eyes on the fortress yard. Da, I want to see you again. "Danuka's eating now. When she's done, they'll most likely lead her to the bridge. The ballista will go first. Those that work it will always keep her in their sight.

"Look. They're moving the ballista."

Danuka's head and neck came into view. Yogari was walking alongside, the iron hook in hand, guiding Danuka to the main outer gate of the fortress yard.

Da will mount her once they're through the gate.

Rumandor's men were continually jockeying the chains into position from one set of rings to another. The ballista and its escort moved out of the fortress onto the road leading to the bridge. They kept it aimed at Danuka as she headed for the fortress's main gate. Archers on each side of the ballista held bows and arrows at the ready. The fortress's remaining soldiers pulled the ballista.

Rumandor manned the tower as predicted. His men controlled the chains as they followed well behind Danuka. Soon the fortress would be empty, except for Rumandor and Dangor's raiders.

The raiders went into action as soon as the last of the soldiers went through the gate. Nagora, Dangor, and Trowan skirted the courtyard wall all the way to the gate that opened onto the fortress yard. From there, it was a short run to the vent house.

Nagora found the vent house empty except for the handcart the guards had used to bring Hag there last night. "We'll put the tools for Da in this one." The chain on the oak cylinder was at its end. She and the others went to their knees to peer over the stone-rimmed vent hole. Far below, in the dim red glow of the vent hole, the cage was empty.

Dangor opened the vent-house gate a crack. The bridge tower from where Rumandor would watch operations was on the other side of the main fortress yard's outer gate, which had been left open. From the vent-house gate to the outer fortress yard wall, it was a quick dash. They ran to the wall and hugged it as they moved closer to the main gate.

Dangor placed a hand on her arm. "Nagora, keep an eye on Danuka from here. Trowan and I will wait under Rumandor's tower. When the soldiers have completed their job, signal me. With your signal we'll go up. By the time you join us we should have him under our control."

She gave her uncle a nod.

Yogari rode on Danuka's back. Rumandor's men had attached Danuka's chains to the chains on the bridge, which ran from the big bollards at the entrance to the key on the middle of the bridge and back. Danuka was only a quarter of the way to the key. As Danuka advanced, Rumandor's men pulled the chains to the bollards and made one turn around each. From there, the chains ran through a series of iron rings set in the island's stone ground behind the bollards.

The ballista's escort slowly backed it up the slope of the bridge. A crowd had gathered on the mainland along the cliff near the other side of the bridge's exit.

Da, you look so confident. Soon we'll join you on the bridge.

The murmur and commotion of the crowd on the mainland increased. Danuka and Yogari must have come into full view. Just then, the dragon spread her wings and flapped them slowly in the air above the bridge. The crowd on the other side, as one, stepped back. Danuka must make an amazing and frightening silhouette.

The soldiers working the chains on the bollards looked up before continuing to haul and lock the chains in place.

The dragon flapped her wings faster. Tar piss! Danuka's lifting and straining against her chains.

If it weren't for the chains, she would fly.

The dragon slowed her flapping and folded her giant wings against her sides.

Nagora waved to Dangor and then ran past the gate to join him.

Nagora reached behind her back, grasped the handle of her big blade and pulled it free. She crouched as she came through the trapdoor of the tower platform.

Dangor held a knife at Rumandor's back just below the waist of his leather armor and he pressed the tip of his big blade below Rumandor's ear where it met his jaw. Trowan had her bow drawn, an arrow nocked and aimed at Rumandor.

"Now! Get down on your knees or Edana will cut your tendons so you never stand again," said Dangor. "Take his sword."

Nagora pulled Rumandor's sword from its scabbard as he went to his knees,.

"Now left hand behind your left knee. Right hand behind your right knee. Good. Sit back on your hands and listen."

Rumandor had his head leaned over to the left as far as he could under the relentless pressure of Dangor's blade. A trickle of blood seeped down his neck.

"Don't think of trying anything. My companion has an arrow aimed at your back. Understood?"

Rumandor managed a "Yes."

"Do you have a signal to call your men back to the fortress?"

"A green flag. But if they've finished their work I don't have to use it."

"So help me, if you lie, you'll die and so will all your men. If you cooperate, you'll live. Choose now for yourself and your men."

"I'll cooperate."

"And your men?"

"They'll obey."

"Good." Dangor withdrew his big blade.

Rumandor straightened his neck and turned to glimpse his attackers.

"There are more of us. Many more. You may stand now. Go back to your window.

"What signals are you expecting to get from the other side of the bridge?"

"A red flag. Within a count from the time it is shown, the dragon will be slain. We're to be ready and in position to keep it under control. If it's killed and falls dead on the bridge, we have to throw it over the side of the bridge."

"Any other signals?"

"No. No others."

Raganora, I hate you, you bitch! You want to create a spectacle of Danuka's death.

Rumandor pointed. "Look. My men are done their work. They're on their way back."

"Down to the yard. Edana, go first. Ready your bow," said Dangor.

Lars appeared at Nagora's side as she nocked an arrow. "Get the other archers ready. The men from the bridge are on their way back."

Dangor nodded to Lars to do as Nagora had asked. He was right behind Rumandor on the ladder. Trowan crouched on the walkway near the tower with her bow at the ready. Nagora also had Rumandor in her sights. Dangor guided Rumandor to the center of the yard opposite the tower he had been in.

As Rumandor's ten men casually marched into the fortress yard, Nagora and the other archers had them covered. "Go join your commander. If you try anything, you'll all lose your lives," said Nagora as she waved them over to Rumandor, where Dangor again had his big blade at his neck.

Rumandor kept calm. "Men, drop your weapons. Fall in behind me. If you want to live, do as I tell you."

Rumandor's men threw down their swords and spears, and his two archers threw down their bows and quivers. Then they lined up behind Rumandor.

"Anything else you want to tell them?" asked Dangor.

"Lads, looks like we've been relieved of our task. From now on, we take our orders from Edana here."

Nagora spoke. "Follow your commander into the courtyard. Line up at the jail door."

Rumandor made his way as ordered. His men followed. Nagora's force followed with their arrows drawn.

Rumandor's men halted outside the jail.

Nagora waved her big blade. "We're going to need your uniforms. I want you all to strip naked as the day you were born. Leave your clothes in a neat pile on the ground on top of your boots. As soon as you're done, make your way to the cell."

They did as she ordered.

...

Once Nagora had locked the jail door, she joined Dangor's raiders who were choosing the helmets and light body armor they needed to appear as Rumandor's men from a distance. She found what she needed and put it on.

Then they brought the useful items they had found into the courtyard.

Dangor pointed to the tower. "Lars, tell Tommassen to get up in the tower and watch for a red flag from the other side. He's to warn us as soon as he sees one being waved. Tell him it'll be like the one in the tower.

"Then take Tsimor and Kymasen and get the big cart outside the main gate. I'll check the stables and the smithy. Nagora, get the handcart."

Back in the courtyard, the raiders sorted the items. Into the handcart went a big hammer, the big axe, two smaller axes, the pry bar they had brought, and another Dangor found in the stable.

He also added a few lengths of rope, a brush, a big chisel, and tongs.

Lars threw in several swords, knives, and spears for Yogari to choose from.

"On the way out, we'll stop for buckets of water at the stables, and we'll bring the six hens that are there," said Dangor.

Into the big cart, they slid two big tables on their sides. These came from Raganora's throne room. They put in their bows, extra bows, quivers, and two bundles of fire arrows.

"We can't get the two carts in position on the bridge at the same time, but we can get the handcart in position close enough to Yogari so he can take whatever tools and weapons he needs. Lars could wheel it into position close to Yogari. Nagora, you and I will crawl close to him to make sure he has everything he needs."

"We'll leave the big cart near the bridge entrance, ready to pull it into place at the last moment. After we empty it, we'll tip it over on its side. We'll stand the two tables on their sides to give us cover.

"Soon as we set up our position, we signal the start of the attack. First we want to take out the ballista. We'll set it on fire and take out anyone near it.

"Okay, let's get these carts to the bridge in nice, orderly fashion. We take our time."

At the main entrance, both carts were ready. Tommassen remained in the tower. His orders were to come and join them right after he shot a fire arrow skyward to signal that the raiders were launching their attack. He would loose his arrow when Lars waved a green flag.

If he were to see a red flag in the meantime, he would signal with a red flag also and prepare his fire arrow.

Lars led with the small cart. Dangor had the traces of the big cart. Nagora and Trowan pushed from the rear of the cart. Tsimor and Kymasen pushed from one side and Jared and Derk, the other.

When the raiders reached the bridge entrance, five of them took eight spears from the handcart and took up positions as guards at the entrance. Nagora and Dangor crouched behind the cart, ready to follow it as Lars pulled it.

Nagora judged it was a full two-hundred-and-fifty-stride climb to the middle of the bridge, still out of sight of the ballista unit at the bridge exit on the mainland. Close to the middle, they crawled on hands and knees the rest of the way, thanks to the cover of the side walls of the bridge. Closer to Yogari, they would keep to their bellies, out of sight.

Lars brought the cart within reach of Yogari's chain, and before leaving said, "Your brother and daughter are here."

Yogari turned slowly to glance and smile in their direction. He didn't gaze directly down at Nagora or Dangor. He took his time as he approached the cart, obviously making sure he was still visible to the guards watching him from the ballista's position. "Dangor! My brother! Nagora! My daughter! You warm my heart. You make me proud this day. You have control of the fortress and this side of the bridge."

He looked into the cart. "Now we stand a fighting chance. You've done well."

"Yogari, is there anything else you need?" asked Dangor.

"You've chosen well. I'll need help from one of you."

Dangor said, "We have a lookout in the fortress tower watching for a red flag. It signals that within a count of its showing, they'll try to kill Danuka. We'll warn you if we see it. We hope to start the battle before they do. We're aiming for just before noon, the time of Edana's ultimatum for Raganora to free the dragon. Raganora is possibly thinking to use the same time to order the execution.

"If, once you've taken what you need, you can bring that cart to the other side of Danuka, we'll be able to move another, bigger cart into position and give you cover fire. We'll move it when you give us the signal."

"Good. I'll raise my fist. While the others bring the big cart into position, I want Nagora to help me get Danuka and I free of these chains."

Nagora smiled.

Dangor gave Nagora's shoulder a gentle punch as he smiled at her. "As soon as our defensive position is set up on the bridge, we'll flag to our warrior at the fortress to shoot a fire arrow to signal the start of our attack. That should bring support from archers on the other side. They'll create a diversion and help us attack the ballista's position."

From his prone position, Dangor looked up at Yogari. "What's your plan for after that?"

As he answered, Yogari walked from the cart to the wall of the bridge, looking up at Danuka. "While you do that, if we are free of the chains, I'll turn the key and unlock the keystone. I'll prepare to remove it with Danuka's help. The bridge will fall apart within moments of the stone's removal. When I give the order, get off the bridge."

"But Da, what will happen to you and Danuka?"

He gave her a quick glance and smiled. "We'll lift out the keystone. I'll fly away on her back. I'll have something to deliver to Raganora."

Yogari removed all he needed from the cart and then pushed it past Danuka, beyond the middle of the bridge and out of the way, as far as his chain would allow.

Nagora crawled ahead and raised her head to watch her father. On his way he made a great show of keeping Danuka away from the hens. Once the cart was in place, he fed Danuka one live hen after another until none were left.

Then he poured water from the bucket he had left in the cart into Danuka's open mouth.

After, Yogari made his way back to the center of the bridge. He leaned against the stone rail of the bridge as Nagora joined Dangor. Her father pretended to be looking off in the distance. "There's so much we could talk about, but not at this time or in this place. Someone could be counting heads on the fortress side. Your being a couple short would draw suspicions. Soon we'll all be together to talk. Best you head back."

Crouching all the way, Nagora and her uncle made their way back to the bridge entrance, where they stood with the others.

"Grab a spear, Nagora," said Dangor as he took one from Lars. "We're going to march in formation in case someone over there is counting heads. Let's hope they think the man we're missing is in the tower with his commander." Dangor led the disguised raiders along the road, back toward the fortress. The sun seemed to stand still instead of climbing toward noon.

Tar piss! I can't wait for this to start. I want to free Da.

"Patience has its rewards." Uncle's wise words echoed in her mind. "Try to see targets or situations as if you're seeing them for the first time. Doing so will help you take a better shot than if you're looking for what you expect to see. Take in a scene from right to left rather than left to right. Look from the bottom up rather than from the top down. Look from the shadows to the light rather than from the light to the shadows. You'll catch the unexpected if you do. That could spell the difference between life and death."

When they turned around to march back, she looked at the bridge. The same nagging question came back to her. Why is Da going to destroy the bridge?

Nagora admired the bridge's arch. Yogari had helped design it and had built it with the help of the dragons. The Isle of Smoke was their exclusive home once upon a time. Queen Raganora had destroyed their island and stripped it of all its trees. She broke the trust Yogari had established with the dragons.

Is he doing it to get revenge because she held him and Danuka as prisoners on the island all these years? Is it to protect us so Queen Raganora can't get to us? With the chains severed he could fly away on Danuka's back. Why destroy the bridge he built? The key? From the outset he must have designed the bridge with this possibility. Why?

Admire it while it's there. You'll only ever see it again as a memory of this day.

When they reached the bridge entrance again, Nagora had a question. "So Uncle, which side of the bridge do we make for when Da unlocks the keystone?"

"If we go this side, we can make it back to the boat. Or we can go for the other side and join the fight there. Our force will need every warrior if we're going to win this battle to put Raynhard back on his throne. Besides, your mother and sister will be fighting there. I don't want her to be lost in battle because we weren't there to make a difference. If Danuka is strong enough to fly for a good length of time, Yogari will be able to help us. If not, he'll have to land her in a safe place."

"I haven't trained all these years for nothing," said Nagora. "We go to the mainland."

"Aye, we will, as long as we don't run into odds we can't handle. I've got your back, Nagora. They will see what Edana can do."

"We'll live to fight another day, Uncle."

The Bridge
Âsokan

Finally, Yogari raised his fist. It was time for the raiders to make their move. They rolled the big cart up the bridge, ten paces from Yogari. He had the huge axe in hand. He spoke to Danuka. She spread her wings and gave them cover. The pry bar, a hammer, a chisel, and tongs lay near the keystone and next to three buckets of water, and a brush. "Dangor, my brother!" Yogari embraced him.

"We've got a battle to fight, Yogari," said Dangor as he slapped his brother's back.

"Dangor, you can help your raiders with the cart. Nagora will help me."

Yogari wasted no time. "Here! Nagora, hold my ankle chain over the side of the hammer's head. Pull tight and keep that link resting on the hammer." She did as she was told. With one swing of the big axe, Yogari cut the link in two. "Now Danuka's chains." He severed them too, with a single powerful swing of the big axe.

Then Yogari knelt on his left knee. He rested the edge of the shackle on the side of the big axe head. "Nagora, just hold the shackle in place with the tongs." Yogari placed the corner of the chisel on the shackle pin, struck it with the hammer. The shackle pin popped out.

"Bring the tongs. We'll do Danuka's shackles." After a few well placed blows, Yogari pulled the shackle pins free, and the shackles fell open.

"Da, they must hear the axe blows."

"Surely, Nagora. Before they get word to Raganora and she gives the order, we have time to ready the keystone."

"One chain to go." It was the one that went through the handle on the bridge's key. Nagora placed the side of the hammer under one of its links. Yogari swung the big axe and split the link open.

Tar piss! How long will it take Raganora to signal to fire?

Dangor and his raiders were pulling the big cart past Danuka. They had doffed the soldier uniforms and were now their warrior selves. The archers had strung their bows and pulled on their full quivers. If they needed more fire power, spare bows awaited Lars, Tremon, and Kymasen.

Nagora stripped off her soldier uniform.

Yogari talked to Danuka. He patted her. "Soon, Mother, we will be away from here. First, I need your help, Danuka, to remove the keystone. I will tie a length of chain to the keystone and you will hold it with your claws. I will tell you when I am ready."

Lars and the others had maneuvered the cart past Danuka. They had pulled the big tables from the cart before heaving it onto its side across the bridge way, just ahead of the small handcart. Then they stood the tables on their sides.

Nagora got a quick glimpse of troop activity near the ballista. "They're onto us, Da."

Yogari knelt on one knee next to the key's handle, which lay in the recess on top of the keystone. He took the big axe, swung it broadside, and hit the top of the pin several times. Finally, the oblong hole at the top of the pin went down until its top end rested on the key handle, allowing the handle to pivot up or down.

"The key is in the lock, Nagora. Now we just have to turn it."

He pried with the chisel and levered the key handle up enough to tap it into a vertical position.

"Stick the grid cleaning hook through the handle."

Nagora did so.

"Now, join me on this end." Yogari was on one knee. "Hold here." He showed the big metal loop handle of the grid cleaning hook. He held onto the bar just below the loop. "When I say pull, we pull together to turn the key." He adjusted the bar so it rested snug against the opposite sides of the key's handle. He looked at Nagora.

"I'm ready, Da."

"Pull!"

Orders were being shouted in the distance.

"It didn't turn, Da."

"To be expected." He pulled the bar out and threaded it through the other side. "Now we push."

"Ready."

"Push!"

"Da, we're not strong enough."

"We are. You'll see. Trust me." He switched the bar again.

"I know, when you say 'pull'. I'm ready."

"Pull!"

They both fell on their backsides. "See, I told you so. We just have to turn it a little more. I can do it."

"Nagora! We need you here!" It was Dangor.

Yogari touched her arm. "Go. I can do the rest."

"They're onto us. We've flagged Tommassen. They're going to fire a bolt soon. Grab a fire arrow. We have to hit the ballista." Nagora took one from the bucket her uncle had made a fire in. "We'll try to make every arrow count. On two we fire at the ballista. One, two!" called Dangor.

Their arrows drifted away from the ballista. "Shit. It's the wind in the strait here. We have to adjust."

"Archers, did you see that? We've got wind gusts to gauge," yelled Dangor. "Fire at will. Do your best to make them count."

Lars added more fire arrows to the bucket.

Nagora climbed up onto the side of the wagon with her arrow. Just as she let it fly, so did the ballista. The giant bow flexed then straightened. The giant bolt jumped forward and raced through the air over the bridge. It shot past, an arm's length to the left of Nagora, missing her and Danuka behind her. "Shit! That was close. They have to adjust too." Nagora's arrow landed to the right of the ballista at the feet of one of ballista operators.

"Get down from there, Nagora," Dangor yelled. "Take cover." A volley of arrows headed their way.

When it stopped, Lars pointed. "Fires in the stable tents. We've got help coming on that flank."

Soldiers cranked the ballista. Dangor let fly his arrow and it took out the man on the crank. Another took his place. Trowan's arrow struck him. The third man hesitated. Grallimdor was yelling at him. Nagora's arrow hit the man in the arm. Grallimdor pushed a fourth man in place.

"I'm ready to pull the keystone," yelled Yogari.

Nagora ran to her father.

"Are you sure you're ready to destroy the bridge?"

"I made a promise a long time ago, and I intend to keep it."

"Da, can you hold off pulling the keystone until we hold the entrance to the bridge? We want to give a hand to our warriors on the mainland. The nine of us can make a difference."

"If you can keep them pinned down over there and stop the ballista from firing, I'll be able to hold on until you can secure a position off the bridge you can defend. Soon as you do, I'll pull. If I decide before, I'll warn you to head back."

A shower of arrows sailed their way. They all ducked for safety behind the cart and tabletops. Any arrows that struck Danuka bounced off her scales.

Dangor pulled a fire arrow from the bucket. "All of you. Get a fire arrow and line up behind me. Judge your aim by the flight of my arrow. Hit the ballista." As soon as his arrow completed its flight, seven other arrows followed in quick succession. Four of them struck the ballista and Nagora's hit a soldier operating it, setting him on fire. Arrows from the flank were reaching the ballista's position. The ballista's support archers pulled back. The ballista was in flames, but with a bolt on board ready to fire.

"Set the cart on its wheels. Grab as many arrows as you can. We're moving to a new position," ordered Dangor.

Dangor led the way toward the ballista, nocking arrows on the run and stopping long enough to aim and release. The wind had helped spread the molten tar from the fire arrows, turning the ballista into a brazier.

And then, the unexpected happened. The last bolt loaded on the ballista leaped out of the flames, struck a stone on the bridge bed, careened to the bridge rail on one side, and changed direction.

It happened as if in another time in another place. If only what was happening was not in fact happening; yet it happened and it made her sick. Nagora tried to scream, but could not.

And then it was too late, even if her uncle had tried to jump out of the way, the giant bolt caught him just on the inside of his right leg above the knee. The bolt pushed and spun him into the stone rail of the bridge where it stopped.

Nagora ran to him. He was unconscious. His lower leg was twisted the wrong way, attached to his thigh by a frayed piece of muscle. Nagora pulled his belt from his waist and tied it around his thigh as tight as she could.

"Brother!" Yogari had come running with the handcart.

A hand touched her shoulder. It was Lars. "We've secured the position. We'll find a medic. I'll find Tagnuska. Yogari, I'll help you put him in the cart."

This isn't happening. It can't be.

"I'll bring him over there. We'll cover him. He'll be safe with us. Take care of Danuka," said Lars.

"Nagora." It was Yogari. He was lifting her from her knees. "There's nothing more you can do. What you did will probably save his life. You've been strong today, Nagora. It's not over yet. You're still needed. You can save more lives."

Nagora swallowed, nodded, and bent to pick up her bow. "Are you still going to destroy the bridge?"

"Like I told you, I made a promise and when I make a promise, I keep it."

"What did you promise, Da?"

"I promised Danuka a long time ago that her eggs would be in a safe place."

"Her eggs? How can that be? Does she have a mate?"

"She had a mate a long time ago. There's no time to explain now."

"Where are her eggs?"

"In the cave, in the vent hole beneath the fortress."

"Oh! Shit! Tar piss!"

"What's wrong, Nagora?"

"Hag is down there! Raganora wanted to be rid of her. Raganora had her sent down last night."

Yogari grabbed her shoulders. "Nagora! We can't let her find the eggs! Perhaps she hasn't found them. They're hidden in a limestone seam I was digging, hoping to find a way out. Nagora, we have to protect them. We have to save them! We have to bring them out and find another cave, a secret place to hide them, so Danuka can care for them."

Nagora held onto his arms. "Da, I'll go. I can handle Hag. Trust me. I'll protect them with my life. And I know just the place to hide them. But I want you to promise me something. Before you destroy the bridge, find Mum or Geirador. Bring either one of them to help Uncle. Once you've done that, you can destroy the bridge."

"I promise."

Nagora ran for the fortress without looking back.

I've got an experienced crew that's going to help me.

The Cave
Kawihkwehcipayik

Nagora rapped on the cell door Rumandor was in and yelled through the small barred window. "Rumandor! Get over here! You've got a chance to save yourself and your men. The decision is yours. Right now! Move it!"

When Rumandor stuck his face in the window, Nagora said, "Tell the others to stay back against the wall. I'll unlock the door. You're coming with me."

As she unlocked the cell door, Rumandor's men behind him pleaded with him to get their release.

Rumandor stepped from the cell, not trying to hide his nakedness. Nagora had her blade drawn. "Follow me."

Nagora led him to the outer fortress yard and up the tower ladder. On the wall, she pointed to the bridge, the severed chains that no longer held Danuka, the burnt carcass of the ballista, the stable tent fires, the warrior riders routing fleeing soldiers, the rabble of onlookers that was pressing forward with every imaginable tool in hand, and Yogari on Danuka's back, flying over the plain.

Rumandor looked at the scene then looked at Nagora. "What's the deal?"

"Freedom from punishment and imprisonment for you and your men if you help me. And I promise I'll do my best to get you all a just reward for helping me."

"What do we have to do?"

"Lower me into the vent hole and bring me back up alive."

"Fair enough. Right now?"

Nagora looked into his eyes. I can trust you.

"Right now." Nagora gave him the jail key. "Bring your men to the vent house."

When he returned with his men, Nagora was turning the crank.

"We'll take over now," Rumandor said. With rope loops attached to the big crank wheel, Rumandor's men had the chain singing as they brought up the empty cage.

When it reached the end of its run and they had locked it into position, Nagora grabbed onto the bar above the cage entrance and swung into it. "Rumandor, you're a good man. You can let me down fast, but keep it controlled."

"Will do."

The cage jerked and the rapid clicks of the crank gear faded as the cage dropped. Nagora hung on and the drop rate of the cage slowed. The entrance of the cave approached. The air in the vent was hot and humid. Below the cage in the distance was a reddish glow.

The cage stopped in its descent. Tar piss! I didn't ask for information about the cave. She stared into the pitch black entrance. *Of course Hag's not in sight. Did she hear or see the cage go up?* Nagora listened.

For what? Breathing? The sound of movement?

She let her eyes adjust. She scanned the bottom edge of the entrance as far as she could see. Her eyes moved up along the right side, along the top edge, and then down the left side.

Is the floor of the cave level? Does it rise upward or go downward? I hear nothing, smell nothing. I taste and feel fear.

Why didn't I bring a fire arrow? Nagora spit, strung her bow, and pulled an arrow from her quiver. Holding her bow across her waist, she nocked the arrow, pulled it back, and released it.

The arrow struck stone, bounced, and fell onto a stony surface.

Fifty to sixty paces.

Then a soft orange glow appeared in the distance on the left side of the cave, followed by a shuffling sound and a stick striking stone. The glow disappeared, along with the sounds.

Nagora jumped across to the entrance and disappeared in the darkness.

Nagora held her bow out in front of her and swept it back and forth in the darkness as she crept forward. She hit something on the floor. It was a v-notched branch. One side was short, the other much longer.

To hook the cage and pull it to the cave entrance.

She pushed it aside.

Nagora arrived at the wall where the arrow had struck and bounced. The cave opened to her left and eight long, rough steps led to a softly glowing entrance to the right. Nagora stopped, bent, and picked up her arrow from under her foot.

Did Hag hear my arrow bounce from the stone wall and come to investigate? Possibly.

Nagora stuck to the right wall as she made her way down the stone steps.

Near the entrance, Nagora bent down to look. A hazy, smoky glow filled the chamber. A strange odor hung in the air, not unpleasant, yet unfamiliar. That part of the cave was a much bigger space.

She glimpsed the cave's high, vaulted ceiling. Drawings of dragons of every imaginable size and shape covered it, all of them in flight.

Hag was not visible from where Nagora crouched.

Nagora pulled her blade from its sheath and led with it pointed ahead of her. She stepped into the lit chamber, casting her eyes about.

Nagora ducked and rolled forward just in time to avoid the approaching whoosh sound. In an instant, she was on her feet and facing Hag who was standing at the top of the steps carved into the wall, next to the chamber entrance.

Hag had swung her snake-headed staff at Nagora and missed. "The Dragon Warrior Princess the sea would not have. I know now who you are. The Rider's daughter. Daughter of Tagnyoriva. I killed all your brothers and sisters in your mother's womb before they were born. Today, I will kill Tagnyoriva's grown daughter. And I will kill the dragon's babies. I have found the dragon mother's eggs. That is what brings you here, is it not? You've come to save the dragon's eggs. You are too late."

"No! That can't be!"

"How unfortunate for you, Edana."

Hag pulled back the hood of her black cloak, released the clasp at her neck, and let the cloak fall behind her. Hag's face was not as wrinkled, and her white hair was now grey. She was naked except for a red silk scarf that adorned her now straighter, fuller body.

The middle loop of the red silk scarf hung between her legs from a knot tied just below her belly. From the knot, the long scarf ends snaked around her hips to cross behind her and reappeared again at her front where they rose and crossed between her breasts to go find her neck.

There, the scarf ends wrapped around Hag's now longer, slender neck three times before sliding over her shoulders, across the tops of her breasts, and under her arms.

From there, the red, silken snakes wound around her arms to her wrists and finally around the palms of her hands from which the scarf ends hung as limp red flags.

Nagora looked from the red-veined blue egg in Hag's left hand to Hag's face.

Dare I believe my eyes? Hag looks so much younger than the first time I met her.

The egg Hag held was the size of a man's head. "You look surprised, Edana. I am the witch, Alizarine, cursed by my mistress with the name of the color I dyed my silk scarves because I seduced her lover with a scarf such as this one." Alizarine waved her staff and the trailing end of the scarf hanging from her hand.

"Today though, I rid myself of the curse by drinking the blood of the dragon's eggs. With the death of the last dragon, I will regain my youth and beauty forevermore. I am honored that I have you, Edana, to witness my final transformation."

Alizarine held the egg above her head. "This is the last of the dragon's eggs." She stood her snake-headed staff on the step so the intertwined snakes rested against her cheek.

Alizarine tilted her head back to look at the egg. Then in one swift motion, she brought her right fist up with her long thumbnail extended so it pierced the bottom of the egg.

She opened her mouth to catch the red blood from Danuka's egg as it poured over her face into her eyes, nostrils, and mouth.

As Alizarine gulped the blood, she grew taller, younger, and stronger. The silk scarf tightened as Alizarine's body grew taut. Her breasts swelled, the muscles in her abdomen rippled, and the muscles of her thighs and calves carved themselves under her smooth skin. The hair on her head went from a scraggly, dull grey to a luxuriant black mane.

Nagora brought a hand to her lower lip. She could feel the slap. Now she remembered the momentary image she'd had when Hag had grabbed Acindor's hand to stop him from striking her again. This was who she had seen in the shock of that slap to her face.

Alizarine!

Alizarine lowered the empty egg and cast her gaze upon Nagora. She licked her lips and then tossed the empty shell at Nagora's feet. Then she kissed the snake heads on her staff and they came to life.

Alizarine held out her staff, pointing its amber eye at Nagora as she came down the steps. Its three snakes hissed at Nagora.

"Well, Edana? Where are your powers now? Show me your fire. My snakes are hungry. They'll feed on your blood and grow, and then devour you and grow some more, and feast on your very own mother and grow some more, and then feast on your father and grow even more so that in the end, they'll feast on the dead body of the last dragon. Poor you, Edana, the dragons will be no more."

Nagora was lightheaded, slow in her thinking. She held out her blade and backed into the center of the chamber. Her eyes tried to scan for another exit. The painted images on the wall and ceiling of the cave had come alive. Dragons flew in circles above her.

Alizarine jabbed with her amber-eyed staff and waved her snakes before her as she smiled her blood-red smile. Her red eyes laughed at Nagora.

Nagora shook her head. She was helpless. Her blade weighed heavier and heavier in her hand. She had to fight to hold her arm out before her.

"Edana, you have no more fire here in my presence. It's time for you to give yourself up. Bare your breasts so my snakes may feed upon you. It'll be so much easier if you offer yourself to them freely. It will be painless. You'll marvel at how they grow as they suckle your blood."

Nagora could no longer hold onto her blade. She let it fall at her feet and staggered backward inside the circle of five tallow lamps on the floor. The same odor as earlier was more pungent there. Still pleasant, relaxing. She had to defend herself, but she was powerless.

Alizarine approached. Before Nagora's eyes, the three snakes danced around the amber eye of Alizarine's staff. They called to her as infants. I'm helpless. Nagora crossed her arms beneath her breasts and just as she reached up to pull open her sheepskin vest, the whole cave shook.

Nagora fell to her knees and looked to the ceiling of the cave where a fissure had opened. At one end of it, a trickle of water poured in. Above the trickle the dust and haze from the cave was sucked up into the crack.

Nagora placed her left hand on the stone floor that still trembled. Cold air caressed the back of her head. The lamp flames about her danced and flickered.

Alizarine had stepped back. She was whirling around, about ten paces from Nagora, looking wildly at the ceiling of the shaking chamber. Tiny pieces of stone fell from the fissure.

Nagora breathed in deep. Her head cleared, and the lethargy left her. She stood on her feet with her knees flexed, absorbing the tremors that rode up her legs. She shook her head and breathed in deep again.

Two of the lamps blew out. Nagora got her bearings.

Before her, Alizarine stopped whirling. A naked, withered old woman stood before her holding her staff with three silver snakes wrapped around an amber stone at its tip. Hag leaned on her staff with both hands for support. Her legs were spread.

Nagora's blade lay at Hag's feet on the trembling stone floor. Nagora pulled a small knife from its sheath.

Hag's wide-open, bloodshot eyes filled with terror. "We're going to die in this hole," she hissed.

"No! You're going to die in this hole, you witch!" Nagora ran toward Hag.

Hag flung her staff at Nagora, knocking the knife from her hand. Then she crouched and grabbed Nagora's big blade, raised it above her head with both hands, and ran at Nagora.

Nagora grabbed Hag's snake-headed staff and jabbed its amber eye at her Skystone blade.

"Nooooo!" screamed Hag, as the amber stone of her staff touched Nagora's blade.

First, a light flashed like lightning striking. It illuminated the cave and Hag. She appeared to glow in that light and become transparent. The dragons on the ceiling above beat their wings. Then an explosion threw Nagora back ten paces onto the floor.

Where Hag had been, a cloud of black, acrid smoke hovered. It rose and disappeared through the fissure in the cave ceiling. Did a bat fly into that same crack? I'm sure.

Nagora stood and looked at the burnt end of the stick that lay on the floor as she picked up her blade and put it in its sheath.

So this is all that's left of Hag's staff, and hopefully of her.

Nagora walked over to the broken eggshell on the floor. She picked up two pieces of shell and examined them. Da is going to be disappointed. I can't imagine what Danuka will do. This blue egg with red veins was the last dragon's egg? Wait! A dragon's egg, yes! But not a fertilized egg!

Sagora's telling of the story came back to her.

Fertilized eggs are blue with red and gold veins! This was not the last egg! I'm not guessing! I'm sure of it!

Alizarine, you thought your punishment was over. Wherever you are, you're still cursed!

Danuka still lives! I'm sure of it! I can feel her! Her fertilized eggs are in here somewhere. I have to find them.

Nagora bent to pick up one of the tallow lamps. She strode up the rough steps carved in the stone wall. At the top, she stepped over Hag's cloak into the small chamber. Nagora had to bend so as not to bump her head on the low ceiling.

It's a sleeping loft. This pile of skins must be where Da slept. Looks like Hag went through here earlier.

Nagora found a recessed shelf on the chamber wall not far from the steps. She set the lamp there. Methodically, she went through the animal hides. Underneath the hides, she found more hides rolled tightly on themselves, laid side by side, and tied together to create the surface onto which the unrolled hides could be thrown.

These must have come from all the animal carcasses sent down to them as food. He passed a good amount of time scraping and cleaning the hides. No eggs up here.

Da said he was digging in a seam.

Nagora brought the lamp back down the steps with her. She looked at the flames of the lamps on the floor. They're still flickering. Air from outside has to be coming in. I feel cool air.

Nagora walked past the lamps in the center of the chamber to the wall opposite, where the cooler air came from. As she came closer to the wall, a cleft in the stone surface opened into a narrow passageway.

Nagora held the lamp ahead of her as she went. She could feel the cool breeze on her face as she walked forward.

She came to a small excavated area with a recessed shelf on the wall on which another tallow lamp rested. Nagora lit it and squeezed over to the other side of the passage, where she crouched down to look at what her foot had touched.

Hide buckets. That one contains a stone axe. The handle is made from bone. Dirt and stone chips in one bucket. The other one is empty. He was digging here. Did he dig all this way? Da was surely set on finding a way out.

She raised the lamp to see where Yogari had chipped away the pieces of stone. And then her lamp was blown out.

The air comes from there.

Nagora stood up to light her lamp from the one on the shelf.

I'll be careful where I hold it when I bring it back there.

This time she held it away from the crack. A big chip of stone had obviously come off when the crack appeared.

Here too? This crack must have happened today.

Nagora found a wider spot in the crack, and sea air wafted in.

This cave is on the side of the strait between the island and the mainland. Da was trying to dig his way out. I wonder how long he had been digging.

Where are the eggs? I'm at the end.

Nagora headed back with the lamp.

Ah! Ha! I missed this on my way in because its entrance is facing the other way.

Nagora went to her knees and placed the lamp on the stone floor ahead of her, just inside the entrance to a small crawlspace to her left. She pushed the lamp ahead of her into the space.

The eggs are here!

She wore a big smile as she wiggled her backside out. In one hand, she pulled the lamp. In the other, she had leather straps. She set the lamp aside, sat back on her knees, and pulled the leather straps. A first pouch appeared.

Nagora undid the four leather straps that had been threaded through slits in the big leather flap. It covered four pockets that contained eggs. The eggs were blue, with red and gold veins. Was it the light from the lamp? The eggs seemed to glow intermittently.

Nagora closed the pouch before pulling on the other straps. She had three pouches in front of her.

Are there more?

She pushed her lamp back in and soon she was wiggling back out with a last pouch.

Nagora set the four pouches in the passageway. She brought them to the main chamber, two at a time. She set two pouches on each of her shoulders, with the carrying straps crossing each other. She picked up a tallow lamp and walked of the big chamber and up the steps to the cave's entrance at the vent-hole shaft.

Nagora set down her lamp, picked up the stick, and reached out to the cage, hooking it and pulling it to the edge of the entrance. She moved the stick over to the center of the cage entrance and let it swing free across the vent hole. She timed her jump across into the cage and made sure she had steadied herself and taken a good handhold on the bars.

She looked up. No one above was watching. She hollered and ran her blade back and forth across the cage bars.

Then someone whistled. The cage started on its climb.

The Lesson
Wapahtihikosiwin

Is the battle still raging on the mainland? How's Uncle doing?

The cage rose. Nagora looked up as it climbed. Rumandor's face appeared over the stone edge of the vent hole. He had a big grin on his face. "For a while we thought we would never see you come out of this hole. Things shook something fierce up here."

She waved a hand. "My thoughts exactly. Things shook something fierce down there too."

When the cage came to a stop, she handed a first pouch to Rumandor. "Be very careful with these pouches. There are eggs in them."

Rumandor's eyes grew wide. "Dragon's eggs?"

"Aye, and don't drop them or you'll be a dragon's breakfast. I'm watching you."

Rumandor was extra careful in finding a spot on the floor where he bent to one knee before lowering each pouch. Once they had unloaded the four pouches, he offered a hand to Nagora. She took hold of it and he helped her up over the stone lip of the vent hole. "Well, this place is still standing fine."

"One of the advantages of a wood timber structure. The bridge, though, fell, and that's what caused all the shaking. I saw it fall myself, right from the wall." Rumandor was pointing to the fortress yard wall.

"Tell me about it," said Nagora, as she shouldered the pouches once again.

"An amazing sight. The Rider was on the dragon's back urging it to fly up. Its big claws gripped a chain tied to the bridge's key. At first we didn't understand that it was trying to pull the keystone out. It was flapping its huge wings as fast as it could."

Nagora and Rumandor were on their way to the wall where three of his men watched. Rumandor and his remaining crew followed Nagora up the ladder.

"Then the keystone came out. The dragon lifted into the air as it circled and rose higher and higher above the bridge. The keystone had four tapered sides that end in a flattened point.

"Suddenly, we heard a grating sound and saw the bridge twist in the middle. It looked like each half of the bridge pushed against the other, twisting inward more before falling down to its own side of the cliffs.

"The next thing we knew, everything shook. We had to hold onto the wall."

"Where were the dragon and the Rider by then?" asked Nagora.

"They were high above the bridge. The dragon was flapping its wings in huge, graceful sweeps, climbing higher with the Rider on its back and still holding onto the keystone.

"The tremors must have been felt on the plain as well. It was pandemonium over there. The queen's force was in a rout, most of them trying to surrender. The queen and Grallimdor were hacking their way through the crowd to get to the road.

"The dragon stopped climbing." Rumandor made accompanying gestures, illustrating his words. "It spread its wings and turned and circled above the plain a few times. We don't know if it was the Rider who saw the queen and Grallimdor, but the dragon swooped down out of the sky in their direction. When it rose into the sky, it no longer had the keystone hanging from its claws."

His spread hand stretched out at his side and then reached in the direction of the mainland. "It soared up over the plain again, circling, only beating its wings now and then. Then it dove down onto the plain to land near Edana, who was riding her unicorn." Rumandor paused, stared at Nagora, and scratched his head. "Say, how many of you are there?"

Nagora looked at him and smiled without answering.

"Well, anyway," he continued, "the unicorn's rider dismounted and joined the Rider on the dragon's back. The dragon flapped its wings and was in the air again flying higher and higher as it circled over the plain. On its last pass over the plain, it came down gliding and disappeared between the cliffs where the bridge used to be. Then it flew on toward the forest hills there in the distance and set down. We haven't seen it fly since."

"I wish I could have seen all of that."

"I for one will never forget it."

"Rumandor, I'm grateful to have heard what you witnessed today. It's the next best thing to seeing it with my own eyes."

"I'm just grateful to be alive so I can tell what I saw."

"Well, you could be witness to more before the day is done," said Nagora.

Rumandor smiled, stood straight, and pointed. "As you can see, the battle is over. There are details rounding up the dead. The wounded are being taken care of. Weapons are being sorted and tallied in carts. Prisoners are being led to a compound. Onlookers are being recruited for different tasks. A new camp is being set up on the plain."

Nagora took in the scene before her, searching for ones she could recognize from a distance, not an easy task with smoke still drifting around and over the plain.

Is that Gabe? I can't be sure.

Everyone is busy.

I'm no use to anyone here.

"Say, Rumandor, what happened to the children?"

He gave a quick glance to his men, standing along the wall, and lowered his voice. "That was not right what the queen did. Not all of us were loyal to her. Most of us made out like we were so our families could survive these times. Those of us who were on the plain last night snuck the children out, past the ditch and into the forest. By the stars! Some of our own were among them." He wiped at the tears that spilled from his eyes onto his cheeks.

Nagora patted his back. "Your heart's in the right place." Then she pointed and asked, "Did you or your men see a boat sail by at the mouth of the strait down there?"

Rumandor nodded. "We all did. It anchored there for a full count before sailing off."

"Looks like we missed our ride off the island," said Nagora.

"You said we would get safe passage off here."

"I did. I just have to make new arrangements, but it won't be easy. What's our best way to get someone's attention on the other side?"

"Go down to what's left of the bridge entrance. Stand there. People haven't stopped showing up on the other side to have a look at where the bridge used to be. Chances are you'll see someone you know."

Nagora reached back to her quiver. "I've got a whistle arrow. That should get their attention. Want to join me? We'll fly across on the dragon."

Rumandor's jaw dropped, but then he regained his composure.

"Queen Raganora was always afraid the bridge would fall. She had a rope bridge made as a way of getting off the island. It's made of three stout ropes to be set in a v-shape with netting on two sides. People hold on to the two side ropes as they walk across on the third. The idea was to use the ballista to shoot a rope to the other side so the rope bridge could be hauled over by a mounted unit on the other side. Then it would be tied to the bollards on each side of the strait."

"Can you get that rope bridge down to the bridge entrance?"

"Sure, if we can put the wheel with the broken spoke back on the cart in the stable, we can haul it to the bridge entrance."

"What are you waiting for?"

Nagora stood in the middle of the entrance and waved her bow. I don't know any of them. Maybe a whistle arrow will bring someone I know. She released it into the air so it would fall into the strait.

Not long after, Trowan pushed her way to the bridge remains and waved to her. She gestured to Nagora. Good, she's going to get word to Da.

When Rumandor and his men arrived, Nagora gave him the news. "It shouldn't be too long. I'm guessing two, maybe three full counts, and the dragon will be here. We'll cross with the rope the ballista would shoot. Once the rope bridge is rigged on both sides, you and your men will be free."

"Thank you, Edana."

"Just paying back what I owe you. A reward is yet to come your way."

Wow! Danuka is magnificent. She was flying over the plain in Nagora's direction.

The last dragon in the land with the last Dragon Rider on her back, my da. Da.

Nagora said the word over and over as the dragon's giant wings flapped and then held their shape to glide toward her. She had longed for her father to return and had never given up hope that he would. Now she was like a little girl. She wanted to hold him and say to him: Da, I'll never let you go. But she would never say that.

After all, I've just helped free you. I won't let my words become a prison for you.

Most of the people on the plain stopped what they were doing. Many pointed and followed the dragon in her flight.

Her magnificent wings shimmered with flashes of iridescent colors as she glided across the strait. Danuka looked about with graceful, controlled movements of her neck. She looked majestic, as did Yogari.

She sailed overhead past Nagora, circled above the fortress, and returned with slow, controlled flaps of her wings to set down on the road about fifty paces from the bridge bollards.

Yogari slid down from his rope saddle and pointed to the pouches that hung from Nagora's shoulders. "My daughter, you kept your promise." Then he took Nagora in his arms and held her.

She held onto her father. If this moment could last and my questions didn't press ... "Have you seen Mum and Sagora?"

"Briefly. They're busy caring for the wounded. The battle was short, with much confusion on the plain. Many were wounded, especially among the untrained fighters who joined in the fray."

"How's Uncle?"

Sadness cast a shadow on Yogari's eyes before he answered. "In Geirador's care."

She swallowed. Uncle, you're in good hands. I hope you'll survive. Your wound is terrible. May the stars allow you the strength to heal.

"What of Raynhard? Have you seen him?"

"He's leading a force to Windhaven with the leader of the force from the Land of Skulls."

"Gabe."

Yogari nodded. "And they have Raganora with them."

He pointed to Rumandor, who was standing next to a cart near the bollards. Nagora explained the help Rumandor needed.

...

Yogari and Nagora went over to him to have a look at the rope they would bring across. Yogari tied a loop at one end of it for Danuka to hold on to. Then he made sure the rope would travel freely as they flew across the strait.

While he was doing this, Nagora explained how Rumandor had helped her.

Yogari paused to look at Rumandor. "From a distance, we've gotten along well over the years, haven't we, Rumandor? You're the one I have to thank for the extra salt and the variety of food you were able to send down to us. I could have lost more than my two back teeth."

Rumandor looked to the ground, away from Yogari. "Just did my best to treat you fair."

Yogari smiled. "No hard feelings. We appreciated the extras you sent down to us.

"Okay, Rumandor. This rope looks ready. Give us a count or so with the dragon. Leave the loop where I put it. We'll come get it when we're ready. We'll tie it off on the other side and then get someone to bring horses to haul your rope bridge across and secure it to the bollards there."

"Thank you, Rider."

Yogari led Nagora back to the dragon. "Come, Nagora. Show the egg pouches to Danuka."

Danuka brought her big head down in front of Nagora. Her red eyes looked into Nagora's. Nagora stared back into them.

"She wants to inspect her eggs. Set the pouches down. Take off your vest. Set it on the ground in front of you. Sit crossed-legged before your vest."

As Nagora did as Yogari had instructed, Danuka spread her huge wings, brought them forward and around Nagora and Yogari. She rested her wing talons on the ground behind them, creating a tent around them, except for the opening to the daylight above them.

Nagora looked up at Yogari.

Yogari touched Nagora's cheek with a finger. "Fear not. She's only protecting us and her future children. Time for me to give you a Dragon Talker lesson."

Yogari sat on the ground behind Nagora with his legs bent and spread out on each side of hers. He leaned his head forward to whisper more instructions. "Pull one of the pouches closer. Open it."

Nagora unfastened the straps and pulled open the flap to reveal the four blue eggs with red and gold veins.

"Take one egg out at a time. Hold it with both hands and slowly turn it over." Yogari's breath was on her ear and neck. That most rare of scents she had first inhaled in the dark beneath Danuka's wing returned, welcoming and comforting her at the same time, making Nagora feel protected and wanted. Is this how a Dragon Talker feels?

Her mouth went dry as she focused on learning her new task.

The recessed, vein-textured surface of the egg gave Nagora a good grip on it. She spread the fingers of one hand over the big end of the egg and the fingers of her other hand over the small end. At least another hand's length separated the finger tips of one hand from the other. It must be slightly bigger than the size of a man's head and as heavy as a small iron cooking pot.

The gold veins, about the width of a dozen strands of hair laid side to side, were recessed deeper than the red and blue veins, which made up the major part of the dragon egg's surface. The smooth bulge on the surface of the gold veins reminds me of the tender shoots of new leaf stems on a grape vine.

As Nagora turned the egg over in her hands, Danuka lowered her head and smelled its entire surface before examining it with one big red eye.

Yogari placed his hands on Nagora's forearms just below her elbows. "That's it. Slowly, so she can smell and eye the whole surface."

"Da, did another dragon mate with Danuka in the vent hole? Was there another dragon?"

"No, Nagora. She had mated just before being captured. Mother dragons have a receptacle inside them, where they can keep the seeds of the dragons. The mothers can decide when to release the seeds to create eggs that will have hatchlings. They do that when conditions are right."

"But were the conditions right down in the cave? I don't understand."

"Conditions would have been right had she been able to fly in and out of the vent hole at will."

"So why did she create these eggs?"

"Because there's a time limit on how long she can hold seed in her. Past that time, the seed will die."

Yogari pointed to the open pouch. "Replace the egg. Take another."

As she did, Nagora's body began to surprise her with a new awareness. The muscles in my neck, shoulders, and back feel so warm. That warmth is spreading down my arms into my hands. It's not just warmth, but strength too. Yes, I definitely feel stronger. The second egg seems lighter.

"So Da, how long before the eggs hatch?"

"Again, Danuka has a time limit in years she can keep her eggs before she begins the process that will make them hatch. She'll only start that when she's sure she and her hatchlings will be safe."

Nagora's whole body grew warmer, like when she would lay down naked on the hot sand in one of the dips of a dune on her beach, warming up after a summer swim in the cool water of her bay. I don't feel sleepy like on the sand in the sun. Instead it's like I'm aware of every detail of everything within reach.

"Once she starts the process, how long do the eggs take to hatch?"

"Dragons usually start the process with the onset of winter. Usually, by the first days of summer, the babies hatch."

Nagora lost track of time as her body seemed to meld with the task into a single moment. She could no longer count.

"What about the other eggs without the gold veins?"

"Danuka lays several eggs each month, but when close to hatching time she will lay many more. They will be to feed the hatchlings. They're good to eat too. They greatly helped to keep me healthy over the years."

Now she was handling Danuka's eggs without thinking, just as when she tied knots to bind hides to the frames of the curraghs she used to build with her uncle. Even the questions she had for her father did not count time. "How is it Danuka can fly despite being confined to the cave for so long?"

"As soon as Danuka's wounds had healed, we took short flights within the vent shaft daily. As you saw, the vent shaft is wide enough for her to spread and flap her wings. With the cage up and out of the way, we could fly up and glide back down with ease. There are smaller caves further down. They became stopover points for us to cool off in before flying back up. One of those even provided us with water for a good part of each year."

Nagora had just finished fastening the buckles on one pouch and was pulling the last pouch nearer to open it. Danuka watched her every move, and Yogari followed each of her movements as if he were her very own shadow. I'm lucky. I have Da all to myself. His closeness is like a reward for all his years of absence. "Da, you must be so happy to be free now. Surely, you can't wait to be aboard the Sea Wolf, far out of the sight of land."

Yogari hugged Nagora to him and kissed her cheek. "I never dreamed my daughter would give me the gift of my freedom. Nagora, I am happy to be free and happy to hold you. And, dreaming about being at sea on the Sea Wolf helped keep me from going mad. It's true, I can't wait to be on board her again.

"But duty calls. My king will need my help to rebuild his country. He will need Danuka's help. He will need your help too. There will be much to do before we can be together as a family. The coming days, months, and perhaps even years will have us all working to rebuild. Let us hope that during that time, we'll be able to be together as a family to share good times."

Nagora made it to the final egg in the fourth pouch, marveling at the warmth and newfound strength that had invaded her body during the inspection lesson. Yogari's spicy, leather-wrapped scent seemed to have intensified within the confines of Danuka's wings. Had it combined with Danuka's scent for a reason? Why has it made my body feel so warm and strong and aware?

As she turned the last egg for Danuka's benefit, the dragon paused and shifted the gaze of its eye to Nagora's. If I were to tell someone she is looking inside me and can read my thoughts, they would not believe me. But I know she can, and she can do so much more. She can control me in ways I can never imagine. And I know that if I'm to be her Dragon Talker, I must submit. Someday I'll understand why.

After she had replaced the egg and buckled the flap of the pouch, Yogari rested his cheek against hers and held her close for a moment. "Well done. Danuka has finished her inspection."

The dragon lifted her giant wings.

Yogari stood and held out a hand to Nagora.

She took his hand, grabbed her vest, and let him help her up. The warmth and strength she had felt beneath the tent of Danuka's wings began to fade.

Yogari brought her to him in a close embrace and whispered, "Danuka is going to speak to you now. Don't be afraid. Listen and believe what you will hear her say inside of you." He let go of Nagora and turned her to face Danuka.

Danuka had folded her wings to her side. The talons of her giant wing joints supported her as she lowered her head in front of Nagora. Her eyes locked onto Nagora's, and then ever so slowly, she brought the tip of her snout to Nagora's Tiwaz symbol on her forehead.

"You saved my children. You are their protector. Protect them, and I will protect you. Take us to a safe secret place." The words, in the language of The People, rang clear in Nagora's mind as if she had heard them with her ears.

"Mother, I will take you to a *kâtanohk*, secret hiding place, where you and your children will be safe. I will protect your children there."

Before Danuka pulled her head away, she said, "Lone Wolf, I trust you."

It was confirmation. Now I too, like Da, am a Dragon Talker. I still have much to learn.

Yogari helped Nagora pick up the egg pouches and lift their straps over her head and lay them across her shoulders. He took Nagora's hand and led her to Danuka's side. Nagora listened as Yogari spoke to Danuka. "Mother, lower your wing so I can bring Nagora to the saddle."

Danuka's left wing talon came down and settled on the ground next to Yogari's feet.

"Stand just behind the talon."

Nagora stepped on.

Yogari kept hold of her hand and stepped on behind her. "Up, Mother."

Danuka slowly raised her wing.

"Grab both the bridle and the saddle ropes with your left hand. Left foot through the loop. Swing your other leg over. Find the loop. When you do, and you're comfortable, pat Mother and tell her."

"Thank you, Mother." She patted Danuka. "I'm on your back, Mother." Nagora's spread her legs wide and bent them at the knee as she sat at the base of the dragon's broad neck. It was like sitting bareback on a giant horse. She was five times higher off the ground than on a normal horse.

"Up more for me, Mother. Good, Mother." Yogari reached for the saddle rope between Nagora's knees and swung up behind her. He placed a hand on each of her knees. "Are you okay?"

"Aye."

"You see. You can talk to Danuka, like you've been doing. Though for a good while still, she must touch your forehead to talk back to you. Eventually, you'll be able to hear her without touching. You can't force it. It will just happen."

"Like when she spoke to me in the dream?"

"Like that, yes. But you won't have to be asleep.

"Today, you felt your body being taken over by Danuka's scent. It might have worried you. It is how Danuka ensures you are receptive to me as my apprentice, and to her, to what she needs you to do to protect her and her eggs. But I want to warn you. When I am not with you, Mother's scent will have an even greater effect on you until she gains complete trust in you. Fear not.

Also, at times Danuka will not have words to convey what she wants to tell you. She will use images. She'll convey them to you in dreams."

"But how will I know they are meant as messages for me? How will I know the difference from other dreams?"

"You will remember them clearly. They will seem so real you'll believe they truly happened. They'll be unlike any dream you've ever had. You'll question why she showed you those images. The reason often will not be apparent right away. Trust what she shows you. It will always be for a reason."

He reached for her hand. "You are strong, Nagora. Your will is your own to govern. Trust Danuka, and she will grow to trust you. She knows so much more than we'll ever know."

Trust. I have to trust Danuka. May the stars help me. "Da, I feel I have so much to learn."

"True, and now you'll learn to fly Danuka."

Nagora swallowed. "Da, no. I've never done this."

"Nagora, you are a Dragon Talker. Trust me. No training is necessary. Speak to Mother calmly. When you are on her, you just have to think where you want her to take you. Soon we'll have a true saddle and bridle for her. It'll be more comfortable for you then."

"Are you sure?"

"I'm most sure. Danuka can't wait for you to bring her to your secret place to hide her eggs so they'll be safe."

"But it's far away. I don't know how long it'll take to get there."

"Can you tell me what place it's near? Not necessarily the nearest."

"Cairnmase."

"If you leave right after we've delivered Rumandor's rope, you'll be there before sunset. Take your time. Come back tomorrow."

He placed a hand on her shoulder. "Nagora, I must tell you. Only if Danuka is completely sure your secret place is safe will she let you come back without the eggs. If she thinks it's not, you'll have to stay to guard the eggs, or bring them back with you."

He gave her shoulder a squeeze. "One more thing, my daughter. Danuka inspects her eggs every day. You will help her as you did today. It's one of your duties as a Dragon Talker. As Danuka's protector, her future, the future of her children, and the future of the people of the Land of the Danu now rest with you."

In Nagora's mind, Hag's prediction surfaced—Child, a dragon awaits you. No more waiting, Danuka. I am here, with you, for you.

Then further back to the first time she had heard the voice speak *Ka Peyakot Mahihkan*. The language was strange, but yet so familiar, as if it were a part of her. I understood the meaning of those words—Lone Wolf, the name my dragon gave me.

Nagora reached for the dragon tear amulet at her neck. Danuka, if this is my path, I will follow it. I have no choice.

✝

✝

Dear Reader,

Thank you for reading *BETRAYED*. For the benefit of future readers and to help me as an author, you would truly warm my heart by leaving an honest review at:

www.hnhenry.com/testimonials

OR wherever you purchased this copy of *BETRAYED*.

Sincerely,

H. N. Henry

P.S.: Here's a **SPECIAL OFFER** for you:

Get the first chapter of *BRED* for **FREE**:

Find out how on the next page.

First Chapter for FREE

A dragon rules Nagora's future. Her submission is total ... no matter the cost.

Duty to her king and her dragon call Nagora to a secret mountain cave. As apprentice dragon talker, Nagora is to protect the eggs of the last dragon in the Land of the Danu. A simple enough task, but fate does not make life easy for those who share darkness with a dragon.

Her king's unannounced visit of concern is a prelude to a royal offer that will bear unimaginable consequences for Nagora.

So will Nagora's failure in her duty to her dragon when the forces of her nemesis threaten the last dragon and its eggs with death and destruction.

What unthinkable price will lone-wolf warrior Nagora pay for a single solitary chance to risk her life to save her dragon and her king? To find out...

Come. Escape with Nagora into her dragon's world.

To learn more about the other books in this series, visit the author at: www.hnhenry.com

BRED *The Dragon's Game*

Book IV

H.N. Henry

ISBN 978-0-9958419-2-5

9 780995 841925 >

Go to the link below to get the FREE first chapter of BRED The Dragon's Game BOOK IV:

https://www.hnhenry.com/bredchapteronefree

ABOUT THE AUTHOR

Other than writing, his passions include kayaking, baking bread, and trying to learn how to play guitar. He shares the profits of his work with a local community cause, *Point de Rue.* They help homeless people on the streets find meaning and passion in their lives. Learn more about it here: http://www.pointderue.com/point_de_rue.html.

To learn more about the author and the other books in the series, please visit: http://www.hnhenry.com.

✝

Titles in THE DRAGON'S GAME series:

BANISHED BOOK I

BRANDED BOOK II

BETRAYED BOOK III

BRED BOOK IV

BLAMED BOOK V

ACKNOWLEDGMENTS

The Dragon's Game books wouldn't have come about without the generous and invaluable support of these people throughout the creative process.

From the beginning, Staecy-Lee, my editor, gave my manuscripts tough, honest critiques. Her hard questions made me see my stories with fresh eyes for the benefit of my readers.

Randi, my proofreader, closely read the final formatted-for-publication texts, finding inconsistencies in details, descriptions needing clarification, and grammatical errors my own eyes could no longer see.

Staecy and Randi, avid readers of this genre, also offered truly valuable and insightful comments that have made me a better writer. Learning from them has been a pleasure and a privilege.

My passionate beta readers of the first original brick, in first name a-b-c order, Ann, Daniela, Danielle, Maria, Marie-Josée, Randi, and Staecy-Lee generously delivered invaluable feedback and constructive criticism that helped spawn *BANISHED*, Book I, and from the volume they read, give birth to Books II and III of the series. I am forever in their debt for their support and encouragement.

I am grateful to the stained glass window artist, Guido Nincheri (1885-1973), who over ten years (1924-1934) created the beautiful windows in the Cathedral of the Assumption in Trois-Rivières, QC, Canada. From the photographs of those windows that I took on February 27, 2006, I was able to digitally manipulate images from two of the panels to create the unique dragons that appear on the covers of the first edition of my books, a humble homage to Nincheri's masterful work.

Though not referenced as Cree in the context of my stories, I have used Cree, in Roman orthography form, for the chapter titles and chapter numbers throughout the books in the series. More importantly, it is the " ... strange yet familiar language ... " Nagora, the main character, a.k.a. *Ka Peyakot Mahihkan*—Cree for *Lone Wolf*, hears in her mind and eventually uses to communicate with her dragon and other characters. At those times, when used, Cree is referred to as the *Language of the People*, in reference to the *First People* of *The Land* where my story is set.

The *Language of the People*, or "dragonspeak" as some readers of The Dragon's Game books call it, in a way, reflects the status of the Cree language in our land today. Though Cree is the most widely spoken Native language still spoken in Canada, it has yet to be recognized as one of this country's official languages. Similarly, in the fictional setting of *The Dragon's Game* books, the *Language of the People* is now only spoken by a few in a divided and renamed land where two different languages (those of the invading Outlanders) have become dominant in use.

To the Online Cree Dictionary Team: *Kinanâskomitin*. *Thank you*, I am grateful to you for making this resource available to all. It has been indispensable in helping me lend realism to that second language in my stories. I hope my readers will have as much pleasure as I do in discovering the living Cree language.

In the end, what appears on the pages of my books is mine, and I take full responsibility for any errors that show up in the final versions.

www.ingramcontent.com/pod-product-compliance
Lightning Source LLC
Chambersburg PA
CBHW031212120726
47905CB00002B/304